Praise for Our Authors

USA TODAY Bestselling Author B.J. Daniels

"*Cowboy Accomplice*...is a masterful blend of humor and suspense."
—*RT Book Reviews*

"Strong familial ties and several compelling secondary stories make B.J. Daniels' *Shotgun Surrender* a heartwarming tale...with fast-paced Western intrigue and lots of cowboy action."
—*RT Book Reviews,* 4 stars

USA TODAY Bestselling Author Delores Fossen

"*Wild Stallion* by Delores Fossen... is one long thrill ride with bullets and kisses running neck and neck."
—*RT Book Reviews,* 4.5 stars

"Sharply drawn characters...and bone-melting sensuality combine in a riveting, tangled tale... that keeps readers on edge until the end."
—*Library Journal* on *Christmas Guardian*

Favorite Author Julie Miller

"A story that starts with a bang only gets better in Miller's capable hands as she delivers a page-turning story of medical ethics, murder and blackmail and a romance that sizzles."
—*RT Book Reviews* on *Beauty and the Badge*

"*Up Against the Wall* is one novel designed to keep you up reading past your bedtime."
—*Cataromance,* 4.5 stars

USA TODAY Bestselling Author

B.J. DANIELS

USA TODAY Bestselling Author

DELORES FOSSEN

JULIE MILLER

TORONTO NEW YORK LONDON
AMSTERDAM PARIS SYDNEY HAMBURG
STOCKHOLM ATHENS TOKYO MILAN MADRID
PRAGUE WARSAW BUDAPEST AUCKLAND

Daniels, B.J

ISBN-13: 978-0-373-83765-6

PLEASE RECYCLE • THIS PRODUCT IS RECYCLABLE •

Recycling programs for this product may not exist in your area.

This edition published by arrangement with Harlequin Books S.A.

For questions and comments about the quality of this book please contact us at Customer_eCare@Harlequin.ca.

www.Harlequin.com

Printed in U.S.A.

CONTENTS

GONE COLD

B.J. Daniels

CHAPTER ONE

"Is everything all right, honey?"

Morgan Sinclair stirred from her dark thoughts as Tom turned off the highway onto a snowy narrow road. She suddenly felt anxious as she looked at the glistening, cold white mountains ahead.

"I didn't realize this resort was so remote," she said, voicing her sudden misgivings. "When you said it was less than fifty miles from home, I didn't realize how much of that was on a narrow gravel road way back into the mountains."

Tom slowed the SUV, looking disappointed. "If you've changed your mind about my plans for our honeymoon..."

"No, it's not that." It was that stupid text message. A hard knot formed in Morgan's stomach at the thought. How she wished she'd never seen it on Tom's phone. Worse, ever since then she'd been questioning whether she'd jumped into this marriage too quickly. Did she really know the man she'd married?

Her friends had certainly been shocked when she'd announced she and Tom were getting married after dating for only a couple months.

"It does seem a little...fast," her friend Luke had said with the quirk of an eyebrow. "What's the hurry?" Leave it to Luke, her best friend, to come out and ask.

"No hurry." She knew what everyone was avoiding

saying. *Isn't it too soon after your mother's death?* But her mother had been fighting cancer for over two years.

Also, her friends didn't know Tom the way she did. Once they got to know him, they'd realize what a great guy he was, and it would put all their fears to rest.

It wasn't as if she'd gone into this blindly. Because of the large inheritance her mother had left her, she'd asked Tom to sign a prenuptial agreement, and he'd readily agreed.

She reached over and touched his hand, wishing she could put her own fears to rest. His skin felt warm and she reminded herself how he'd swept her off her feet. He was the most romantic man she'd ever met, and he loved *her*. He didn't care about the money—he didn't even know how much she'd inherited.

If he had, he would have known that they could afford to go to Hawaii or Fiji or anywhere they wanted for their honeymoon. Instead he'd insisted on something more affordable closer to home, and just for a weekend. Tom had said he couldn't get any more time away from work, but she suspected he couldn't afford more right now. He'd only recently moved here and started his new job.

"Ice Lake is said to be Montana's best-kept secret," Tom had said when he'd proposed the idea. "Imagine a warm fire, a nice bottle of that wine you like, a cozy cabin in the woods, all nestled in the Rocky Mountains. Doesn't that sound perfect?"

It did. *Just like Tom,* she had thought at the time.

"Honey, I'm going to make this honeymoon something you will never forget," he'd said. "You do trust me, don't you, Morgan? Now that you're my wife, all I want to do is take care of you."

"Morgan? What's bothering you?" Tom asked now, bringing her back to the present, his voice edged with irritation, and something else that only increased her anxiety. When he was nervous or upset, he spoke with a slight Southern accent.

The first time she'd heard it, she'd kidded him about it. Tom had acted almost insulted, saying he couldn't imagine why she would say such a thing. He'd never lived in the South. She hadn't brought the subject up again.

"It's not that text message again, is it?" he asked now, then let out an annoyed sigh. "It was just a wrong number. It obviously wasn't for me."

"No, it isn't that," she said. It wasn't *entirely* that. "It's those clouds over the mountains ahead. Winter storms always make me nervous."

That seemed to appease him. He smiled over at her and squeezed her hand, before letting go to concentrate on his driving. "You have nothing to worry about. I'm going to take good care of you."

He'd taken care of her after her mother had died. Morgan had desperately needed someone during that time, and he'd been there for her. But since then she felt as if he was hovering over her. She hated that she felt that way. He was so sweet and caring. What was wrong with her?

She stared at the clouds hunkered over the tops of the mountains. They felt as ominous as the odd sense of foreboding she'd awakened with this morning.

The weather didn't help. Dark shadows filled the snowy canyon as Tom drove into it. Tall snow-covered pines towered over the narrow road. Only a slit of silver-gray sky showed high above the trees.

Why hadn't she just told him about her inheritance and tried to talk him into a real honeymoon someplace warm? But even as she thought it, she knew Tom would still have insisted on something he could afford. That was the kind of man he was.

So why was she having doubts about him? Because of some stupid text message that was, just as he'd said, an obvious wrong number?

"We need this, honey," he said, his voice thick with emotion as he took his attention off the road for a second to look over at her with a smile. "And we can afford this weekend away. I promise we'll have a real honeymoon one day, when I can afford to take us."

She heard the pride in his voice and quickly said, with more enthusiasm than she felt, "Ice Lake Resort is a wonderful idea. I'm just nervous about the weather."

She tried to relax, but couldn't stop thinking about the text message she'd seen on his phone.

Eric, I know you're screening my calls but we have to talk about this. Unless you want me to tell your wife everything, call me. A

"It's obviously not for me," Tom had said when she'd held up his phone and said, "What's this?"

But she'd caught something in his expression, just for an instant, something that set her heart pounding and filled her with the sick feeling that her friends had been right. She really didn't know this man she'd married.

"What do you know about Tom for certain?" her friend Luke had demanded, and she'd instantly regretted going to him after seeing the text. Luke was an investigative reporter and her best friend at the local newspaper where they both worked. The head photographer, she loved her job, loved the excitement of working in the media.

"I know I love him," she'd said, sounding defensive.

"If the guy is on the up-and-up, what would it hurt if I did a little checking into his past?" Luke had said when she'd tried to backpedal and put an end to him investigating her husband. She'd argued that she trusted Tom.

"Then there's nothing to worry about," Luke had said. "I know you, Morgan. Let me relieve your mind, okay? I'll just check him out and then you can relax and enjoy your honeymoon. So tell me everything you know about Tom Cooper."

Reluctantly, she'd given him the information, knowing he would be discreet, and wanting very badly to be reassured. It had scared her though, when she'd realized how little she *did* know about Tom.

They'd met just before Christmas. She'd been shopping, had dropped one of her packages, and Tom had picked it up for her. They'd talked for a few minutes, he'd made her laugh and they'd ended up having coffee at a little bistro.

What had followed was a whirlwind courtship and a small, intimate wedding in a church. Tom liked to say it had been love at first sight.

"Isn't this beautiful?" he said now, dragging her back to the present. She looked out the window at the pines heavily mantled with snow and the creek beside the road crusted in cold blue ice.

"Oh, stop," she cried, as a breathtaking section of the creek came into view.

"Honey, there really isn't a place to pull over. This road is pretty much single lane."

But she had already grabbed her camera bag and was opening her door.

WITH A MIXTURE OF impatience and awe, Tom watched his beautiful wife doing what she loved most. When

Morgan had a camera in her hands, she was like a different person. There was a strength in her when she held one, a confidence that he hadn't seen when he'd first met her. She knew she was good at what she did, and she didn't need anyone to tell her.

"You have such an intensity about you when you're shooting photos," he'd told her after the first time he'd seen her like this. "You change before my eyes. Your work completes you, Morgan."

She'd been touched. He'd felt guilty, but would never have admitted to her that he was often jealous of the relationship she had with her art. When she was shooting photos, nothing else mattered to her. He had known even then he would always play second fiddle to her work.

Now, though, he was hit with a rush of pride to think this woman was his wife. He'd seen the way other men looked at her. Just as he had the first time he'd seen her. It really had been love at first sight. He often marveled at how lucky he was that she'd dropped that package the day before Christmas and he'd stopped to pick it up. He'd thought he couldn't get any luckier. But he'd been wrong about that.

He glanced in his rearview mirror, wishing she'd hurry up, though. "Morgan, it's freezing." She'd left the door open and he was impatient to get to the cabin and be completely alone with her. Since they'd gotten married, it seemed something was always coming up with her work, or her mother's estate, something or someone always calling her away. That's why he'd chosen Ice Lake. Here he could have her completely to himself. "Honey?"

She turned to smile at him, then took a couple more shots. He looked at the scene and knew he wasn't seeing what she was through her camera lens. He watched her study the way the winter light played on the snow, the angle of the dark shadows beneath the pines, the way the wind had sculpted the drifts. He often wondered what she saw when she looked at him.

Her cell phone rang.

He stifled a curse and guarded his words. "I thought we agreed to leave the phones at home?" he said, still unable to keep irritation out of his voice.

When they'd left her apartment, which had become their home for the time being, he'd asked her not to bring her phone.

"Cell phone coverage at the resort is sketchy at best," he'd said. "Anyway, I want this to be just the two of us, curled up in front of the fireplace, snow falling outside, a thermos of hot buttered rum, with no interruptions." No damn calls from the newspaper. Or her friends—worse, her best friend from work, Luke.

Morgan had agreed, but at the last moment must have tucked the phone into her camera bag.

"It's my grandmother's fault," she called over her shoulder as she snapped another photo of the creek. "She told me she never went on a date without having a dime to call home. I've always taken her advice to heart." Morgan sent him a grin over her shoulder.

It was hard to be irritated with her. The woman was so adorable. "This isn't a date. It's our *honeymoon*."

"I know." Her phone rang again.

"Don't answer it," Tom said as Morgan pulled out the device. He watched her check to see who was calling and felt his stomach roil as he saw her expression. It was that damned Luke; he'd bet money on it.

Luke was one of the reasons Tom had asked her to leave her cell phone at home. There always seemed to be something going on at the newspaper that the handsome investigative reporter just had to talk to her about.

Tom started to demand that she give him the phone so this didn't happen again, but stopped himself. He had no reason to worry about Luke anymore. Morgan had married *him*. It didn't matter how Luke felt about her.

Tom needed to keep his cool. He couldn't let anything ruin this weekend. It had to be perfect. With any luck, her cell phone wouldn't work once they got where he was taking her.

AS MORGAN CHECKED her phone, she saw that it was Luke calling from his cell phone. That meant the call wasn't about work.

She felt her heart jump. He must have gotten some information for her, something that would relieve her mind and let her actually enjoy her honeymoon. She desperately wanted to take the call, but knew if she did, Tom would be upset.

Hopefully, Luke would leave a message she could check later. As anxious as she was to hear from him that there was nothing to worry about it, she couldn't let her husband know that she'd had him investigated.

Nor did she want to spoil their honeymoon over one silly phone call.

So she let it go to voice mail, and tossed her phone back into her camera bag. "There," she said, and climbed into the SUV.

Tom looked relieved she hadn't taken the call. He glanced toward her bag as she put it on the floor at her feet, but when his gaze returned to her, he smiled and seemed to relax.

She felt guilty, part of her wishing she hadn't asked Luke for his help. Tom would be devastated if he knew she'd gone behind his back. Worse, that she had *Luke* checking into his past.

"Thanks for being so patient. I love you." Morgan hated that it sounded as if she was trying to convince herself as much as him.

He gave her a tight smile, and she could see she'd upset him by not leaving her cell phone at home. Or was it that he suspected the call was from Luke?

It seemed so silly for him to be upset over such a small thing. Morgan felt heartsick. Their relationship hadn't been the same since that text message. Tom had been distant. Or maybe it was because just as he'd said, that he was worried about something at work.

As much as she hated it, she'd found herself watching her husband more closely. She'd even gone through his chest of drawers in the bedroom, feeling horribly deceitful. She'd found nothing incriminating. Why couldn't she accept that the text message had simply gone to the wrong phone? It had been for a man named Eric—not Tom.

It was that look on his face when she'd asked about the text that was causing her suspicion. Something had crossed his features, something like guilt?

She shivered now at the memory as she saw him steal a look in the rearview mirror.

When she checked her side mirror, she saw a dark SUV some distance behind them. It was too far away to see the driver. Glancing at Tom, she saw his brows furrow as he checked his rearview mirror again.

"Is there a problem?" she asked, glancing behind once more.

"Honey, I told you, it's about work." He sounded aggravated with her, and she wondered if he was still mad that she'd brought her cell phone. Or could it have something to do with the SUV on their tail?

Morgan tried to corral her suspicions. She'd been like this ever since the text message, and she had to stop. "Is the problem at work something you'd like to talk about?" she asked wishing Tom would open up to her. Maybe that would still these crazy thoughts she'd been having.

He shot her a look. "Yes, Morgan, there is nothing I'd rather talk about than work on our honeymoon." He sighed and softened his tone. "Everything is fine. You know me, I just worry too much."

But she didn't know that about him. The Tom she'd known until the text message never seemed to worry about anything.

She was the one who worried. Like now. As she tried to concentrate on the beauty of the winter landscape around her, she couldn't help noticing how dark the clouds over the peaks had become. It really did look as if a storm was blowing in.

"I just need to relax for a couple of days with the woman I love," Tom said, but he glanced in his rearview mirror again.

This time when Morgan looked back, the road was empty. As she turned around, she heard Tom say, "There's the lodge."

The rambling log lodge appeared out of the pines. It was wonderfully Western, clearly old and so picturesque that she quickly reached for her camera.

"I knew you'd like it," Tom said, sounding pleased.

She put down her side window and snapped a couple photos, the cold mountain air rushing in, then grinned over at her husband. "I *love* it. Thank you. This is perfect," she said as he parked in front.

"You want to come in while I get the key to our

cabin?" he asked, but she was already out the door, her camera bag hooked on one shoulder.

He shook his head, smiling at her as he hurried up the steps and disappeared into the lodge.

Morgan took a few more photographs before entering the mountain lodge. As she stepped inside, she saw Tom at the front desk. She was about to take a photo when she remembered the call she'd gotten earlier from Luke. Convinced he had found information that would save her honeymoon, she stepped around a large log post, out of sight from Tom, and played Luke's message.

"We need to talk. I was waiting to hear back from some of the inquiries I'd made, when I ran into a man at the coffee shop who works at Vi-Tech. I asked him if he knew Tom Cooper. I thought he'd say, 'Sure, Tom's a great guy.' Instead, he said, 'Who?' Morgan, I called Vi-Tech. The receptionist checked. There is no Tom Cooper employed there."

"Obviously there is some mistake," she said under her breath, and turned to see Tom headed in her direction. She quickly deleted Luke's message and stuffed the phone back in her coat pocket.

She'd been disappointed when Tom had taken an instant dislike to Luke. "You're *jealous?*" she'd said with a laugh, since she and Luke were just friends.

"The guy has a crush on you, can't you see that?" Tom had said.

"That's ridiculous."

Tom had pulled her into his arms. "Doesn't matter, because you're mine and no one is stealing you away from me now that I've found you."

She'd felt a thrill at the passion she'd heard in his voice, and thought what a lucky woman she was. It wasn't until later that his jealousy began to bother her.

"Ready?" Tom asked now as he joined her.

All she could do was nod. That terrible feeling in the pit of her stomach was back. Of course there had to be an explanation, because otherwise where did Tom go every morning when he said he was headed for work? Not to mention he'd insisted they couldn't have a longer honeymoon because he couldn't get the time off work. Had that been a lie, too?

The drive to the cabin was up an even narrower road, through dense woods. Morgan had expected it to be within sight of the lodge. But when she looked back she could see nothing but the darkness of the pines. She glanced down at the map Tom had handed her when he'd gotten into the SUV.

The Mountain Badger Cabin was circled. Heart dropping, she saw that it was the farthest from the main lodge. She'd had no idea that where they were staying would be even more isolated.

"I heard some good news at the lodge," Tom said without looking over at her as the car snaked up the mountainside. "It's supposed to snow."

She could have told him that. She'd smelled snow in the air and had known it was probably already snowing at the top of the peak where the clouds had settled in.

"Can't ask for anything more romantic than snow, right?" he said, smiling as he drove.

Morgan agreed. There was nothing more beautiful than falling snow, especially large, lacy flakes. She reminded herself that this was her honeymoon. She couldn't let a wrong number text message and an obvious misunderstanding about his job spoil it.

But still, her heart ached. She'd been so sure Luke's message would be good news. Now she fought her disappointment—and worry. First the text message and now this? Tom had said there was a problem at work. Or had he said *with* work?

She couldn't remember. But he'd been anxious and distracted lately. As she watched him drive up the slope through the dense pines, she debated asking him about the job.

Or should she just wait until the weekend was over? She didn't want to spoil their honeymoon. Also, how could she ask about what Luke had told her without giving away how she'd found out? She couldn't even imagine what Tom would do if he knew it had been Luke she'd turned to. But as she looked out at the wintry scene, she felt even more anxious.

"So I assume you checked your messages while I was getting the key and map," Tom said, startling her. He smiled over at her as if she should know that he knew her too well for her to fool him. "Anything to worry about?"

"No, why do you ask?" She hated that she sounded a little breathless and a whole lot guilty. He'd caught her flat-footed. Of course he would have known she would check her messages. He probably even suspected it was Luke calling, given his jealousy.

"I ask because you're sitting over there gripping the edge of the seat and frowning."

She released her death grip and let out the breath she'd been holding.

Tom brought the SUV to a stop in the middle of the snowy road and looked at her, his handsome face suddenly serious. "Morgan, I don't want us to have any secrets," he said, his gaze locking with hers.

"I feel the same way," she said around the lump in her throat. She almost confessed everything right then. "I just want you to know that you can tell me anything."

His eyes narrowed for a moment, then he sighed. "I didn't plan to get into this now, but...I have been keeping something from you. I didn't know how to tell you, and I'm sorry. I lost my job. It turns out the position I came up here to do was already filled. I've been looking for another one and didn't want to say anything until I found something."

Morgan felt such a wave of relief she laughed. "That's all?"

"That's all?" he repeated mockingly. "I take providing for my wife a little more seriously than that."

She wanted to throw herself into his arms. They had plenty of money. "We'll be just fine until you find another job." She leaned over and kissed him tenderly.

"I don't want to let you down, Morgan."

"You could never do that."

He gave her a weak smile. "I hope not." Then he got the SUV going again.

She couldn't believe how much better she felt. Simple explanation for what Luke had learned about her husband.

But as the SUV climbed higher up the mountain, she studied the storm clouds over the peaks and felt a little of her earlier apprehension coming back.

She'd had no idea they'd be staying in a cabin so far from the lodge. What if they got snowed in and couldn't get out once the weekend was over? Tom might not have a job, but she had photographs that needed to run in next week's newspaper.

"How much farther is this cabin?" she asked, unable to keep that growing uneasiness out of her voice. He didn't know about Montana winters in the mountains. He was probably hoping that they *did* get snowed in.

"Just a little farther." He glanced at her. "Try to relax.

Do I have to keep reminding you that it's our *honey-moon?*"

She attempted a smile. A moment later, she was glad when the trees opened a little and the cabin appeared.

It was charming. She quickly put down her window to snap a picture, imagining the shot pasted in their first photo album.

As Tom parked and she climbed out, she heard him say, "This snow is great. You know what we should do? We should make a snowman before the next storm hits. What do you say?"

She hadn't built a snowman since she was a kid. She smiled, hearing the enthusiasm in his voice. He acted as if he'd never seen snow before, she thought with amusement. That couldn't be the case, though, since he'd grown up in Seattle and it snowed there occasionally. Maybe like her, he just never lost his sense of wonder.

"Come on," he said. "I'll unpack the car later." He was already making a large snowball in his gloved hands. He laid it down in the snow and rolled it toward her, the ball growing in size as the soft snow stuck to it. She loved the huge smile on his face. He was so boyish, so young and happy-looking. She fell in beside him to help.

Morgan quickly got caught up in the creation of what Tom began to call their "Honeymoon Snowman." They positioned it right in front of the cabin window so they would be able to see it when they looked out.

"I'll get a hat," she said, and hurried back to the car. She was digging in the back of the SUV when her cell phone rang. She hurriedly pulled it from her coat pocket, realizing belatedly that she'd forgotten to turn the darned thing off after listening to Luke's message.

When she checked, she saw it was him calling again.

Tom apparently hadn't heard the phone, since she kept the ringer set to a low volume. Debating whether to let the call go to voice mail or answer it, she clicked it on.

She needed to tell Luke that Tom had never even started the job at Vi-Tech, so it was no wonder they hadn't heard of him. Nothing to worry about. She also needed him to stop investigating her husband.

"Hello?" she said, stepping behind the SUV and keeping her voice down.

"Morgan!" Tom called, making her jump. "I'm going into the cabin to see what I can find for the snowman's face."

She waved, hiding the phone behind her and waiting until Tom was inside the cabin before she said, "Luke, are you still there?" There was a lot of static on the line and she thought for a minute she'd lost him.

"Yes. Did you get my earlier message?" he asked, sounding worried.

"I did, but I talked to Tom—"

"I'm afraid I have more bad news, Morgan. Tom Cooper never graduated from Puget Sound High School in Seattle, Washington. According to school records, there was no Tom Cooper enrolled in any of the schools in Seattle. I'm checking other schools in the area and waiting to hear back from the University of Southern California, but I'm having a hell of a time finding any information on this guy. I have a bad feeling about this, Morgan."

She heard Tom come out of the cabin and call to her that he'd found something they could use, and to hurry up with the hat.

"There has to be a mistake," she said, shocked by this news. There would be an explanation, just like with the job.

"I'm worried about you," Luke said. "I wish you weren't up there. But at least you should be all right at Ice Lake Lodge with other people around—just in case."

Just in case? What was he saying? That Tom might be dangerous? She thought of her husband busy making their honeymoon snowman. Luke was wrong. She should never have told him about the text message. There was a logical explanation for all of this.

"I have to go." She clicked off, stuffed the phone into her pocket and tried to swallow the lump in her throat as she looked at the remote cabin Tom had rented for the weekend.

"Did you find a hat?" he asked, suddenly appearing next to her, startling her. "Something wrong?"

"You surprised me, that's all," she said, and handed him the old hat she'd found in the back. "Let's see how our snowman looks."

Slamming the back door of the SUV, she walked toward the cabin through the snow, her mind racing as she tried to remember everything Tom had told her about his past. He'd been vague, the details sketchy. That's why she'd gotten the information wrong. It was the only explanation.

Tom perched the hat on the snowman's head and looked at her, his blue eyes shining with excitement that quickly turned to desire. He pulled her close. She buried her face in his warm wool jacket, breathed in his familiar scent and felt the first falling snowflake land on her cheek.

This moment should have been perfect as he swept her into his arms and carried her up the cabin steps. Snow began to drift down from a big sky thick with the cold breath of winter. The mountains disappeared as the storm moved in.

Morgan glanced in the direction of the lodge, but knew she wouldn't be able to see it through the dense trees and snow even if it had been closer. To her surprise, though, she thought she glimpsed the corner of another cabin roof in the distance before Tom opened the cabin door and carried her inside.

She tried to put Luke's call out of her mind, telling herself Tom would be able to explain everything—just as he had about the job at Vi-Tech.

But at that moment, the only thing she was sure of was the distinct chill in the air, before he closed the door behind them.

CHAPTER TWO

MORGAN WOKE IN THE large king-size bed. She didn't open her eyes at first. She could hear Tom breathing softly beside her, his naked body warm and familiar.

He had been so wonderful when her mother passed away. Since her father had died a few years earlier, when she was in college, she was now an orphan. It seemed so wrong to lose them both so young. But Tom had helped her through the mourning. He'd offered her a shoulder to cry on and encouraged her to talk about her parents, and seemed to enjoy hearing her stories about growing up in Montana.

Her eyes slowly opened as she tried to remember stories he'd told her about *his* childhood. When she'd questioned him about his parents, he'd said, "It was a *Leave It to Beaver* kind of childhood, dull compared to yours." Then he would get her to talk more about her past.

Restless with the return of her doubts, she slipped out of bed and padded across the cold pine floor, closing the bedroom door behind her.

There was kindling beside the fireplace and, growing up in Montana, she was no slouch at building a fire. She got a small blaze going, then added more wood. Sitting on the hearth next to it, she told herself she was being ridiculous. She had to stop being suspicious of everything about Tom.

"What about your family?" she had asked when he'd insisted they get married right away. "Are they going to be able to make the wedding?"

"I told them we couldn't wait, but they promised to come out this summer. I was thinking we could have a big reception. They would like that. I don't want them to have to travel in the winter. Not on these roads."

"I'm anxious to meet them," she'd said.

"You will. But when you do, I want to introduce you as my wife."

She hadn't said more, but now realized she and Tom had never gotten a call or a card congratulating them. She could understand her in-laws not sending a present because they would be coming out this summer, but not even a call to talk to their new daughter-in-law?

Had Tom lied about more than where he'd grown up and gone to school? She thought about that Southern accent she swore she sometimes heard in his voice, and hugged herself feeling a cold chill that not even tossing more wood on the fire helped.

Morgan shivered, reminded of last night's lovemaking. Tom had been so tender and yet so passionate. Her heart beat a little faster at the memory of the way he'd looked at her, at the way he'd touched her, as if he still couldn't believe how lucky he was.

It had been the perfect honeymoon night, just as he had promised. Outside, huge snowflakes had drifted down from a black velvet sky. Inside, a fire had crackled, filling the cabin with warmth and golden light. Not even Fiji could have been more romantic. Just after midnight, they had stood at the window, Tom's arm around her, and admired the snowman they'd built together.

She smiled now at the memory, and went to the front window to look at it again.

A cry of shock and disappointment escaped her lips. The snowman was gone! All that remained were footprints in the snow, where someone had trampled it.

Hurrying to the front door, Morgan flung it open, appalled and outraged that anyone would do such a thing. She stumbled to an abrupt stop as she saw what the vandal had left on the porch.

The snowman's hat sat just outside the door. The vandal had filled it with snow and had made a face from the produce Tom had used to make the honeymoon snowman's smile. This face, though, was anything but smiling. It stared up at her with a grotesque, twisted expression that made her shudder.

Morgan started at a sound behind her.

"Hey," Tom said as he wrapped an arm around her waist. "What..." The rest of his words died on his lips.

"Someone destroyed our snowman."

He cleared his throat as he reached down, picked up the hat and dumped out the horrible face someone had left for them. He turned and pulled her into his arms. "Damn kids."

"You think it was kids?"

"Had to be," he said. "Come on. It's freezing out here."

She let him draw her back inside. The fire crackled, but she couldn't shake off the even deeper chill that had settled over her. She remembered thinking she'd seen the roof of another cabin through the trees. Finding the map Tom had handed her yesterday in the car, she checked.

The Mountain Lion Cabin. It was fifty yards or so through the trees. Was that where the kids had come from? It seemed inconceivable. The snowman had been fine at midnight so when had kids destroyed it? Surely not this morning, since it was still early and it had been snowing hard all night.

"I'm going to take a hot shower," Tom announced. "Want to join me?"

She could tell he was trying to get her mind off the snowman. "In a minute."

"I'll be waiting for you," he said, and headed for the bathroom.

The moment he closed the bathroom door, she hurriedly pulled on her coat. There would be tracks in the fresh snow, tracks that would lead her to whoever had done this. What upset her was the vindictiveness of the act—and the violence.

They hadn't just knocked down the snowman, they'd trampled it, kicking the packed snow all over the front yard.

Tugging on her boots, she slipped outside. The air had a bite to it. Snow fell in a silent shroud around her as she stepped off the porch. The tracks were still visible, even though fresh drifts had started to fill them in.

She put her boot next to the track to measure the footprint, and felt a sliver of ice run the length of her spine. No kids had made these tracks. It had been one person, and from the size of the print, it had been an adult.

Morgan heard Tom calling as she started to follow the tracks into the woods. The lone set of boot prints ran along the edge of the cabin and woods, and returned the way they had come, into the cold dark shadows of the pines.

Morgan stared through the falling snowflakes. Who was staying in Mountain Lion Cabin? And what possible reason could they have had to destroy the snowman?

A sense of dread filled her as she thought about the

hat she'd found on their doorstep, the gruesome face left like a message. A threat.

A crazy thought crept in along with the cold. What if these tracks belonged to "A," the woman who'd left the text message on Tom's cell phone? The message had sounded threatening. Morgan felt a flash of fear as she considered again the violent way the snowman had been destroyed.

"Morgan?"

She spun around, heart in her throat, to find Tom standing in the cabin doorway wearing only a towel.

"Honey, it was just a snowman." Their *honeymoon* snowman. "Come inside. I left the shower running."

Shivering, Morgan hurried up the steps and into the cabin. Locking the door soundly behind her, she followed Tom to the bathroom, needing the heat of the shower and the reassurance of his strong arms around her.

WORRIED ABOUT MORGAN, Luke hadn't gotten much sleep last night. This morning he'd spent half the time mentally kicking himself for not telling her how he felt about her before Tom Cooper had come into her life.

The other half of the time he'd spent worrying about Tom Cooper, and how to find out the truth about the man. Hadn't he known there was something not quite right about him?

Okay, Luke had to admit maybe he wanted there to be something wrong with Tom Cooper. He'd wanted Morgan to realize her mistake, but the whole romance and marriage had happened so quickly....

It was his own fault. If he'd just spoken up before Tom appeared on the horizon... All the reasons why Luke hadn't seemed so inconsequential now.

But when he'd met Morgan he'd been coming out of a heartbreak. His high school sweetheart, whom he'd dated through college, had decided to take a job in France. He hadn't wanted to leave Montana; she couldn't wait to hop on the plane.

Luke had seen it coming, the two of them growing apart, wanting entirely different things. But still, it hurt.

So when he'd met Morgan, he'd been gun-shy. Soon she had become his best friend, and then he was afraid of trying to change that. He'd feared he might lose her if he told her how he felt about her and she didn't share his feelings. He couldn't bear the thought that it might destroy their friendship.

"You should have told her, man," he said now to his empty apartment. "You should never have let her marry that guy. You knew he was all wrong for her."

That was water under the bridge. He had to concentrate on what to do now. He hadn't told Morgan the worst of it. As far as he could ascertain, the man she'd married hadn't existed until eleven years ago. Luke was still trying to find out who Tom Cooper had been before then.

Luke told himself that she'd hung up too soon and hadn't given him a chance to share everything. But he knew he'd feared putting her in even more danger by doing so.

This morning, as he'd showered and dressed for work, he'd questioned whether he should have told Morgan anything until she returned. He feared what might happen if she decided to confront Tom.

Meanwhile, Luke had to find out what Cooper was hiding, and just how dangerous the information might be. He assured himself that Morgan would be safe. Whoever Cooper was, he wouldn't try anything with a lodgeful of people around.

But Luke still couldn't bear the thought of her up in the mountains with a man who could be...well, just about anything.

Picking up his phone, Luke tried her cell again. It went straight to voice mail. He didn't leave a message, knowing that anything he said might make the situation worse—not to mention possibly be overheard by Morgan's husband.

What also worried Luke was that there were believed to be two serial killers on the loose. He'd been covering the story since the last murder and was at least relieved that neither of the two profiles the FBI had done resembled Tom Cooper.

Then again, the personality sketches were based on known serial killer profiles and could be dead wrong. The latest victim, Special Agent Leah Gray, had survived, but didn't get a look at her attacker.

Luke checked his watch. He had to get to work. But he knew he wouldn't be worth a damn all day. He'd be waiting to hear what his private investigator friend had found out about Tom Cooper's past, and worrying about Morgan. That is, when he wasn't beating himself up for letting her marry the wrong man. Maybe if he had—

He shoved the what-ifs away. He'd blown it. He hadn't told Morgan how he'd felt and now it might be too late.

He was startled when his cell rang as he entered the newspaper office. He snatched it from his pocket, hoping it was Morgan.

It was his P.I. friend, who often helped him out when he was working on a story.

"Did you find out anything more about Tom Cooper?" Luke asked after a hurried hello.

"I hope you're sitting down."

CHAPTER THREE

MORGAN INSISTED they go over to the lodge for brunch, even though Tom had brought food so they wouldn't have to leave the cabin.

"Whatever you want," he said, surprising her. She'd expected him to put up a fight. Or at least look disappointed. But he seemed to realize she was still upset about the stupid snowman and needed a change of scenery.

"Oh, shoot, I forgot my wallet," he said as they got into the SUV. "I'll be right back."

Morgan looked toward the other cabin, but the woods were too dense from this angle and the falling snow too heavy to see it. An eerie silence seemed to envelope the SUV. She was glad when Tom returned and they headed for the lodge.

They ate in the large dining room. She surreptitiously studied the other guests, wondering who was staying in the cabin closest to them. Morgan didn't lie to herself; she was searching for "A." That was silly, she knew, but she couldn't help it.

No one in the lodge dining room was paying any attention to her or Tom, nor did she see a woman who looked as if she had gotten up in the middle of the night and hiked all the way to an adjacent cabin in a snowstorm to destroy a snowman.

But then again, what would a woman like that look

like? Morgan knew she was being foolish. It *was* just a snowman.

Tom was quiet during the meal, reaching for her hand occasionally and smiling over at her, but neither of them talked much.

Morgan couldn't help noticing that the lodge was only half-full. She overheard guests talking about the winter storm warning, and how they might leave after they ate. Apparently some guests had already taken off.

"Maybe we should go, too, if this storm is going to get worse," she suggested.

"Is that really what you want?" Tom asked, sounding disappointed. He seemed disappointed. "A Montana girl like you afraid of a little snowstorm?"

"You don't realize how dangerous these storms can be, since you grew up in Seattle. Unless you never went up in the mountains. I know you said you don't ski, but didn't you ever go up to that ski hill on the pass? What was the name?" she asked, pretending interest in her food because she couldn't look at him.

"Steven's Pass," he said. "I don't ski, but I have seen snowstorms. You should try my walnut encrusted trout, by the way. It's delicious. We should make it sometime. I assume you're an old hand at trout fishing, right? We could go fishing in the spring. Where's a good place to go?"

She noticed how he'd changed the subject, as he always did when she asked about his past. "What kind of fishing did you do out in Seattle?" she pressed, not taking the bait.

"My family didn't fish. So you're going to have to teach me. I think I'd like to take up fly-fishing. Is it hard to learn?"

"No. I think you'll catch on quickly." Just as she had

caught on to how he maneuvered out of telling her anything about himself.

Her stomach ached as she moved her food around on her plate. Thankfully, Tom began to talk about the lodge and its history as he finished his meal.

"Would you mind if I checked my email? I want to make sure some photographs I sent out arrived," she said, wondering if lying was contagious.

She'd expected him to be upset, but to her surprise, he said that would be fine.

"I'll meet you in the bar, if that's all right," he suggested, and she quickly agreed.

The moment he disappeared through the door to the lounge, she went to the main desk and asked about the other cabin she'd seen in the woods.

"Is Mountain Lion Cabin available? I heard some of the guests are leaving because of the storm," Morgan said, quickly improvising.

"I'm sorry, there is a guest staying there," the clerk replied. "It appears she's staying through the weekend."

She. Morgan felt her pulse jump. And the clerk had said "a" guest. The woman was staying there alone?

All Morgan's doubts rushed to the surface again. Why would a woman want to stay out in the woods alone? Even crazier, why would she get up sometime after midnight and tramp through the woods to an adjacent cabin to destroy a snowman?

Unless she was a woman scorned and looking for a way to get back at the man she called Eric.

With a start, Morgan remembered the way Tom had repeatedly checked his rearview mirror. Had he been worried that someone was following them? Someone whose name began with *A?*

It seemed to always come back to that text on his

phone. The threatening message had left little doubt in Morgan's mind that "A" was a woman scorned.

She had to stop this. She knew her whole theory was crazy. Just because the boot prints had come from the direction of the cabin didn't mean its occupant was the snowman killer.

But what were the chances that whoever had destroyed the snowman had come from even farther away, in a blizzard in the middle of the night?

You are letting your imagination run wild, Morgan Sinclair. Morgan Sinclair Cooper, she reminded herself.

In case Tom left the bar rather than wait for her, she went to a corner of the large lounge and began to check her emails on one of the computers for guests. The moment they came on screen, she saw a recent one from Luke. She hurriedly opened it.

Morgan, call me. It's urgent. Luke.

She checked to make sure Tom was nowhere in sight. Even though she now suspected that her husband had lied to her, she still felt guilty and disloyal as she took out her phone and tapped in the number. The line buzzed with static and for a moment she didn't think the call was going to go through. She was relieved when Luke answered, more relieved than she knew she should have been, just hearing his voice.

"I saw on the news that there's a winter storm warning, especially for the mountains," he said the moment he heard her say hello. His voice sounded so good that tears welled in her eyes and her heart lifted. "You really need to get out of there while you can," he insisted.

"I can't do that—"

"Everything Tom told you about his past is a lie. He

was *never* employed at Vi-Tech. He's from a small town in Arkansas and his name isn't Tom Cooper. At least it wasn't until eleven years ago."

She felt as if an elephant had stepped on her chest. As she fought to draw a breath, she whispered, "If you're going to tell me that his name was Eric before he changed it—"

"It's worse than that, Morgan. He—"

Static suddenly filled the line.

"Luke?"

No answer. He was gone.

CHAPTER FOUR

IT'S WORSE THAN THAT.

Morgan tried to call Luke back, but couldn't get through.

It's worse than what?

What had he meant?

She put her cell phone in her pocket and stumbled up from the computer. What was clear was that Tom had lied about his past and for some reason had changed his name eleven years ago. Didn't he realize he'd get caught?

No, she thought. He would never suspect the woman he loved would investigate him.

She felt sick, her food fighting to come up as she rushed to the ladies' room.

Once inside the bathroom stall, she closed the door and leaned against the cool tile wall until she felt better.

She heard several women come in, but didn't pay any attention to what they were talking about until one said in a pseudowhisper, "That woman we saw earlier, with the cast on her wrist and all the bruises? She's the victim who was attacked by one of the Big Sky Stranglers, those serial killers they're looking for."

"Oh, my gosh. I got a glimpse of her when she checked in. That's where I'd seen her before. In the newspapers."

"I heard one of the employees say she's here to recuperate."

"Here at the *lodge?*"

"She has a room down the hall from ours. The poor woman."

Morgan thought of the cabin she'd glimpsed through the trees. If she was right and a woman was staying in that cabin alone, Morgan could eliminate the serial killers' victim, Special Agent Leah Gray.

The newspaper had been chasing the story, calling the duo the Big Sky Stranglers because they choked their victims. She'd never heard of a serial killer in Montana, let alone two. Agent Gray had been lucky. Unfortunately, the other woman hadn't.

Morgan shuddered. First a winter storm. Now the victim of a serial killer duo was hiding out here? Not to mention Morgan herself was honeymooning with a man who didn't seem to have a past—at least not the one he'd claimed.

When the bathroom cleared out, she tried Luke once more, but again couldn't get cell phone service. Back in the lobby, she thought about using the landline guest phones, but they were all busy and she knew Tom would be looking for her soon.

What was it Luke had been about to tell her? She thought of the special agent, the Big Sky Stranglers latest victim, who just happened to be here at the lodge. Surely he wasn't going to tell her that he thought her husband was one of the stranglers.

The idea was so outrageous it made her laugh. Tom had lied to her, but she *knew* him. He was sweet and gentle and loving. He wasn't some deranged killer. He was her *husband.*

Her earlier queasiness passed, and she felt anger

surface. He was also apparently a liar. Mad at herself for involving Luke in this, and at Tom for lying to her, she went to find him. As much as she hated to do it on their honeymoon, it was time to confront her husband.

In her heart, she knew she was clinging to the hope that Tom would have a logical explanation for everything. He had to, she thought, as she walked toward the lounge.

Out of the corner of her eye, she noticed a man who appeared to be watching her. He was nondescript, from his plain brown hair to his build—except that one of his legs was in a cast. A skiing accident?

But if he had been watching her, he quickly looked past her, to a short man with shaggy blond hair, dressed in work clothes. The blond man had stopped in the middle of cleaning one of the windows in a large bank of glass along the lodge wall.

"Excuse me."

Morgan turned in midstep at the sound of a man's raised voice. She came face-to-face with the brown-haired man who she'd thought had been watching her.

"I believe you dropped this," he said.

She stared at his smiling face, her heart pounding hard. The man was average in every way, which made her wonder why his being so close scared her.

Looking from his face to what he was holding out to her, she saw it was a black knit glove.

"I thought I saw you drop this." His smile had an edge to it.

She shook her head and took a step back. "No, it's not mine."

"Sorry to have bothered you, then." His smile faded.

She turned and hurried away, chiding herself. This wasn't like her, being so paranoid. No one at dinner had paid her any mind. Nor had anyone since then. The man hadn't even been looking at her—until he'd thought she'd dropped her glove.

With a start, she realized she hadn't noticed the glove on the floor when she'd walked toward the lounge. Nor had anyone else passed her before the man approached her with it.

She fought the urge to look back, then caught her reflection in the window glass and felt her pulse leap. Both men were watching her.

Shivering, she quickened her step, telling herself this whole thing with her husband had her spooked.

CHAPTER FIVE

THE LIGHTS SUDDENLY flickered and went out as Morgan reached the entrance to the bar. With the dull gray storm clouds outside, the old lodge was left in darkness. She stopped, waiting for the electricity to come back on.

To her relief, the lights came back on a moment later. She looked around for Tom, but didn't see him. At least not at first.

Then she spotted him at the back of the bar, talking on one of the guest phones. The anger on his face made her freeze.

When he saw her, his expression instantly changed. He said something into the phone and hung up. As Morgan walked toward him, she noticed that he was pale and sweating. He wiped his brow and attempted a smile, but could do little to hide the fact that he was upset. Upset at the person on the phone? Or at Morgan for catching him?

"What's going on?" she asked.

"I was just checking on a job I interviewed for. I didn't get it." He couldn't even look her in the eye as he said it, or as he sat down at the table, where an almost empty drink glass had left a wet circle on the lacquered wood.

Her husband was a liar.

Luke had already told her that, and yet it finally hit

her. The truth brought shock, disappointment and anger. She had held out hope…for what?

Tom downed what was left in the glass, and Morgan realized it hadn't been his first drink.

"You checked your emails?" he asked, clearly trying to change the subject. No wonder he'd been fine with her checking in at work. He had needed to make a phone call, one that had nothing to do with a job.

"I take it everything at the newspaper is fine?" There was that slight edge to his voice, reminding her how jealous he was of Luke.

She nodded as she sat down. He had started to rise so they could leave, but now returned to his chair as he saw she had no intention of going just yet.

"Do you want a drink? Or would you like to go on back to the cabin?" he asked, clearly hoping she would agree to the latter. "I brought your favorite wine, remember? Or we could open that bottle of champagne from the wedding."

The barmaid had come over to their table. Morgan ordered a vodka collins. Tom looked resigned and ordered another black velvet and water.

"A ditch," he added, and then smiled at Morgan. "I sound like I'm from Montana, ordering a ditch, huh."

As the waitress left, Morgan studied her husband. He was perspiring heavily and nervously rattling the ice in his empty glass.

No, she thought, *you sound like a man from down South, say from Arkansas.* "Who was really on the phone?" she asked quietly.

He slowly put his glass down on the table. "Why don't we finish our drinks and take this convers—"

"Who is A?"

He looked as if he was having a hard time breathing as he raised his gaze to hers.

She didn't give him a chance to lie to her again. "I know everything you told me about your past isn't true," she said angrily, fighting to keep her voice down. She really *didn't* know the man she'd not only fallen in love with, but had married. "You never intended to work at Vi-Tech and you aren't from Seattle. Apparently you're from a small town in Arkansas, which would explain the Southern accent you say you don't have."

"How did you—"

"Does it matter how I found out?"

"Maybe." He looked away, the muscle in his jaw bunching. "It might matter if you got this from your friend Luke, the investigative *reporter*." Tom turned back to her, his blue eyes cold as ice chips and just as hard. "Morgan, you can't trust anything he says when it comes to me, don't you realize that? He doesn't like me because he's crazy about you, and I wouldn't be surprised if you weren't half in love with him. You can't go even a day without talking to him. Don't you think I've noticed?"

She wasn't going to argue, even if she could have. How she felt or didn't feel about Luke wasn't the issue. "This isn't about him."

"He's who told you that I lied about my past, isn't he?" Tom didn't wait for a reply. He must have seen the answer on her face. "Why would he investigate me if this wasn't about his feelings for you?"

"Because I asked him to."

Tom leaned back, his expression so filled with shock and hurt and disappointment that for a moment she wanted to reach out and comfort him.

The barmaid returned with their drinks. Tom downed

his in one gulp and then got to his feet. "You can take that with you," he said, nodding toward her drink, which she hadn't had a chance to touch.

"I'm not going anywhere with you until you tell me the truth."

He stood looking down at her, anger distorting his handsome features. After a moment, he seemed resigned and slowly sat back down. "Do you really want to talk about this in a bar?" he asked quietly.

"Why did you lie to me?"

He groaned. "I had my reasons, which I will be happy to share with you if you'll come back to the cabin with me. Morgan, I'm your *husband*. I love you. Does anything else matter?"

"It might. I know you changed your name." Just as she knew in her heart that his name before he'd changed it had been Eric, even though Luke hadn't confirmed that. "Who *is* A?"

He looked away.

"Are you having an affair with her?"

Swearing under his breath, Tom turned back and raked a hand through his thick, sandy-blond hair. He was a good-looking man, funny and smart. She'd thought she was the luckiest woman in the world to have met him, let alone to have him fall in love with her.

"How can you ask me that?" he demanded.

"You've lied about everything *else*." The words came out choked with emotion. She took a gulp of her drink. It was heavy on vodka and burned all the way down.

"I'm not having an affair," he said, enunciating each word. "You're the woman I love, the woman I married for better or worse, till death do us part. Do you really think there is anyone else?"

Morgan felt him cover her hand with his, and closed

her eyes. Her body remembered his tender touch. Her heart pounded, making it hard to draw a breath. She had fallen in love with this man. She'd married him. She couldn't be wrong about him.

"Why did she call you Eric?" Morgan asked.

He sighed. "Because that used to be my name. Can we please go back to our cabin now? I promise I will explain everything. I planned to tell you this weekend, anyway. I know I should have told you before we got married, but Morgan, I was so afraid of losing you...."

She took another gulp of her drink. "And A?"

"Allison Stuart. She was my high school girlfriend until a terrible tragedy—" His voice broke. "I can't talk about it here. Please, Morgan." He stood up and reached for her hand.

"A tragedy? And that's why you had to change your name, lie about your past?" She hated that her own voice broke with emotion and that her heart filled with hope that Tom would give her the reasonable explanation she so desperately needed.

"You can be the judge of that after you hear what I have to tell you. But I can't, not here." He glanced toward a group of people sitting nearby. "Please, Morgan. If you ever loved me..."

She heard the vulnerability in his voice, saw his blue eyes fill with tears.

He squeezed her hand. "Please don't make me tell you here."

She downed the rest of her drink, the alcohol firing in her veins, but it was with a chill that she let him lead her out of the bar and lodge.

Snow was falling harder as they crossed in front of the lodge and walked toward his SUV. They passed a couple who were talking about trying to leave the lodge, but were afraid they would be forced to turn back because of the storm.

Morgan thought about Luke pleading with her to get away from Tom, away from Ice Lake before the blizzard blew in.

Too late, she thought, feeling the effects of the wine she'd had with brunch and the strong vodka collins she'd just finished.

Her friends had always told her what a smart, reasonable woman she was.

Until she married Tom so quickly.

Why had she done that?

Because for the first time in her life she was in love with a man who couldn't wait to marry her. She'd been so flattered....

Was she really going to leave the safety of the lodge now, with other people close by, to go with this man she feared she couldn't trust?

She saw Tom staring at someone and turned to look. "Do you know that guy?" she asked him. It was the man who'd been watching her earlier, the short, nondescript one.

To her shock, she saw that he now had the single black glove. Two fingers of it stuck out of his jacket pocket. But it had been the other man who'd approached her with the glove...

Tom frowned. "Why would you think I knew *him?*"

Morgan glanced again at the man, who quickly looked away. Was there something else Tom wasn't telling her? Or did she suspect everything and everyone now?

She stopped walking and pulled her hand free of his as she breathed in the cold, wintry air and tried to think straight. Her head ached, and she felt confused and scared. The clouds were lower, the thick flakes of falling snow almost suffocating.

She realized she was trembling from the cold, from her fear and hurt. "I don't know you."

"You *do* know me," Tom said, moving closer to thumb away her tears and the snowflakes that stuck to her cheeks as she looked up at him. "You know me like no one ever has. You know the man I was always supposed to be."

She gazed into his blue eyes. When he took her hand again, his was warm. She clutched it, wanting desperately to believe she hadn't been wrong about him as she let him lead her to his car.

He opened the passenger side and helped her in. Before he closed the door, he brushed more melting snowflakes from her cheek, smiling almost regretfully as he closed the door.

She touched her cheek as she watched him walk around the front of the car, then slide behind the wheel. She knew if Luke were here, he'd be telling her what a fool she was, and she feared he'd be right.

But when she looked over at her husband, she saw how vulnerable he was, how frightened. How could she not trust this man? She'd shared his bed. She'd married him. Didn't she at least owe him a chance to explain?

She hugged herself, fighting to stop the trembling as he started the engine. Snow blanketed the windshield. The wipers cleared it away, only to have the glass instantly covered again. Snowflakes were falling so hard that even with the wipers on high, she could barely see the road ahead as they headed for their cabin.

Between the clack of the wipers and the wind whipping around the SUV, they couldn't hear each other talk even if they'd wanted to. Feeling numb, Morgan stared out at the storm. It was the worst one she'd seen in a long time. She realized that Tom had to have known about it before he'd brought her up here. Was he hoping they would get snowed in? Was that another reason he'd picked such an isolated place in the mountains in the middle of winter?

While he focused intently on his driving, she tried to make sense of what he'd told her. He had admitted that he'd lied to her not only about his past, but about the text message, about a woman he'd been in love with, and even about his real name, because of some tragedy.

Morgan tried to imagine what. A dozen scenarios flashed through her mind—none of them warranting lies and deceptions, let alone changing his name. And at the heart of it, she feared what else he might have lied about.

Hadn't "A" threatened to tell his wife *everything?* About his past? Or was there something even more damaging?

The memory came at Morgan like a freight train, even though it had only been a scent. When she'd opened the door to her apartment a week ago, Tom had been standing at the far window, his back to her. She'd frowned as she'd sniffed the air. Perfume. Just not hers.

"Morgan? I didn't expect you back so soon," he'd said, turning in obvious surprise to look at her standing frozen in the doorway. She'd seen something cross his expression. Guilt? Or just concern? "Is something wrong?"

"Sorry, I just smelled…perfume. I was trying to place the scent."

"Oh, that," Tom had said as he'd gotten up to come toward her. "A neighbor stopped by earlier asking if I'd seen her dog. She reeked of perfume."

Morgan had forgotten about it until this moment. The scent had permeated the apartment—and when Tom had hugged her, she'd smelled it on his shirt.

But back then, she'd still been the trusting girlfriend. Now she felt like a fool—the foolish wife. Why hadn't she questioned his story about someone in her building looking for a lost dog? Pets weren't allowed, but then Tom probably didn't know that.

He was on the last switchback to the cabin when the SUV fishtailed, the rear tires sliding into the shallow, snow-filled ditch next to the trees. He tried for a few minutes to get the vehicle unstuck. But Morgan had already realized that was futile. They wouldn't be getting it out anytime soon.

She had never felt so alone. Or so terrified. It had been a mistake coming back here with him. But she had only herself to blame for ending up deep in the woods, in the middle of a blizzard, with a stranger. Possibly a dangerous stranger.

It crossed her mind that if she was going to need saving, she was going to have to do it herself.

LUKE TRIED REPEATEDLY to reach Morgan again. He was running scared. After what he'd learned about Tom Cooper, there was no doubt in his mind that she was in danger.

Another blizzard warning came over the scanner on his desk. A *series* of winter storms were coming in, one after another, with blowing and drifting snow, below zero temperatures, and avalanche warnings in the high mountains. Morgan was *in* the high mountains. The thought shook Luke to his core.

He couldn't help but remember the first time he'd seen her. She'd been only a few years out of college, with very little experience, but he'd instantly recognized her talent as a photographer. There was also something about her that had attracted him from the start.

They'd begun going to lunch together, their first interest in common being unusual foods. They'd tried different restaurants, and over these lunches they'd talked about everything. Morgan had laughed at his jokes, and he'd gotten hers.

He'd never met anyone who was so fun and enthusiastic—about life and her career as a photographer. He had loved spending time with her.

It was funny. At first everyone at the paper was positive they were having an affair since he and Morgan had their heads together so much.

They'd both laughed about that. Maybe that's when he'd realized he would do anything to keep the relationship they had—even if it meant keeping his feelings to himself.

Then along came Tom Cooper.

Luke still cringed when he thought about what he'd done when he'd heard Morgan was planning to marry the guy.

"Step into the darkroom for a minute," he'd told her. The space, now out-of-date because of digital photography, was used for storage these days, but it was the only private place in the newspaper office.

"Is something wrong?" she'd asked, appearing concerned.

What was wrong was that she was marrying a man she'd known for less than two months. The *wrong* man, Luke had wanted to say. True, he and Tom hadn't liked each other from day one.

He had seen how possessive Tom was of Morgan, putting his arm around her shoulders the first time they'd met, as if staking his claim. But it was more than that. Tom had perceived Luke as a threat from the beginning. Had Tom sensed Luke's feelings for Morgan? Luke didn't think the guy was good enough for her. Then again, he would have thought that of any man.

After that first meeting, Tom had kept Morgan away from newspaper events. She'd promised to come, but would call later to say Tom had surprised her with something else planned for that night.

Luke had struggled that day in the darkroom to find the right words, but unable to, he'd stepped close to her, grasped her shoulders and kissed her.

Without a doubt, it had been the stupidest thing he could have done. He was a reporter, a man who worked with words for a living, and yet he didn't know how to tell Morgan that he'd fallen madly in love with her and didn't want her marrying Tom.

As he'd drawn back after kissing her, he had tried to read her expression.

"What was that?" she'd whispered.

He'd stammered for a moment, then said, "Something I've been wanting to do since the first day you walked in here. Morgan, I—"

"Luke, I'm getting married Saturday."

He should have done his damnedest to talk her out of it. But he'd seen her shocked reaction to the kiss, so he'd said, "Then I wish you all the best." What a jackass he'd been. Instead of telling her how he really felt, he'd wished her the best?

On impulse, Luke dialed the number of the Ice Lake Lodge and was surprised when his call went through. "I wanted to check on a guest staying there. She was going to try to leave before the storm got worse. I need to know if she made it out. Her name is Morgan Sinclair."

"We don't have a Sinclair—"

"Sorry, I should have given you her married name." He gritted his teeth as he said, "Cooper. Mrs. Tom Cooper."

"Oh, yes, here it is. Mr. and Mrs. Cooper."

"Could you please ring their room?" Luke knew there was a chance Tom would answer the phone and be furious he had called, even if Luke pretended it was about work. But he had to know that Morgan was all right.

"I'm sorry, the Coopers are staying in the Mountain Badger Cabin, where there is no phone service. Can I take a message? They might stop by the lodge at some point."

Morgan was alone with the man at some cabin, instead of at the lodge? Luke hung up and quickly looked up Ice Lake Resort on his computer. It took him only a moment to find the map of the place, and he swore under his breath.

Tom had rented the cabin farthest from the main lodge?

Apprehension washed over him. He tried Morgan's cell phone one more time, and when he couldn't get through, he printed out a copy of the resort map and headed to the managing editor's office.

"I need to take the rest of the day off," he said. "I know it's my weekend to work, but there's a good chance I won't be in tomorrow, either."

His boss frowned. "Are you sick?"

"It's…personal. I need to go somewhere. It could be a matter of life or death."

The man's eyebrows rose. "Where, exactly, are you going?"

"Ice Lake."

The editor leaned forward and lowered his voice. "Isn't that where your friend at the police station said the stranglers' victim is recuperating?"

"This doesn't have anything to do with that." At least Luke hoped not. "I also need to borrow your snowmobile."

CHAPTER SIX

TOM TRIED ONCE MORE to get unstuck, but the tires spun and the SUV didn't budge. As he turned off the engine, he glanced over at Morgan, as if about to apologize.

She realized how little she trusted him now. Had he gotten the SUV stuck on purpose, so she couldn't leave him once he told her the truth?

"You don't think I got stuck on purpose, do you?" Tom asked, no doubt reading her expression. He let out a curse as he opened his door and got out.

Morgan opened her door, too, and was instantly forced to hang on to it to keep the wind from ripping it from her hand. Once out, she slammed it, struggling against the blinding snow as she headed up the road in the direction of the cabin.

She waded through the drifts, understanding how easy it would be to get lost out here. She knew of ranchers who used a rope system to get from their houses to their barns in blizzards like this. Suddenly, she realized she hadn't seen Tom's tracks in the snow ahead of her. Was he back at the SUV, trying to get it unstuck?

A gust of wind whirled snow around her for a moment, and then she caught a glimpse of the cabin. There was a light on in the living room. Morgan frowned. She didn't remember leaving one on. Tom must have turned on a lamp when he'd gone back for his wallet earlier.

Stumbling up the steps and into the chilly unit, she shrugged off her coat and hat, then moved to the fireplace. The embers had died while they'd been gone.

Always practical, she began to build a fire, even though she doubted it would warm her. She was shivering uncontrollably when she heard Tom come in. He stomped snow off his boots at the door. She didn't turn, couldn't look at him right now.

"Here, let me do that," he said from behind her.

"I have it," she snapped, still not looking at him. She heard him take off his coat. He didn't try to touch her, didn't even come near her, as if he knew it would be the wrong thing to do right now.

She'd been so busy working and taking care of her mother, she hadn't had time to date much before meeting Tom. No wonder he had been able to sweep her off her feet, she thought as she heard him head toward the bedroom.

Reminding herself of all the lies he'd told her, Morgan wondered if he was finally going to tell her the truth—or merely come up with more lies. That Luke was the one who'd found out the truth about Tom made it worse. Luke must think her such a fool. All her friends had tried to warn her that she was moving too fast, especially him.

She couldn't bear to think of him right now, or that kiss in the darkroom. Had a part of her wanted him to stop her from marrying Tom? Hoped that he'd tell her he loved her, wanted her, couldn't live without her?

With a shock, she realized that she would have cancelled the wedding. As much as she'd believed in her heart that she loved Tom, one word from Luke that day and she would have called off everything with Tom.

She would have had to until she resolved her feelings for Luke.

Feelings for Luke? She laughed to herself. Tom had picked up on them. Probably everybody in the newsroom had. As it turned out, Luke had simply wanted to wish her luck with her marriage. Clearly, he hadn't been trying to stop her from marrying Tom. Right? He was a good friend, she thought, remembering how worried he was about her now.

Morgan turned only when she heard Tom let out an oath. He was standing in the bedroom doorway, shoulders slumped, head down. The sight of him sent a dagger of icy fear up her spine. With the memory of the snowman fresh in her mind, she demanded in a tight, strained voice, "What is it?"

As she took a step toward him, he motioned for her to stay back. But she was already moving, unable to stop even though she knew, whatever it was, she wouldn't want to see it.

The far wall of the bedroom was smeared with what looked at first to be blood. But she quickly realized it was too red for that. Words appeared out of the mess, vulgar angry words scrawled with venom and spray paint across their bedroom wall.

A cry escaped Morgan's lips as she stumbled back from the horrible sight. Her eyes filled with tears of both fear and anger.

Tom hurriedly closed the bedroom door and stepped toward her. He was shaking his head as if he couldn't believe this any more than she could.

But she knew that wasn't true.

"This has something to do with your past," she declared, and saw her accusation hit its mark.

He stopped inches from her, his face filling with anguish as he said, "I'm so sorry. You can't know how sorry I am."

Morgan dropped into the nearest chair. Her limbs felt as if they were made of water. And while her brain was screaming, *"Run! Get out of here before it gets any worse!"* she couldn't move, could barely speak. "It's her, isn't it? The woman who sent you the text message. Allison Stuart."

He slowly lowered himself into the chair across from Morgan and dropped his head into his hands. "It has to be, and yet I don't understand how she could have found us."

Morgan fought for breath, feeling as if all the oxygen in the room had suddenly been sucked out. "Why is she doing this?"

Tom lifted his head, and she saw the guilt in his eyes. He knew exactly why. "You have to believe me. I hadn't seen her in years—not until last week. I thought she was out of my life."

Morgan wanted to throw up. "You were in love with her?"

He nodded. "In high school. We were going to get married, but then, like I told you, something horrible happened." He seemed to struggle with his next words. "My parents and siblings were murdered."

She stared at him, aghast. For a moment she didn't know what to say. Why would he lie about his identity unless… She felt her eyes widen, her heart take off like a rocket. "Tell me you didn't—"

"How could you even think that?" He gave her an incredulous look. "Don't you know me at *all?*"

"Apparently not. Why didn't you tell me this? Why would you keep it from me if you had nothing to hide?"

Because there is more to the story, she thought with a sinking feeling.

"I was out with Allison the night they were murdered. When I came home, I found them."

She saw his pain, felt it at heart level. It melted her anger a little. "I'm sorry. I can't imagine..."

"If that wasn't bad enough, the media descended on the small town where we lived. It was a circus. Reporters were constantly pushing microphones into our faces."

The small town in Arkansas. Something flickered in her memory. Some news story about ten years ago. "So you left the South and changed your name."

He nodded, giving her a guilty smile. "I thought I'd put it all behind me, including the accent. I guess I was wrong. But you have to understand. Everywhere I went, I was the kid whose family was slaughtered."

Slaughtered. She shivered, trying to block out the thought of what it must have been like for him to come home and find his family...gone.

Seeing her shiver, Tom went to the fireplace and threw more logs on the blaze as he talked. "It only got worse when Allison's older brother was arrested for the murders," he said, his back to her.

Morgan couldn't help gasping in shock. "Why would he hurt your family?"

"Apparently, because my father had kicked him out of the hardware store we owned in town. He had tried to steal some tools, but Dad caught him and told him never to come back. Dad didn't call the cops, I guess because I was dating Allison. I wish he had."

If he had, maybe Tom's family would still be alive. "You said siblings?"

"A sister and brother. Joey was six. Melody four."

"Oh, Tom, I'm so sorry. They're sure it was Allison's brother?"

He nodded. "Allison adored her older brother and was very protective of him. She was inconsolable. And his arrest made it impossible for us to see each other, what with the town crawling with reporters, all wanting to turn our tragedy into tomorrow's headlines."

The way he said "reporters" made her think of Luke, and Tom's instant dislike of him. Maybe it had never been jealousy. She tried to imagine what he'd gone through, but couldn't.

"I went away to college. Allison still had another year of high school. She couldn't have left, anyway. Her parents needed her. I took the coward's way out. I ran as far away as I could, and changed my name. I couldn't stand the way people looked at me when they recognized the name Eric Wagner."

Morgan's eyes widened with recognition. Goose bumps skittered over her skin as she recalled the media stories. She hugged herself. "Oh, my God."

LUKE DROVE HIS editor's snowmobile up onto the back of the four-wheel drive pickup and then headed for Ice Lake. The trip normally took less than an hour, but with the weather…

His every instinct told him Morgan was in terrible trouble.

"Why Ice Lake?" he'd asked her when she'd told him about their plans for the short honeymoon.

"Tom thought it would be nice," she'd said. "He said the lodge is beautiful."

She hadn't sounded that excited about the prospect of spending her honeymoon there. But what stuck in his mind now was that *Tom* had chosen it. Luke hoped to hell it was just a coincidence that the surviving victim of the Big Sky Stranglers was staying there.

As he drove through the snowstorm, he tried to tamp down his fear. He reminded himself that Morgan was smart and capable. But even as he thought it, he couldn't forget that Tom had fooled her from the moment they'd met. The man had conned her into falling in love and marrying him. What would he do when he realized he'd been caught?

Luke shook his head as he recalled something that had happened at the wedding. Morgan had invited only a handful of friends, including a few from college. Tom, who was new to town, claimed his friends and family from Seattle couldn't make it on such short notice. He'd added that he and Morgan would throw a party in the summer and get all his relatives and friends out to Montana. Another lie.

But it was what one of Morgan's college friends had told him that now kept Luke's foot nailed to the gas pedal as he raced through the storm toward Ice Lake. She had been with the soon-to-be-bride before the ceremony, helping her dress, when Morgan had suddenly looked as if she was going to pass out.

"Did she explain what was wrong?" Luke had asked.

"She said she hadn't eaten breakfast and was just feeling a little faint." The college friend had dropped her voice. "Then Morgan said, 'Tell me I'm not making a mistake.'"

"What did you tell her?" Luke had asked.

"I didn't know what to say. You're closer to her than I am. Do you think she's making a mistake?"

He had. But he'd answered, "I just want Morgan to be happy."

Now Luke wanted to kick himself. The signs had

been there all along. Not only was something terribly wrong about Tom Cooper, but Morgan had sensed it on some level. Tom had rushed her to the altar, no doubt realizing she was having misgivings.

If any of her friends had just spoken up, they could have stopped this. If *he* had spoken up… Luke shook his head. It was far too late for what-ifs.

But he couldn't help remembering that day after the wedding, how cold her hands had been when she'd thanked him for being there.

"Promise me we will always be friends," she'd said.

He'd smiled and squeezed her hands. "Always."

But Luke had known he'd lost her. Tom would see to that. Especially if he ever found out about that darkroom kiss.

CHAPTER SEVEN

ERIC WAGNER.

Morgan's mind whirled like the snow outside the cabin as she pictured shots of the murder house, the bodies. It had been a massacre and on all the news about ten years ago. More like twelve.

Here in the cabin, the fire licked at the logs in the grate. The soft crackle of dry pine was the only sound in the room. Tom stood silhouetted against the blaze, his head down. He seemed to be waiting for her reaction to everything he'd told her.

Still in shock, she glanced toward the closed bedroom door, remembering what she'd seen scrawled on the wall. "Why would your old girlfriend..." Morgan stopped as she realized what could have made a woman react in such a way. "You broke her heart."

"I deserted her when she needed me the most," he said, his voice tight with some strong emotion. Guilt? Regret? "I was planning to marry her, but after what happened..."

He looked beaten, broken, his back to her as if he could no longer face her. This man, her *husband,* had been through something so horrible she couldn't even comprehend it. What that must have done to him...

Morgan rose and went to him, wrapping her arms around his waist and pressing her face into his warm back. "You can't blame yourself."

She felt him flinch, and drew away as he turned to face her. One look at his expression and she knew. "There's more, isn't there?"

"We fought about her brother," he said. "I wasn't very understanding."

"How could you be? He *killed* your *family*." *Slaughtered them.*

"He was sick—that's how she saw it. She didn't want him to go to prison. She was afraid for him because of what the other inmates would do to him, and the whole time he kept denying what he'd done. Maybe if he would have unburdened himself…"

Morgan shook her head. "I can see how awful this was for both of you, but still that doesn't excuse her—"

"Allison was pregnant with my baby when I left."

Morgan felt all the air rush from her lungs.

"She miscarried and wasn't able to have any more children."

It took Morgan a moment to realize there was only one way he could know that. "She told you this recently. How many times have you seen her?"

He dragged his gaze away and Morgan's heart fell. As she dropped into the chair again, he said, "Three times. I wanted to tell you—"

"Before we got married. Yes, that would have been a good idea."

His gaze came back to her and she saw why he'd continued to lie even before he spoke. "I was afraid you would call off the wedding."

With a start, Morgan remembered the "ushers" Tom had hired to stand outside the church. "You thought she might try to stop the ceremony."

He didn't have to reply.

"Did she threaten you? *Us?*" Of course she had.

Morgan covered her face with her hands for a moment. "The brother was homicidal and now his crazy, vengeful sister is after us, and you didn't think to tell me? Better yet, call the police?"

"She's just *hurt*."

"No, Tom," Morgan said, getting to her feet. "Someone who is 'just hurt' doesn't follow us on our honeymoon and stomp our snowman flat or write obscenities all over our bedroom wall." A thought struck her. "How did she even know we were coming here?"

He shook his head. "I swear to you I don't know. I certainly didn't tell her. She must have followed us."

Morgan remembered him checking his rearview mirror yesterday. She realized now that he'd been worried that Allison would tail them.

"We have to call the sheriff." Morgan pulled out her cell phone. Earlier, Luke had been able to get through, but they'd been cut off. With the blizzard howling outside… "No service." She snapped the phone shut and looked toward the front window and the driving snow, wondering where Allison was.

Only a crazy person would go out in a snowstorm like this.

"Honey, I should have told you," Tom said, reaching for her. "I tried so many times."

She sidestepped his embrace. "You didn't try hard enough."

"I didn't want you to see me as Eric Wagner. I only wanted to be Tom Cooper to you. Can't you understand that?"

Actually, she could. She wished his past had never come up, but he'd been naive to think that he could keep such a secret. Especially when there was an ex-girlfriend in town with a need for vengeance.

"I am the one person on earth who needed to know who you really are," Morgan snapped.

"You know who I really am. I'm *not* Eric Wagner. He died the night he opened the door of his house to find his family murdered. I had to put all of that to rest. I didn't want to spend my life defined by that horrible tragedy. I knew it would destroy me."

"Why has it taken her more than ten years to come after you?" Morgan asked, as she had another thought. She'd been pacing, angry and scared, but now stopped to face him.

He shrugged. "Well, last I heard, she'd been in and out of mental hospitals. Until recently. And I was thinking it must have been the marriage license that led her to me now. It's the only paperwork that left a trail to me."

Morgan remembered how surprised she'd been when she'd realized that Tom didn't have any credit cards and always used cash. Even when he bought a car. Was it possible that their marriage license was how the woman had found him?

Tom looked sick. Morgan stared at him, weakening as she saw the pain in his face. How could she not feel compassion for everything he'd been through? He was a victim, just as much as his family and his high school girlfriend and her family had been.

"Maybe if we talked to Allison—"

"I wish it was that easy," Tom said. "Her brother was killed last year in prison. She's made it clear she will never forgive me."

"She can't blame you for that."

"At her brother's trial, she pleaded with me to beg the judge for leniency for Louis. I didn't. I couldn't. If you had seen my little brother and sister..."

"What does she want, Tom?"

He shook his head. "I'm not even sure she knows. I've told her how sorry I am. I've offered her money, which in retrospect was a mistake. I don't have enough to make up for the past."

"She wants *you*."

He fell silent.

"And she wants me…what?" Morgan's eyes widened as she saw the answer in his own.

"I won't let her hurt you," he said quickly as he stepped to her, drawing her gently into his arms and cradling her against him.

"What are we going to do?" Morgan hated the trembling in her voice.

"We're going to get out of here and go to the police. That's what I should have done in the first place."

The strength she'd loved about Tom returned to his voice and his demeanor. He'd been so capable and caring after her mother died. Was it any wonder she'd entrusted her love and her life to him?

"I have a set of chains in the back of the SUV," he said. "You pack up our things. Even if we can only make it as far as the lodge, you'll be safe there." He let go of her to return to the bedroom.

Morgan looked toward the front window at the raging storm, remembering the hateful words scrawled on the bedroom wall. With chains on the SUV, they should be able to get to the lodge, where Allison Stuart couldn't harm them. Maybe they could even get to town and the police.

"Here," Tom said, pressing something cold into her hand.

She stared down at the gun, then up at him in surprise.

"It's loaded. I'm assuming you know how to fire it, being a Montana girl."

She could only nod. *He'd brought a gun?* He'd been more than worried that there was a chance Allison would follow them—he'd been ready.

Tom gave her a quick kiss. As he drew back, he said, "Coming here was a terrible idea. I'm sorry. But you have to believe me. I was going to tell you everything this weekend and let the chips fall where they may, I swear."

She wanted to believe him. There'd been a point when she'd had misgivings, right before the wedding. But she'd thought it was simply cold feet. Hadn't she wanted to believe that together they could overcome anything? She hoped that was true now.

"Are you sure you don't want to take the gun?" she said as she watched Tom dress to head down the road in the storm to put the chains on the SUV. "Maybe I should go with you."

"No, you're safer here with the doors locked and a loaded weapon. I don't want to have to worry about you."

She checked the safety on the handgun and stuffed it into her vest pocket as he moved to the front door.

"Lock up behind me." He hesitated for a moment, as if there was more he wanted to say. "Don't open the door. No matter what. And if you have to, use the gun."

The moment he stepped out, she fastened the lock, then checked the back door, as well. From the window, she watched Tom disappear into the blizzard, swallowed up by the whirling snow as he stepped off the porch.

She quickly turned away. Restless, she threw more logs on the fire. The gun felt heavy in the pocket of her winter vest. As she started toward the bedroom to pack, she saw that Tom had brought all their belongings out so she wouldn't have to go back in there.

He had always been thoughtful and protective. She suddenly felt a paralyzing fear for him. He was unarmed, and with the snow falling as it was, he wouldn't hear or see Allison coming.

On impulse, Morgan grabbed her coat, moved the gun from her vest to her coat pocket and headed for the door. She opened it cautiously and scanned the porch before stepping out. It was empty. No Allison.

But as Morgan headed down the steps, she saw something in the snow that made her stumble to a stop, her heart in her throat.

Tom's tracks, while filling in quickly, were still clearly visible. She stared at them, shaking her head in both shock and disbelief.

Tom hadn't headed back down the road to where they'd left the stuck SUV.

Instead, his tracks disappeared in the same direction as the ones Morgan had found earlier, after discovering their ruined honeymoon snowman—toward that nearby cabin in the woods.

She felt so betrayed and alone she almost sat down in the snow and cried. Tom had known all along where Allison was staying. He'd lied yet again. He hadn't gone to put chains on the SUV so they could go to the lodge. He'd gone to see his crazy, vindictive old girlfriend.

CHAPTER EIGHT

LUKE ALMOST MISSED the turnoff to Ice Lake Resort, the snow was coming down so hard. Wind whipped the icy flakes across the road in what locals called "snow-snakes."

He regretted telling Morgan anything. He should have waited until she returned from her weekend honeymoon—if it wasn't already too late.

That thought shook him to his core. The short, close-to-home honeymoon. Was that, too, a sign?

He was terrified Tom Cooper might have chosen the resort for a reason that had nothing to do with a honey-moon escape. Just as he'd chosen the cabin farthest from the lodge for a reason.

As Luke turned up the narrow road, he prayed he would get there in time. He knew his chances of driv-ing all the way to Ice Lake Resort were unlikely, given that the route was deep with snow and drifting badly. But he figured he might make better time on the snow-mobile, anyway.

His cell phone rang. He grabbed it, praying it was Morgan.

It was his friend the private investigator, who'd promised to see what else he could find out about Tom Cooper aka Eric Wagner.

"The sheriff in Oak County, Arkansas, arrested a man named Louis Stuart for the crime. He was convicted and sent to prison for life. But, Luke, the sheriff said he has always suspected that the wrong man went to prison, that Louis was framed."

"What are you saying?"

"There were several suspects. One of them was Eric Wagner. The other was his girlfriend."

Luke gripped the steering wheel, his knuckles white. "The sheriff thought Eric Wagner might have killed his own family?" Luke had been in the newspaper business long enough that he shouldn't have been shocked. But this was the man Morgan had married. The man who was now alone with her at an isolated mountain cabin. Even the thought that Tom Cooper might be a killer…

"Actually, the sheriff said he has always suspected that Eric and his girlfriend, Allison Stuart, might have done the deed together. That's definitely what the older brother who went to prison believed."

"Wait," Luke said, trying to drive through the storm and still make sense of everything. "The man you believed was framed was the girlfriend's older brother?"

"Yep. He was killed last year during an altercation in the prison. For years, he'd claimed he was innocent."

Luke couldn't believe this. "You said Eric was out with his girlfriend that night, so they were each other's alibi." He swore. "No one else saw them at the time of the murders?"

"Nope. It was just their word that they were parked up on some mountain outside of town, doing what teenagers do at that age," his friend said.

"So they might have both lied. What did you find out about this old girlfriend, Allison Stuart?"

"That's where it gets interesting. She flew into Montana last week. Until now, she's been in and out of mental institutions."

Heart pounding, Luke hung up and floored the pickup, even though he knew he was taking a hell of a chance, given the road conditions and the visibility. But he was suddenly terrified for Morgan.

MORGAN STARED AT the tracks in the snow. Tom had lied again. She stumbled back against the steps, grabbing the porch railing to keep from falling. She'd believed him. She'd felt compassion for him. She'd forgiven him for lying to her and had remembered why she'd fallen in love with him.

And what had he done?

Lied right to her face. Again.

Had he ever planned to put chains on the SUV? Or had that just been a ruse?

She pulled herself up the stairs, the wind howling around her. Snow pelted her face and had already formed another drift against the cabin door.

Her hand found the gun she'd stuffed in her pocket—and her cell phone. She hurriedly pulled out the phone, not bothering to wait until she got inside out of the cold before she hit Redial.

Luke would be at work. He would call the sheriff. As she heard his cell phone begin to ring, Morgan realized the sheriff probably couldn't get up the road in his patrol car by now. Even if he could, he wouldn't arrive before Tom returned.

The ringing stopped. She looked down at her phone. Searching for service.

With a cry of frustration, she snapped it shut and shoved it back into her pocket. She looked out through the falling snow toward the other cabin. Tom could be coming back any moment.

Hurriedly, she opened the door, stepped inside and

closed it behind her. As she started to lock it, it dawned on her how stupid she'd been. Not just in trusting Tom, but in bothering to lock the door.

Both doors, front and back, had been locked when she and Tom had left for brunch earlier, and still Allison had gotten in. Either Tom had forgotten to lock it after he'd gone back for his wallet...or Allison had a key to their cabin.

But if that was true...

Morgan turned, knowing she shouldn't have be surprised when she found a woman she'd never seen before standing just inside the back door with a gun in her hand.

CHAPTER NINE

TOM KNOCKED AGAIN at the cabin door, then tried the handle. The knob turned in his gloved hand. "Allison?"

He stepped inside, thinking she must not have heard his knock with the wind howling the way it was. He was lucky he'd found the cabin at all in that blizzard outside. "Allison!"

The place felt chilly, and he noticed that she'd let her fire burn out. He could still smell the smoke as he walked in. The cabin was exactly like the one he and Morgan shared. Except there was no red spray paint on the bedroom wall, he noticed, as he glanced through the open doorway.

The bathroom door was also open. Both rooms were empty.

He let out a curse. He'd told Allison to sit tight, when he'd spoken to her from a lodge phone earlier. He'd asked her to wait, saying he would get away as soon as he could so they could talk.

Though there really was nothing to talk about, and he didn't want to spend time arguing with her. Either she could accept the way things were going to be or he would have to make sure she got nowhere near Morgan.

But where the hell was Allison? Surely she hadn't gone to the lodge for something. In hindsight, giving her money had been a mistake. He knew she'd just want more.

Stepping into the small kitchen, he opened the refrigerator. Empty except for ice cubes. She hadn't thought to bring food?

He slammed the door and headed for the bedroom, wondering what she *had* brought. Allison used to hunt with her dad and brother. Her family had owned all kinds of guns, not that she could have gotten one on the plane. Still, she would know where to get one. Here in Montana, a weapon could be bought at any gun show or from a classified ad in the newspaper.

There would be no record of a gun purchased from a private individual. Allison was a smart woman. She would know how to work the system, and that worried him.

He glanced at his watch. He had to get back to Morgan. But where was Allison? She'd promised she would wait so they could get this hashed out.

At the back door, he looked out. Did he really expect her to come slogging through the drifts from the direction of the lodge? He'd started to close the door when he saw tracks in the snow behind the cabin.

With a shock, he realized there was only one reason Allison would take the back way—in the opposite direction from the lodge.

THE WOMAN WAS PETITE and blonde, with big blue eyes and a small, slightly turned-up nose. The freckles that dusted her cheeks made her look much younger than the age Morgan knew she must be.

Allison Stuart wouldn't have looked dangerous at all if it wasn't for the large handgun she gripped, the barrel leveled at Morgan's heart.

Surprisingly, the gun didn't frighten her as much as the tears in the other woman's eyes.

"Tom went to see you." Morgan wasn't sure why she said that, given the situation. It was just the first thought that popped into her head.

"I know. I saw him and took the back way. That's why I'm here." Her voice was soft and Southern and cracked with emotion. "We don't have much time."

Time for what? Morgan was afraid to ask. She thought of the gun in her coat pocket, but feared what the woman would do if she tried to reach for it.

"So you're his wife."

"And you're Allison." Morgan did her best not to appear as terrified as she suddenly felt. The woman seemed meek—except for the gun. But there was that destroyed snowman, and the horrible threatening words scrawled in red paint on the bedroom wall.

"He told you about me?" Allison asked, sounding surprised.

"He had to, didn't he? After what you did to our snowman and our bedroom wall."

The woman frowned. "I'm sorry. I don't know what you're talking about."

Apparently Tom wasn't the only liar in his former relationship.

Morgan felt anger burn through her veins, hot as flowing lava. "Right. You didn't destroy our snowman, spray paint obscenities on our bedroom wall or follow us here. Next thing you're going to tell me that's not a real gun you're holding on me."

"Oh, the gun is real, but I don't know anything about a snowman or—"

"You didn't write that on the wall?" Morgan demanded, stepping toward the bedroom and flinging open the door.

All the anger died in her as she saw the expression

on the other woman's face. Terror. Morgan frowned in confusion as she thought about the snowman she and Tom had built together, and the obvious violence with which it had been destroyed. Violence and hatred. Just like the words painted on the wall.

"If you didn't do this, then who..." The rest of Morgan's words died on her lips and she felt herself begin to tremble. She shook her head. "Tom wouldn't—"

"His name is Eric Wagner, and you have no idea what he is capable of doing. He let my brother die in prison for a crime he didn't commit," she said, pain shimmering in her blue eyes.

"Your brother killed Tom's family."

"Is that what Eric told you?" She let out a sound, half laugh, half sob.

It sent a chill down Morgan's spine.

"I was with him that night. Don't you think I know what happened? I begged him to at least spare his little brother and sister, but he said they were old enough to testify against him."

This was all wrong. "No, he wouldn't...he couldn't." Morgan thought of Tom. He might be a liar, *was* a liar, but he wasn't a killer.

"He told you he was out with me that night, didn't he?" Allison demanded. "That he dropped me off and went home and found them?" She nodded, as if she knew exactly what he'd said. "That was the story he came up with after he killed them. He took a shower, burned his bloody clothes, then he changed and took me home."

Morgan was shaking her head, fighting the urge to put her hands over her ears.

"I couldn't bear another minute in that house. I started walking home, but he came after me. I remember the feel of his pickup's headlights on my back. I stepped off the road and almost took off through the woods. But I knew he would track me down, and when he did, he'd kill me, too."

"If he is a killer, then why didn't he?" Morgan asked. "Wasn't he afraid you would talk?"

Allison let out a humorless laugh. "I was his alibi. The sheriff would have been suspicious if I had been killed, too. No, he needed me alive and scared. He knew I would lie for him to protect my baby."

The baby Allison lost. "If you're so afraid of him, then why do you want him back? Why follow him to Montana, to Ice Lake?"

Allison looked shocked. "*He's* the one who found *me*. He sent me a plane ticket to come up here. How do you think I knew where the two of you would be? That's why I waited until I saw him leave this cabin. I came here to warn you."

No, this was all twisted to make it look like Tom—Eric—was… "If you came to warn me, then why did you bring that gun?" Morgan glanced from the woman's face to the gun gripped in her hands.

"I wasn't sure you would listen without this." Allison's voice broke. "He plans to kill you."

"Why would he do that? He married me—"

"For your money." She must have seen Morgan's surprise. "He knows about the money your mother left you. He's known almost since he met you. Why do you think he rushed you into marrying him?"

Morgan felt her legs give out from under her. She stumbled back and sat down hard on the hearth. It was one thing to hear that Tom knew about her inheritance. It was another to realize that there was only one way *Allison* could have known about it.

"I don't believe you," Morgan managed to say around the lump that had formed in her throat. It was a lie and Allison knew it.

She moved closer and lowered the gun. "Why do you think he killed his entire family? His father had just come into some money. Eric knew he would never see a cent of it, the way he and his dad got along. His father made him work in the hardware store every day after school, and Eric hated it."

"No," Morgan said, but it was a feeble, defeated sound. "Why would you fly here if you knew—"

"He sent me the plane ticket so I could help him get rid of you. He promised to marry me and share the money with me. You think I don't know what he really has planned?" Allison scoffed at that. "I came because I knew if I didn't, I'd always be looking over my shoulder, knowing that one day he'd be coming after me. The only reason he hasn't before now was because I've been sick."

Sick? "He said you've been in mental institutions." *A good reason not to believe anything the woman says,* Morgan reminded herself.

"I couldn't live with what had happened. I had a nervous breakdown, and when I finally told the truth, no one believed me."

Morgan shook her head. "I don't believe you, either."

"I was there that night. I heard their screams. I'm the only eyewitness. I'm sure Eric's been planning how to get rid of me for years. He just couldn't get to me as long as I was in the mental institution. But now that I'm out...he's figured on a way to get rid of both of us."

Where was Tom? Morgan wondered. He should have been back by now. Or maybe after he went to Allison's cabin, he really did go down to put chains on the SUV.

"You want to know who destroyed your snowman and scrawled those words on that wall? Eric. He wants you to think I'm the one you have to fear. He plans to kill you, make it look like I did it, then kill me. He gets rid of us both and everyone who knows the truth. Then he walks away with your inheritance."

Morgan looked at her. "But he signed—"

"A prenuptial agreement? Except if you're dead…"

"No, Tom—"

"There *is* no Tom Cooper. There is only Eric Wagner." Allison suddenly glanced over Morgan's shoulder, the woman's terror palpable in the small cabin. "He's going to be coming back any minute. You'd better decide who you believe."

CHAPTER TEN

LUKE SAW A VAN STUCK in the middle of the road ahead. He swore and hit his brakes. There was no way he was getting by. Fortunately, he wasn't that far from the lodge, just a few miles. He took the pistol he kept under the seat of his pickup, checked to make sure it was loaded, and tucked it into his coat pocket.

Hurriedly, he looked around and found a place to pull off and unload the snowmobile. He drove the machine off the bed of the truck and onto the snowpack at the edge of the road as fast as he could.

Steering around the stuck van, he saw that the vehicle was empty. The driver must have already hiked down to the highway to catch a ride.

Luke gave the snowmobile full throttle and raced up the road, bursting through one drift after another. Snow billowed up in a blinding cloud around him, with a dizzying effect.

He tried not to let himself consider what might have already happened to Morgan. When he thought of her, he saw her in sunshine, her hair ablaze with the golden light, her eyes bright as diamonds. He smiled at the memory of those sunny days when a group from the newspaper had played miniature golf during their lunch hour.

She'd been good, often beating him. He thought about how fun it had been and how, when Tom came into her life, Luke had known the lunches, the miniature golf, all that was behind them. A lot of other little things were behind them, as well.

Funny how it was often the small things that broke your heart.

Visibility improved once the road narrowed, and he could make out the blur of dark pines through the falling snow. He drove as quickly as possible, feeling time slipping away.

All he could do was pray Morgan was all right. What if he was wrong about Tom Cooper? What if the right man had gone to prison and Tom was merely a victim, and by now Morgan had forgiven her husband for lying to her?

Luke could live with that. As long as Morgan was all right, that's what mattered. As he raced on, the roar of the snowmobile engine loud in his ears, all his instincts told him that the last thing Morgan was doing right now was enjoying her honeymoon.

MORGAN HEARD THE THUMP of boot heels on the porch at the same time Allison did.

"Do you believe me?" the woman cried in a hoarse whisper, her voice tight with alarm.

Morgan didn't get a chance to answer before they heard the key in the lock. The door swung open and Tom stepped in.

"Stay right there," Allison ordered, swinging the gun so it was pointed at him. She stepped back, making it possible to cover both Tom and Morgan if either of them tried anything.

"She knows, Eric," Allison said. "I told her *everything.*"

He nodded. "That must make you feel better." When

he spoke again, it was to Morgan. "She hasn't hurt you, has she?"

She shook her head, although she'd never been more hurt, scared or uncertain.

Tom slowly closed the door behind him and then looked at Allison. "You don't want to do this," he said quietly to her. "This isn't going to accomplish anything."

"I can't let you kill her," Allison said.

"I'm not going to kill anyone."

The woman shook her head. "I told you, she knows *everything*."

He cocked his head, and when he spoke there was sadness in his tone. "You've been in a mental institution off and on for the past twelve years. I understand—you're sick. But—"

"You did that to me," she cried. "I couldn't live with what I saw you do. When I tried to tell the truth, no one believed me. You made sure of that."

He shook his head and glanced at Morgan as if to say, *You see why you can't believe anything she says?*

But Morgan feared it was Tom she couldn't believe. "You told me you were going to put chains on the SUV," she said.

"I'm sorry. I didn't bring any chains. I went to find Allison, to try and talk to her and warn her off. All I was thinking about was protecting you."

Morgan desperately wanted to believe him.

He must have seen her waver. "So who are you going to believe?" he asked. "Your *husband?* Or the unbalanced woman who wants to destroy him? Destroy us?"

"He's lying. He's going to kill us both," Allison cried.

Morgan slipped her hand in her coat pocket. The movement wasn't missed by Allison or wasted on Tom.

He shook his head and she slowly removed her hand without the gun.

"I'm sorry I lied to you about my past, Morgan, but now you can understand why. What woman would marry me if she knew about all this?" He shot a look at Allison, his meaning clear. Then his gaze came back to her. "I'm so sorry, Morgan." He started toward her.

"Don't take another step or I'll shoot you, Eric." Allison waved the gun at him. "You can't talk your way out of this like you did the murders. She knows that you only married her for her money."

"I know about the inheritance," Tom admitted. "But I will support my wife on what I make. That money is Morgan's. She knows how I feel about that."

"How did you find out?" Morgan asked.

"By accident. I wish I hadn't," Tom said. "Remember when someone broke into your apartment back when we first started dating?"

"You wouldn't let me call the police because nothing appeared to be missing." Her gaze swung to Allison. "You—"

"No, I told you, Eric only flew me up here last week."

Tom shook his head. "I checked with the mental institutional in Arkansas. Allison had been released just days before that."

"That's a lie!" she cried. "See how he twists it all around?" Her voice was shrill in the small cabin. The gun shook in her hands. "All he cares about is the money. It's why he killed his family. Why he is going to kill you!"

"Do you really think I would kill my family for a few thousand dollars?" Tom demanded of Morgan. "Honey, Allison couldn't bear the thought that the brother she'd looked up to for years could do such a thing. But Louis had a violent streak and he'd threatened my father in front of several people."

"You egged him on," Allison cried. "You set him up so he would look guilty. You planned the whole thing so Louis would take the fall for you."

Tom shook his head. "She has never been able to accept it. That's why she's been institutionalized all these years."

"Stop talking about me as if I'm not in the room!" Allison cried. She turned a little to look at Morgan. "He's lying. You have to believe me."

Morgan could see the woman was starting to come apart. She was trembling, her eyes shiny with tears.

"I married you because I love you," Tom said directing his words to Morgan as he took another step toward her. "I couldn't care less about your money. Did I hesitate to sign the prenuptial agreement? No. All I care about is you," he said as he took yet another step.

"Don't!" Allison cried.

"You going to shoot me, Allison?" he asked without looking at her.

She was crying. "I don't want to. But I have to stop you. I should have stopped you that night, but I loved you and our baby and I thought… I'll never forgive myself. That's why they locked me up, Eric. Because I tried to kill myself after I lost our child."

Allison pulled back her jacket sleeve with the hand holding the gun. Even from across the room, Morgan could see the scars crisscrossing her wrist.

"When I saw you going back into the house with the gun, I didn't think you would kill them. Even when you started arguing with your father about the money, I…" She was crying hard now, the gun wobbling in her hands.

"If you kill me, they will put you away again, Allison," Tom said as he took another step toward Morgan. "They already suspect you're crazy. But if you shoot me, they'll know it."

Morgan saw what he was doing—trying to get to her, to step between her and the madwoman with the gun. How could she have ever questioned this man's love for her?

"Tom, don't," she cried, fearing that Allison would shoot him if he took another step.

He closed the distance so quickly that Allison didn't have a chance to get a shot off. But it was Morgan who was taken by surprise. She'd been so sure he was trying to reach her to protect her from Allison.

But to her shock, he grabbed Morgan, locking an arm around her throat and dragging her against him, using her like a shield as he reached into her coat pocket and pulled out the gun.

He leveled it at his former girlfriend. "Put down the weapon, Allison."

She shook her head. She was still crying, the gun gripped in both trembling hands now, confusion and fear in her eyes.

"I told you," she said to Morgan in a defeated voice. "Didn't I tell you? If you had just trusted me…"

"Tom," Morgan choked out. "What are you doing?"

"Sorry to disappoint you, Morgan, but I would have sooner or later, anyway."

CHAPTER ELEVEN

MORGAN GRABBED FOR THE gun, but Tom wrenched it away and tightened his grip on her throat. She fought desperately to free herself from his hold, but he was bigger and stronger and her attempts were futile.

"This is what I believe is called a Mexican standoff," Tom said with a laugh. "So what are you going to do, Allison? Wish you'd taken my offer, don't you."

"You planned to kill me either way." There was a flatness in her voice as she leveled the gun at them.

Morgan saw that Tom was hoping Allison would shoot her. Then he would shoot Allison, and do just what the woman had tried to warn her he would. He'd be the grieving widower, with Morgan's inheritance to spend.

Anger bubbled up in her. "I'm sorry I didn't believe you, Allison," Morgan said, her voice hoarse from the pressure Tom was putting on her throat.

Right up until he had grabbed her, she had wanted to believe that she hadn't been wrong about the man she'd married. How many women stayed in bad marriages because they couldn't admit they'd made a mistake?

Tom had fooled her. She saw that he'd been doing that not only to *women* for years, but to himself, as well. He took what he wanted, seeing himself as the victim.

What frightened her most was the planning that had gone into this. Had it been from that first day on the street, when he'd picked up the Christmas package she'd dropped? Had he known then who she was, that her mother had recently died?

Morgan realized that working as a photographer at the newspaper in a small town, she'd often had her photo run for one promotion or another. It would have been fairly easy for him to find out she was an only child, and that her parents had been well-to-do, but were now both dead.

"Don't hurt Allison," she managed to say as she fought to loosen his hold on her throat. "You can have my money. Just let her—"

The boom of a gunshot report thundered in the small cabin. She stared at Allison, waiting for the woman to fall to the floor, believing Tom had fired the shot.

But it was Tom who let out a curse and staggered back, dragging her with him.

"You stupid bitch." As he raised the gun, Morgan tried to throw him off balance, but her effort was wasted. The gunshot next to her ear was deafening.

Allison looked stupefied for a moment as she stared down at the hole in her down jacket. Her head came up. She glanced across the room at Tom, resignation on her face. "I loved you, Eric." She lifted her gun.

Morgan saw what was going to happen as Tom took aim again. She drew her feet up, throwing all her weight forward. The move took him by surprise, driving him off balance as he fought to keep his hold on her.

The report of the gunshot was followed an instant later by Tom's scream of pain. As another blast filled the air, Morgan realized her efforts had been for nothing. She hadn't saved Allison or herself.

The woman dropped to the floor, the gun clattering on the wooden planks next to her.

AN EARLY MEMORY OF MORGAN suddenly filled Luke's thoughts as he raced up the road to Mountain Badger Cabin. It was of her standing in the darkroom doorway. He remembered turning to find her there, and wondering how long she'd been watching him. Since the darkroom was no longer used for anything but storing supplies, he'd been in there searching for one of the older cameras to give to the new intern to use.

"Hey," he'd said, surprised to see her, and equally glad. She'd stood silhouetted against the light of the newsroom.

"So what do you think?" she'd asked.

He'd grinned. "About anything in particular?"

"I'm wearing a dress." She'd sounded mildly exasperated with him. Normally she dressed like the rest of them, in jeans with a shirt, and sometimes a jacket, if they were going to be out covering a story.

He'd stepped closer, taking her in with one glance. The coral-colored dress highlighted her lightly tanned skin. There was a summer glow to her, and he'd noticed a sprinkling of freckles on her cheeks and the bridge of her nose, even though she'd tried to hide them with makeup.

The dress accented her curves in a way that made him ache inside. He'd cleared his throat. "I love it." *I love you,* he'd wanted to say. "You're going to drive the male reporters wild."

She'd laughed then, that wonderful musical laugh of hers.

"I've never seen you looking more beautiful."

She had swatted at him playfully, but he'd sworn that she'd blushed as she'd ducked back out of the darkroom, her last words hanging in the air. "Thought I'd better run it by my best friend before I started driving all the male reporters wild," she'd joked.

Her best friend. He remembered standing alone in the darkroom as the door had closed behind her, wishing he had taken her in his arms and kissed her.

CHAPTER TWELVE

TOM HAD BEEN HIT AGAIN, but Morgan had no idea how badly. All she knew was that this was probably her last chance to save herself. She drove her foot back and caught his shin with the heel of her boot.

He let out a curse and loosened his grip on her throat enough that she could twist in his arms. She struck out at him with her fists as he tried to get his arm locked around her neck again. Bringing her leg up, she caught him in the groin.

Tom let out a whoosh of air and slumped forward. Morgan untangled herself from him and dived toward the door of the cabin.

Clutching the knob, she twisted it frantically, realizing too late that Tom had relocked the door when he'd come back in. Another boom filled the air. Wood splintered next to her as the bullet he'd fired barely missed her.

Morgan turned the lock, wrenched the door open. A gust of cold wind and snow blew in, taking her breath. If she could get out of the cabin and run fast enough—

Tom grabbed a handful of her hair and jerked her off her feet.

"You aren't going anywhere," he snapped as he dragged her back inside, kicking the door closed.

He swung her to him. Blood had soaked through his wool coat, oozing from wounds at his shoulder and left arm. Unfortunately, neither appeared life threatening. Nor had they slowed him down. All Allison had done was make him more dangerous.

His face twisted in pain and rage. Morgan stared at him, seeing the stranger he was—coming at her with a vengeance. He didn't even sound like the man she'd met that day before Christmas. He'd never loved her.

And now he was going to kill her.

She saw it all as she stared into a face she'd once thought handsome. He would use Allison's gun. With him wounded, he would appear to have tried to save his new bride. Allison had only made his plan more foolproof. He would come out of this looking like a hero. A *rich* hero.

"No one is going to believe that Allison killed me," Morgan said, even though she knew better. Tom had set it up too well. Once they saw the spray-painted walls, and Tom told them about the snowman and Allison's past mental problems…

The whine of a snowmobile could suddenly be heard in the distance. Tom froze, the gun in his hand motionless as he listened. It sounded as if the driver of the machine was headed this way. Was it possible?

Morgan thought of Luke. He'd been so afraid for her. No, he wouldn't have come after her. He couldn't have gotten up into the mountains in this storm. And yet she realized that was exactly the kind of thing he would do.

Hope soared in her heart, but quickly crashed as she heard the snowmobile's engine die, plunging the cabin into silence.

Tom relaxed, and she saw the change in him. He smiled through his pain and anger, knowing he was going to get away with this. He was already planning on how he would spend her money.

"I can't believe I didn't see through you."

"You made it too easy," he boasted.

She nodded, hating that it was true. She'd wanted to be swept off her feet, carried away on a big white horse like a princess in a fairy tale, and Tom had been more than willing to play the role.

"Try to understand," he said, sounding more like the man she'd thought she'd married. "This way Eric Wagner finally *dies.* It will be over here, today, don't you see? You are really going to make me the man I was supposed to be."

"Only if the man you're supposed to be is a manipulative, self-serving, egomaniacal murderer," she said.

Tom swore and fired a shot into the ceiling above their heads making her jump. His grip tightened on her arm.

"I knew you would be incapable of understanding. I was always supposed to be more than a salesman in a hardware store. With your inheritance, I can live the life I should have had."

She spat on him.

He snarled at her as he wiped his cheek. "Let's get this over with," he said as he dragged her over to where Allison lay on the floor. Her eyes were open, but Morgan saw no sign that the woman was still breathing.

"Is she…dead?" she asked, forced to look away.

"Fortunately," he said.

Morgan choked back a sob. "Why?"

He finished loading the gun, then looked up at her and frowned. "Why what, Morgan?"

"Why *me?* My inheritance won't last you that long."

He almost appeared sad. "I know. I'll have to find a woman with money to marry. She won't be as beautiful as you."

Morgan tried not to flinch as he reached out and ran the barrel of the gun along her cheekbone.

"It was love at first sight, you know. I really never dreamed I could be married to such a drop-dead-gorgeous woman. It made it all that more enjoyable when I saw how much your friend Luke wanted you." His smile had a cold edge to it.

"Don't do this," she said, knowing she was wasting her breath. But suddenly she couldn't bear the thought that she would never see Luke again. He'd tried to warn her about Tom even before she'd married him. "You need help—"

"I might have tried to make this work, Morgan," he said, as if he hadn't heard her. "But I knew how you would react when I told you about my past. You see me as Eric Wagner now, damaged and flawed. I'm not good enough for you anymore. See why I didn't want you to know? I was certain it would ruin everything."

"You're wrong," she said, realizing he would have to bend down to pick up Allison's hand, then her gun. If Morgan timed it right, maybe she could grab the gun before he did.

His laugh startled her. "Do you think I'm stupid? I look into your eyes and I see that your love has gone cold. Just like my parents' love for me long before that night. Why do you think they had two more children, both much younger than me?"

"You said you loved Allison, were planning to marry her," Morgan said.

"I *did* love her. I loved my family, too. I didn't want to hurt them, any more than I want to hurt you. I'm not a monster, Morgan."

"You *killed* them."

"I had no choice. You think I have a choice *now?*" He shook his head. "You are so naive. You think I'm the only killer on this mountain? The sheriff will have his hands full with those serial killers over at the lodge.

Don't look so surprised. I saw that one watching you. The other one is around somewhere, you can bet. Yes, Morgan, I know killers when I see them."

"Evil recognizes evil," she said under her breath.

Tom's expression changed, and with a start, she realized he was already practicing what he would tell the sheriff.

"I tried to stop Allison from killing her," he said with what sounded like true sorrow. "I would have given my life to save Morgan, and thought I had at one point." His voice broke. Tears welled from his eyes. "I'm not sure how I will go on. I will never get over losing my beautiful, talented wife. Never."

AS LUKE APPROACHED the cabin, he knew the sound of the snowmobile would be heard, so he didn't dare drive it all the way up there. He had no choice but to cut the engine and go on foot the rest of the way.

He'd just stepped from the vehicle into the deep snow when he heard the gunshot. With his heart in his throat, he took off running up the mountainside.

As he plowed through the deep drifts, breathing raggedly, he caught glimpses of the cabin up on the slope. His terror for Morgan increased with each step.

Luke prayed as he never had before. Reaching the cabin, he circled around to the rear. He knew that bursting in the front door would be nothing short of suicide. At the back, he moved along the wall to peer into a window. He saw a bed. Past it, through an open door, he saw a body lying on the floor. His pulse pounded as Tom stepped into view, then Morgan.

He had a handful of her hair. He dragged her over to the body and started to pull her down as he reached for something on the floor.

Luke moved quickly, easing open the back door, gun in hand, a silent prayer on his lips.

TOM DIDN'T DO WHAT MORGAN had anticipated, hoped for. When he leaned down, it wasn't for Allison's hand—but her gun. He picked it up in his own gloved fist and pressed it into Allison's dead fingers.

"You might want to close your eyes," he said, still holding a handful of Morgan's long hair.

She met his gaze, refusing to look away. "Is that what you told your family before you killed them?"

He shook his head, a soft chuckle emitting from his lips. "When I met you, I thought you were a weak, helpless woman. You've proved me wrong. I like that."

Did he? Out of the corner of her eye, Morgan caught movement. She fought to keep her expression neutral as she saw Luke slip in the back door of the cabin.

Luke. Her heart swelled, bringing tears to her eyes. Why hadn't she realized before how much she loved him? He was her best friend, the reason she couldn't wait to get to work each day, and why she hated Fridays and long weekends. It wasn't just her love for photography. *She loved Luke.*

She realized what a fool she'd been not to tell him how she felt, that day in the darkroom when he'd kissed her. But she'd been mere days away from marrying Tom. If only she had followed her heart.

Morgan quickly wiped at her tears as she noticed the satisfaction they gave Tom. He thought they were inspired by fear. He wanted her to beg for her life, to grovel.

Maybe she could make it work for her. Pretending to be weak with terror and having trouble standing, she slumped, even though it hurt because of his grip on her hair.

The move drew Tom to one side, putting his back to Luke.

"They won't believe she shot me," Morgan said, hoping to cover any sound Luke might make as he inched closer. She caught the glint of the gun in his hand, but he couldn't fire as long as Tom was standing so close to her. "Forensics," she added, trying to put some distance between them.

Tom frowned. "I beg your pardon?" He wasn't in a hurry to kill her. He was waiting for her to fall apart. Needing it. She thought of his family. Had they begged for their lives? She shuddered at the thought.

"If you shoot me with us standing this close, they will know Allison didn't kill me," she said. "She couldn't have held on to me and shot me. I saw a case just like this on one of those police procedural shows on television."

"Aren't you the smart one."

"If Allison had pulled a gun on me, I would have run for the door."

"And she would have shot you in the back," Tom said in agreement. "So you want me to let you make a run for it." He chuckled. "You just don't give up. Didn't you learn anything before, when you tried to get away and I caught you? Do you really think you can outrun a bullet?"

"I won't know until I try," she said, lifting her chin in defiance.

He laughed. "Maybe I was wrong about you. Maybe you and I could have been good together." He seemed to be considering it, but then shook his head almost sadly. "I made that mistake with Allison, and look how that turned out. No, you would end up telling that *friend* of yours, Luke, the one you're half in love with."

"I'm more than half in love with him," Morgan said. "I just wish I'd told him. I wouldn't be standing here now if I had."

Tom swore and shoved her away. "Run, bitch."

Morgan turned and launched herself instead for the fireplace, giving Luke a clean shot at Tom.

She heard the report of the gun. Two shots. They sounded louder than all the others, reverberating through her. For a moment, she thought she'd been hit, the painful fear in her chest was so great for Luke.

Something heavy slammed into the floor behind her and she turned to see Tom there. Luke rushed to him, kicking his gun away, then checking for a pulse.

She held her breath. After a moment, Luke shook his head. Tom was dead. No, Eric Wagner was dead. She waited, expecting to feel something for the man. She felt hollow until Luke rushed to her and took her in his arms. He cradled her to him and she finally felt as if she could breathe.

When she stopped trembling, he pulled back to look into her eyes. "I love you, Morgan. I should have told you a long time ago. I'm a damned fool."

She shook her head as tears streamed down her face. "No, Luke." Her voice broke. "You're no fool. You're my hero. You just saved my life."

He drew her to him, holding her for a long moment, as if he never wanted to let her go, then he led her out of the cabin, away from the smell of spilled blood and death, and through the falling snow to the snowmobile he'd left down the road.

When he'd climbed on, she settled behind him and wrapped her arms around him.

"Everything is going to be all right now," Luke said.

Snow fell around them as she hugged him tighter and remembered what Tom had said about there being more killers on the mountain. Serial killers over at the lodge.

Then again, Tom had lied about everything, hadn't he?

* * * * *

COLD HEAT

Delores Fossen

CHAPTER ONE

SPECIAL AGENT LEAH GRAY stared out at the ice-scabbed landscape and thought about the woman she'd gotten killed. She squeezed her eyes shut for a moment, hoping to block out the images.

But she failed.

Six days wasn't nearly enough time for memories like that to soften even a little. Leah relived every moment, every last detail, every mistake she'd made that had led to the woman's crumpled, lifeless body on the floor.

"Look, Mommy," she heard someone say. Leah's attention zoomed across the lodge's sprawling lobby to where a freckled-faced kid was pointing at her. "That lady's got bad boo-boos."

The child's mom went a little pale when she saw Leah, and she whisked away her wide-eyed daughter in the direction of the resort restaurant.

Great. Now, she was scaring small children.

Leah had pretty much avoided mirrors, and people, since her attack, but last she'd checked, there was a purplish-greenish bruise crawling from the center of her forehead all the way to her left cheekbone. It color coordinated with the ones on her neck.

Those bruises weren't just scary. They had nearly left her dead.

And then there was the cast on her fractured right wrist. Her shooting hand, no less. The break had put her on paid convalescence leave. That, and the fact she'd failed her psych exam.

Yeah. She scared little children, all right. Heck, she scared herself, and that was the reason she was hiding out at Ice Lake Lodge in Nowhere, Montana.

Leah had spent most of the first three days of her wound-licking recovery in her room, but just a half hour earlier she'd decided to test the waters and venture to the lobby, to see if a change of scenery would lift her dark mood.

Despite the scared child, it was working.

A little.

Everything on the other side of the wall of windows was frozen. Quiet. No dead bodies. Just a steady blanketing snowfall and happy childhood memories of when she'd come here skiing with her family. Good memories beat those of dead bodies on floors any old day. With her mind and other parts of her bruised and broken, it was exactly what she needed to get her head on straight again.

She settled back in the comfy chair, the fragrant fire in the stone hearth warming her, and she tried reading the first page of the paperback novel. However, a car caught her attention. A black, four-door sedan came to a stop in the parking lot. It had heavily tinted windows, no shiny frills. Not a vehicle that most people would even notice. But Leah did.

She mumbled some profanity, jacking it up a notch when she saw a man step from the car. What the devil was *he* doing here?

Leah got to her feet, and in the same motion tossed the paperback onto the chair and made a beeline for the front door. Thanks to that wall of windows along the way, she could see him doing the same darn thing.

Special Agent Alex McCade.

The last person on earth she wanted to see.

Yet here he was. All six feet two inches of him. Every strand of his storm-black hair. And yes, he'd brought that perennial scowl with him. He was good at it, too. The eyes helped, since they were the same chilly color as the frozen blue-gray lake that gave the resort its wintry name.

Alex opened the door and stepped into the lobby, his scalpel-sharp gaze slicing over the half dozen or so other guests who were milling around, before it finally darted to her.

"Leah," he said in greeting.

His breath mixed with the frosty air and created a split-second filmy cloud around his face. It made him look a little otherworldly, like a vampire who'd just stepped in for a bite. Judging from his especially deep scowl, he intended to take a bite out of something. Her, probably. And it made her wonder what else she'd screwed up.

He shut the door, stepped closer, and she caught his scent. The snow. The pines.

And Alex.

It cut through the cold and warmed her in places that it shouldn't. Always did. She figured one day she would find a cure for him, but she hadn't yet.

Leah braced herself for the worst and refused to give him a friendly greeting. "Checking up on me? Because I doubt you drove all the way from Billings for lunch."

The little voice inside her, belonging to the part of her that wanted her badge and gun back, reminded her that these days Alex was her supervisor and she should put her serpent's tongue in check and beg him for another crack at that psych eval.

Another part of her glared at him because Alex had cut her to the core by taking her badge. He hadn't trusted her. He had put department rules ahead of their four-year past, and that hurt more than the bruises around her neck.

As if he knew exactly what she was thinking, Alex's mouth tightened, and she felt a jolt from a memory of a different sort.

Sheez. Not this, not now. Talk about needing another cure.

That mouth had kissed her, and kissed her well, on many occasions. That mouth, and its owner, also had her hormonal number, and even now with her mentally cursing him, Leah still felt the warmth rev up to the heat stage.

With Alex, there was always heat.

He gave her a once-over, starting at the bruise on her face, lingering a few moments on the ones on her neck and finishing with her cast. His scowl faded, but his forehead bunched up with worry. Or something.

"Yes, I know," she mumbled. Best to take the first strike here, since Leah darn sure didn't want him saying how sorry he was about all this. She couldn't take that from him right now. "I look like death warmed over."

Those icy eyes narrowed, and he snagged her uninjured arm. "We have to talk," he said, his voice husky and low. "Let's go to your room."

Alex always sounded as if he had a cold coming on, but it somehow managed to come off as sexy. That and his easy Montana drawl.

"You picked a bad time to travel up here," she commented. "A storm's moving in. Supposed to be a rough one, too. A lot of the guests left right after breakfast." And that had been the main selling point in her decision to venture down to the lobby again. Fewer guests. Fewer people to gawk at her.

Alex mumbled something she didn't quite catch, but it sounded like— "I didn't have a choice."

She hoped she'd misheard him, and waited for him to clarify. He didn't. He just kept trying to get her to move by tugging on her arm.

Leah held her ground. For a lot of reasons, including that hot persuasive mouth of his, she didn't want Alex in her room.

"Did you bring my badge and gun with you?" she asked, knowing he hadn't. She also figured that the question alone would bring back the scowl. He'd made it crystal clear she was suspended for thirty days minimum.

Twenty-five more to go.

Alex quit tugging at her, and looked around the lobby again, his attention lingering a moment on the acne-scarred clerk behind the rustic log counter, and then on the massive oil painting on the wall behind him. A painting of the lodge's logo: snow-capped mountains and the frozen lake.

That got his forehead bunching up again, and she wondered what he had against that particular piece of artwork.

"My badge and gun?" she reminded him.

But he ignored her. "Let's go to your room," he repeated. He gave her arm another tug.

Everything inside her went still, because that badge and gun question should have earned her another scowl or at least a cocky comeback. Alex was good at those, too.

Something was wrong.

Leah had to gather her suddenly thin breath to ask

him the question she feared most. “Has there been another murder?”

But she wasn’t sure she could deal with the answer if it was yes. It was her fault that the duo serial killers known as the Big Sky Stranglers were still at large. Her fault that the investigation had been botched.

Her fault that the woman’s body had been on the floor.

“No other murder,” Alex said under his breath. “Where’s your room?”

His one-track mind wasn’t doing much to steady her raw nerves, so Leah didn’t put up a fuss or even wiggle out of the hold that he had on her arm. She fished her key card from her sweater pocket and headed up the wide stairs toward the second floor, to room 222. The last one off the long corridor.

Secluded, the clerk had called it.

Leah could verify it was indeed that, since she hadn’t heard a peep from any other guests.

“Okay, what’s wrong?” she asked the moment she stepped inside.

But Alex didn’t give her a quick answer. He released her arm and closed the door, locked it and turned back around to face her. Until he did that little maneuver, Leah hadn’t realized she was standing too close to him. The front of him brushed against the front of her.

Breasts against chest.

Another jolt of memories.

Beneath that coat and suit was a great body. But clearly something was on this sizzling hunk’s mind.

Leah pulled in another breath. “Have you come here to fire me?”

“No.”

Well, thank heaven he didn’t hesitate with that response. Relief flooded through her and turned her legs wobbly. Since she didn't want to disgrace herself by falling, she caught on to the back of the chair that was stuffed beneath a writing desk.

Alex gave a rough sigh when he glanced at the desk and spotted the notepad where she'd doodled a picture of her badge. And a picture of him with devil horns. The likeness wasn't very good, but he probably recognized himself.

"But I have come with bad news," he added.

So much for her relief. Leah just stared at him and waited. She didn't have to wait long, at least not long for him to spring into action.

Alex went to the closet, pulled out her suitcase. He dumped it on the bed and opened it. "You have to leave with me," he insisted, and proceeded to gather her clothes from a dresser drawer and deposit them in her suitcase.

Leah latched on to his arm and used her cast to point to the window, beyond which the snow was falling even heavier now. "There's a storm coming in," she reminded him. "The roads will be closed soon, if they aren't already. So unless you're here to tell me that I need to report to duty ASAP because of some emergency—"

"It's isn't safe for you here," Alex interrupted.

Safe. Now, that was a strange word for him to use, considering she had been a federal agent for nearly seven years and had lived in cold country her entire life. There wasn't much other than nightmares and Alex that frightened her.

"I think I can handle a blizzard," she added for good measure.

Alex made a sound deep within his throat, and reached into his pocket and took out something. Not her badge or gun, but rather a plastic evidence bag. Inside, Leah could see a piece of notepad paper.

"It was in a plain white envelope, addressed to me," he explained. "No prints, no trace. Someone put it on the counter at the diner across the street from the FBI office, and no one could get a description of the person who left it. It's possible it was placed there a couple days ago."

That was a lot of explanation for such a small piece of paper, and she figured it had to be important or Alex wouldn't have risked driving through a storm to bring it to her.

Leah took the bag and turned it so she could study the sheet. Not much to study, though. Just a couple sentences.

You can't save her this time. Just me and her. I'll finish what I started.

She shook her head, not understanding. "You think this is some kind of threat meant for me?"

"Turn it over," Alex instructed.

The chill went through her blood again, but Leah flipped the paper anyway, trying to brace herself for what she might see.

She didn't brace herself nearly enough.

There. On the front side of the note paper was a familiar logo and equally familiar words.

Ice Lake Resort.

Oh, God.

She swallowed hard and met Alex's gaze. Leah tried, but couldn't make herself ask the question.

But he answered it, anyway. "Yes, the strangler is *here.*"

CHAPTER TWO

HELL. ALEX HAD KNOWN this visit and news would be hard for Leah. And it was. Unfortunately, the *hard* was just getting started.

He reached for her, because he knew she would need a shoulder for support. He also knew she would push him away, and that's exactly what she did.

A good thing, too.

Having her in his arms right now might soothe her a little—might soothe him, too—but it would also create a dangerous mix of adrenaline with an old attraction that just wouldn't die. They had enough *hard* without adding that.

"The Big Sky Stranglers are at Ice Lake?" she whispered, moving to the other side of the room, far away from him.

Alex shook his head. "Judging from the way the threat is worded, I'm guessing just one of them is here."

The one who'd actually put his hands around Leah's throat and tried to choke the life out of her. But Alex knew he couldn't rule out that the other one was somewhere around. They worked as a pair, even though the profile said the duo was made up of a submissive accomplice and the dominant mastermind.

And the latter was the one who'd no doubt written that note.

You can't save her this time. Just me and her. I'll finish what I started.

"He's here," she mumbled. The color seeped from Leah's face. Well, except for that god-awful bruise on her forehead and cheek. Her short, spiky blond hair covered some of it, but not nearly enough.

That bruise and the ones on her neck turned Alex's stomach.

So did the bleached expression on her face, and in her eyes, which were an identical green color to that bruise. And despite all those visible responses, Alex knew it was worse inside for her.

It sure was for him.

He could put up a front. The cool facade of a badass federal agent. Unfortunately, a cool facade wasn't worth spit when it came to convincing her that they had to get out of here.

Oh, yeah. Despite what she'd just learned, he was certain Leah would fight him on this.

"I would have called the minute I found out," Alex continued, "but there's no cell service up here. I couldn't risk phoning the resort or lodge." He'd been worried that the strangler was monitoring the calls in some way, and would immediately kill Leah.

Of course, Alex could have called the sheriff in nearby Graniteville and requested assistance, but he knew he was the only person with a chance of talking her into leaving.

"If he's here…" Leah said. She cleared her throat, probably so she could manage more than a ragged whisper, and sound more like a law enforcement officer. "Then I can be bait to draw him out, and this time we can catch him."

That didn't help his stomach either, but Alex had been

expecting it. That's why he had rehearsed his answer. "In theory, we could do that. But you know his profile as well as I do."

Leah and he had developed that profile together. The killers were chameleons, able to blend in. White males. Late twenties, early thirties. And the most critical part of the profile—they were serial killers.

"When cornered, they kill," he reminded her.

Of course, Leah had firsthand knowledge of that. Alex knew the hard way that secondhand knowledge sucked almost as much as the real thing.

"Someone broke into your apartment," he continued. To speed things along, he went into the bathroom, retrieved her toiletry bag and put it in the suitcase. He got a glare for his efforts. "And I think that someone learned you were here by hacking into your personal computer."

She nodded. Sighed. Cursed. "I made the reservations online."

Yes, Alex had figured as much. He had been informed of the break-in after her security company had called him about an intrusion alarm. Later, when he had her off this mountain, he'd tell her that the stranglers had trashed her place so badly it was unlivable. She would have to stay with him until some repairs were done, because he didn't want her alone with at least one of the stranglers apparently out to finish her off.

Oh, yeah. That info could wait. He'd already dumped enough on her for now, and she was wasting a lot of mental energy trying to look as if she was unaffected by everything.

"You're leaving with me," Alex added, making sure he sounded like her boss.

The spark of anger and resistance in her eyes was instantaneous. No surprise. He was straying into touchy territory with that tone of authority.

"You took my badge and gun," she reminded him. "You don't have much leverage in getting me to obey an order."

Alex shrugged. "I have leverage, all right. Because you want your gun and badge back."

Gotcha, he thought. Those two things were at the top of her what-I-want-most list. Once, months ago, he'd been third.

If that.

Of course, first, second and, heaven help him, even third, wouldn't stop her from disagreeing with him. So Alex went ahead and launched the argument they were about to have, anyway.

He took out the folded sheet of paper from his other pocket and dropped it on the bed next to the suitcase.

"The composites." Leah huffed and spared a glance at the sketches of the two men presumed to be the stranglers. "No need for you to show them to me. I see them in my sleep," she added.

Yeah. So did Alex, and he saw them trying to kill her. Again. And again. And again. In each of those nightmares he tried to save her—and he failed. But Alex had no plans to fail this time.

"Look at them one more time," he instructed. "You said you hadn't seen either man's face when they attacked you last week."

"Only one attacked me," she clarified. "Just one." Leah paused, drew in her breath. "I'm not sure what the other one was doing, because as you know, they'd cut the power in the house. No lights."

Not an accident, Alex was betting. But Leah's walking into that ambush had been. She'd been canvassing the neighborhood, showing the composites, when a woman had said the men look like the pair that her elderly neighbor had hired to do some carpentry work. Leah had called for backup. Alex had responded. But Leah hadn't waited. She'd gone over to check out the possible lead, and had been beaten, then choked.

"Do the composites resemble any of the guests you've seen here at the lodge?" Alex pressed. "Look hard."

"No," she snapped in answer. But she did ease closer and comb her attention over those sketched images. "There are at least twenty men in that age range staying here. Or they were before news of the storm. I'm sure some have checked out."

"But not this guy," Alex reminded her. "He wants to kill you, Leah. And that's why you have to leave with me now."

She mumbled something, raked her hair away from her face and winced when she encountered the bruise. That seemed to aggravate her even more. She certainly wasn't grabbing her suitcase and making a run for the door, so Alex went to her and grasped her shoulders.

"This isn't the place to make a stand," he warned. "There are families here. Easy targets. And I don't want one of them getting in this SOB's way."

Leah opened her mouth to argue, but Alex caught her hand, lifting it so the cast was in her line of sight. "Besides, you can't shoot, and if I were going to agree to such an asinine bait plan, then I would demand that the women and children be quietly evacuated. I'd also need backup."

Hell.

There went her color again, and she moved away once more. No doubt because she thought his remark was an admonishment because she hadn't waited for backup six days ago. And it had resulted in a woman's murder and the attempted murder of a federal agent.

"Don't," Leah warned when Alex reached for her.

He ignored her, hooked his arm around her waist and pulled her to him. This time she didn't fight. She melted against him.

Oh, man.

Not good. The melting reminded him of other times he'd held her. It also reminded him of other things that were best left out of this.

Leah made a sound, a muffled sob, and dropped her head onto his shoulder. She fit. Of course. Always had. And in the back of his mind, Alex wondered if she always would.

"You're my supervisor," she whispered, in the same warning tone he'd used.

Yeah. She knew him. Knew what was going through his mind and body. But hey, he knew her, too. And Alex was certain that the guilt was eating away at her like battery acid. There was no way she wanted more guilt by endangering anyone other than herself.

"Leave with me," he insisted. Alex brushed his mouth on the unbruised part of her forehead. "You can heal. Get back your gun and badge. And then we can catch these guys the right way."

He waited for a response, the seconds crawling by before she finally eased back a little and met his gaze. "I'm sorry," she said.

"For what?" he snapped, because he thought she was about to disobey his order to leave. But her apology wasn't about that. Alex could see it in her eyes.

"I killed that woman."

He cursed. "No, the stranglers killed her."

"Because I botched things."

"Because you were doing your job," he corrected.

Alex huffed. "Look, you made a mistake by not waiting for backup, but you couldn't have known what would happen when you went there to ask about her newly hired handymen."

She shook her head. "I should have known."

"Right. Because of the ESP that the Bureau issued you when you became an FBI agent."

Leah gave him a flat look. Good. That look was better than the I'm-sorry attitude, and maybe it meant he'd finally gotten through to her.

"Finish packing," he told her.

And this time she didn't fight back. Oh, she huffed and mumbled something derogatory about him, but she went to the dresser and took out the remainder of her clothes. No. Make that her underwear. Alex got a glimpse of the pink panties that Leah favored.

Always pink.

"Don't say anything," she mumbled.

Alex felt the corner of his mouth hitch a little. During their time as lovers, he'd often questioned her about her penchant for that particular choice. It wasn't a color she wore anywhere else on her body. Yet for some reason all her bras and panties were cotton-candy pink. Finally, just weeks before their breakup, she'd confessed that the girlie undies were her way of rebelling. Something feminine and frilly to clash with the conservative clothes she had to wear to do her job.

Yeah, that was Leah, all right. A woman of contradictions, who had a rebellious side. However, she didn't always hide that rebellion the way she did her pink panties.

Alex's smile went south when he heard sounds outside Leah's door. Footsteps and a frantic shout.

"Help!" a man yelled.

Alex automatically reached beneath his coat to his shoulder holster and drew his gun. "Stay behind me," he ordered, when Leah started toward the door. "This might not have anything to do with the strangler."

He kept that possibility in mind when he opened the door and peered into the hall. The man calling for help was there, and so was a maid in a dust-gray uniform. The woman's eyes were wide with fear, and she was shaking almost violently.

"I'll get the manager," she told the lanky, dark-haired man, then scurried down the corridor.

Using his left hand, Alex pulled back his coat so the man could see his badge. "What's wrong?"

"Look in there...." He tried to say more, but his voice cracked. He lifted his trembling hand and pointed to the room across the hall from Leah's. The door was partially open, but not wide enough to see what was wrong.

"Stay put," Alex warned Leah again, and shot her a glance over his shoulder to make sure she did. If the strangler was in the room, ready to jump out at them, he didn't want Leah in the line of attack.

With his gun aimed and ready, Alex stepped forward and used the toe of his boot to ease open the door.

Hell.

CHAPTER THREE

NOTHING SHORT OF paralysis could have made Leah stay put. Especially after she heard the single word of profanity leave Alex's mouth.

Something was wrong, and even though she wasn't duty-ready, she was better than no backup at all.

Leah grabbed her personal handgun from her purse, and even though it caused a sharp pain in her arm, she gripped the weapon in her right hand and hurried to join Alex. She stepped around a stack of white towels that appeared to have been dropped, and looked into the room. From over Alex's shoulder, Leah could see what had caused his profanity.

Her heart dropped to her knees. Oh, God. Not again. *Please.* Not again.

But it was.

The woman was sprawled on the floor.

She wasn't moving, and her blank, lifeless eyes were wide-open and fixed on the ceiling.

"Get the manager and a doctor down here now," Alex ordered the man in the hall who was wearing a lodge uniform, Leah noted.

The guy nodded and sprinted away as if he couldn't wait to get out of there. She couldn't blame him. Death wasn't pretty.

Then her training kicked in, and she made a mental note of his general description, which she would need to complete the paperwork. She made a mental note of the area, too. And the room.

No. The crime scene, she corrected.

Because that's no doubt what it was. This woman probably hadn't died of natural causes.

Leah glanced up the hall and spotted someone else. A short guy with shaggy blond hair. He wore glasses and was holding a bulky cardboard box, but he must have realized something bad was going on because he froze in place.

"I'll cover you," Leah murmured to Alex.

Thank God he didn't argue—because he didn't have a choice. He had to check on the victim, make sure the danger wasn't still present, and then secure the scene.

Alex eased into the room, pivoting his gun from corner to corner as he scanned the area and the bathroom. Leah checked, too, but didn't see anything other than the dead woman.

The flashbacks came. Brutal and relentless. Knifing through her mind. She saw the other dead woman and felt the life being choked out of her.

Leah gulped in some air and fought to keep ahold of herself. She couldn't fall apart. Not now. Not in front of Alex.

She watched as he knelt down and touched his fingertips to the woman's wrist. "Dead," he verified.

Leah kept fighting to maintain her composure. She inched closer, but stayed in the doorway so she could see anyone who might approach. The short guy with the box turned and ran. She didn't go after him. It was too big a risk to leave Alex alone at the crime scene. She'd already learned that particular lesson the hard way, but she would ask the lodge manager about the man when he got there. She would have to ask him about a lot of things.

Soon, the chaos would come. And the questions. But for now, Leah had one specific question that had to be answered.

Just one.

She waited for Alex to move away from the woman, and that's when she got a look at the deceased's neck. Leah nearly lost her breath again, because she had her answer. She saw the telltale signs of manual strangulation.

Ligature marks.

Like the ones on her own neck.

That wasn't the only similarity. No. The woman had short blond hair, like Leah's. Similar build, too. And then there was the fact that this room was directly across from her own.

Alex looked back at her, and in his eyes she saw the order he was about to give. He could see she was on the verge of losing it big time, and he was about to send her to her room—literally.

"We know who did this," Leah whispered.

The logical thing would have been to tell her to wait for all the facts, but he didn't bother. They both knew who'd killed the woman. But Alex didn't acknowledge it. He kept his attention on the crime scene.

"There isn't much disturbed in the room. The bed's made, nothing's toppled over." Alex's gaze fanned the area before going back to the woman's neck. "There are two small puncture marks just below her right ear. He could have used a stun gun to subdue her."

That would explain why the woman hadn't managed to put up much of a struggle. No time to scream or fight back before his hands were on her throat.

"If she was expecting towels, she would have opened the door readily when the strangler knocked," Alex continued. "If he had the stun gun ready, she wouldn't have seen it coming."

Leah certainly hadn't seen her own attacker before he pounced, and she hadn't been incapacitated, as this woman likely was.

"Maybe he thought she was me," Leah mumbled. "After all, he attacked me in a dark room. He might not have gotten a good look at my face."

The idea sickened Leah. Another woman possibly dead because of her.

"No," Alex quickly disagreed. "He knows you're injured. Even though they didn't put your picture in the newspapers, they reported that you'd suffered a broken wrist. This woman doesn't have a cast or any visible previous injuries." He hesitated. His gaze met Leah's. "Plus, he's probably been watching you, or maybe even saw pictures of you in your apartment. There's no way this is a case of mistaken identity."

Yes. The strangler had watched her, and Leah could feel his eyes on her just as she'd felt his brutal hands.

She heard voices and a commotion in the hall, and looked out. A wide-shouldered bald man was running toward them. Behind him was the maid who'd been there earlier. As Leah had done with the other worker and the box guy, she made mental descriptions that she would need for the report.

"Keep them out," Alex instructed. He, too, backed out of the room and blocked the entry by standing in the doorway.

"I'm Winston Cooper, the lodge manager," the man explained. He was gulping in his breath as if on the verge of hyperventilation. "Rosa said you needed a doctor, that a woman had been hurt. We don't have a doctor. Just a medic, and he's out helping a crew right now."

"We don't need the medic—the woman's dead," Alex explained. "I'm Special Agent McCade." He looked past the manager at the petite maid with the salt-and-pepper hair. "You found the body?"

The woman nodded and crossed herself. She was trembling all over, especially her hands. "I was bringing up towels." Her gaze dropped to the ones on the floor. "She didn't answer when I knocked, so I let myself in with the master key."

"Did you touch anything?" Leah asked.

"No." Rosa shook her head. "When I saw her, I ran out." A hoarse sob tore from her throat, and tears spilled down both cheeks. "Is she really dead?"

Alex made a sound of confirmation and glanced around the ceiling. "No security cameras?"

"Not in this part of the resort, only at the front desk and lobby," the manager answered. "There'd been no need for them. Not until now." He put his hands on his hips, lowered his head, sucked in more air. "I need to tell the sheriff about this. The storm's already taken out the phone lines, but I have a portable CB radio I can bring down for you to use. That way you could talk to the sheriff yourself."

"Do that," Alex instructed. "And keep everyone away from this end of the hall. I'll also need to speak to your other employee, the man who was with Rosa when she found the body."

"David Fowler," the manager supplied. "He's pretty shook up, but I'll let him know you need to see him."

Leah understood that "shook up" reaction. Especially since Fowler wasn't law enforcement. She'd had years of experience and training, and it still ripped her apart to see this woman murdered. If only she'd been able to stop the strangler—

"Focus on this case," Alex whispered to her.

That worked. Well, as much as words could. It wouldn't do the dead woman any good if Leah didn't give this her full attention. That was the way to find the person responsible.

And that person was clearly here at the lodge.

Leah had no doubts about that now. The written threat had been real, and that meant the strangler would come after her next.

Alex gave her one last *hold-it-together* look before he walked closer to the maid and started a string of necessary questions. Did she know the dead woman's name? Had she seen anyone in the hall? Anyone else in the room? Had she heard anything suspicious?

Rosa answered no to each one before Alex dismissed her.

"Go ahead and bring down that CB radio from my office," Winston called out to her. She nodded and hurried away.

Leah tipped her head toward the far end of the hall. "A few minutes earlier there was a man here holding a box," she said to the manager. "Blond hair. Glasses. Wiry build. Did you see him?"

Winston glanced at the spot she'd indicated. "Oh, you must mean Lou. He's a seasonal hire." His eyes widened. "You think he had something to do with this?"

"Right now, I'm just getting information." Though she did already have some doubts about this Lou. He didn't appear the size to be the strangler. Of course, the use of the stun gun could have made up for that. "What's his last name?"

The manager shook his head. "I'll have to find out, and I won't find out from him. Lou went running from the lodge like a man on fire. I just hope he can get to a safe place what with this storm breathing down on us."

That gave her more doubts about the guy's guilt. The strangler wouldn't have just left. No. He wouldn't leave until he had what he wanted, and what he wanted was *her*.

"I'll check on the maid and make sure you get that CB right away," Winston assured them, and he headed out, running back up the hall.

God knew how shaky Leah must have appeared, because the moment that Winston was out of sight, Alex latched on to her arm and moved her to the other side of the hall. "You look ready to keel over."

"I'm fine," she lied.

Alex stared at her.

"*Almost* fine," she corrected. "Besides, we don't have to be fine to do our jobs."

Alex gave a grunt of agreement. "But sometimes the job is best left to others. Once the sheriff arrives to take over, we'll get out of here."

That helped rid her of some of the nervousness. Still, Leah shook her head. "But it's our case."

"We're not doing this," Alex snapped.

He stared at her for several seconds, then his face softened. Well, as much as it could. In the five years she'd known him, she couldn't say she'd ever seen Alex look soft. Even during sex, he was in the alpha warrior mode.

"We *can't* do this," he corrected.

She wanted to argue, but since her wrist and hand were throbbing like a bad toothache, Leah knew it wasn't an argument she could win.

Not that she ever won one with Alex.

"I just don't want to be scared of him," she admitted. She didn't have to clarify the *him*. They both knew it was the strangler. "Leaving feels a little like being scared."

Alex touched her good arm. "Nothing wrong with being scared. But being reckless is a whole different story. I can't allow him to come after you again."

Leah waited, because it seemed as if he wanted to say more. Her suddenly fertile mind filled in the blanks for him. Did he want to say he couldn't allow it because he still had feelings for her?

No.

It couldn't be that. The lust was all that was left. Maybe all that there'd ever been. Except her fertile mind rejected that, too.

She'd cared for Alex once. Okay, even now she cared for him. Some days it was easy to push that completely out of her brain.

But today wasn't one of those days.

"I'll finish packing," she told him, and had turned to do just that when she saw Winston hurrying back toward them. He was shaking his head and wheezing again, and he had both the CB and a piece of folded paper.

"I got Sheriff Quick on the CB," he said. He repeated the news, the anxiety in his voice going up a notch with each word. "He can't get here anytime soon. There was an avalanche, and it buried a couple in their car. It's touch-and-go right now."

Leah understood the lawman's priorities. The couple could be saved, perhaps. There was nothing to be done for this woman, but the sheriff would need to secure the lodge and make sure someone else didn't get killed.

Like her, for instance.

She glanced out the window at the steady sheet of falling snow. Soon the roads would be impassable.

Alex took the portable CB from Winston. "Sheriff Quick?"

"Agent McCade," the lawman answered. "Winston just told me about the dead woman. Do you have the resources there to secure the scene?"

Alex opened his mouth to answer, but there was a flurry of static. "Sheriff Quick?"

Nothing.

Alex tried again. And again. But got the same result.

"This happens during bad storms," Winston explained. He took the CB back from Alex. "But I'll keep trying to get through to him."

"Oh, and someone put this on my desk," the manager added through the wheezes. He volleyed wide-eyed glances at both of them before handing Alex the folded piece of paper. "It has your name on it, so I figured it might be important."

Leah's stomach tightened into a cold hard knot. She recognized that paper. It was from the lodge's notepad.

"I didn't see who left it," the lodge manager explained, "and it wasn't there when I came running down here the first time."

Alex examined it, no doubt to see if there were any visible prints. There weren't any. He used his thumb to brush open the folded sheet.

There was a single handwritten sentence. One that twisted Leah's stomach even tighter when Alex read it aloud.

"'If you leave with her, I'll kill another woman in her place.'"

CHAPTER FOUR

"ALISHA MONROE," Alex mumbled. Age thirty-one. Single. According to the info that Winston had provided Alex, she was from Billings and had come to Ice Lake for a ski vacation.

Her vacation was over. She was dead.

Maybe her murder had been a message. Some sick cat-and-mouse game meant to torture Leah. Or maybe Alisha had learned the hard way who the strangler was. Whatever the case, Alex didn't think it was a coincidence that the woman had been choked to death or that she so closely resembled Leah.

"You're scowling," Leah mumbled.

She was in a chair that she'd pulled up next to him—her shoulder to his—staring down at the items scattered on the desk in her room. Items they'd both been studying for the past hour and a half while they waited for the sheriff.

Included in their stash were the two threatening notes, bagged and tagged using the evidence materials he'd had in the field kit in his car. Alex hadn't wanted to leave Leah in order to retrieve it, so Winston had gotten it for him.

The manager had also given them the hotel guest list and personnel files. They were on the desk next to Alex's phone, which he'd used to take photos of the crime screen across the hall. His own personal notes were there, too. The beginnings of the reports on the murder of one Alisha Monroe and the continued threats aimed at Leah.

"Sixteen men are still registered guests at the lodge," Leah said, dropping her copy of the guest log in front of him. "Seven fit the age range for the profile. That means seven possible suspects."

"Eleven," Alex corrected. He tipped his head to the personnel files he'd been scouring. "There are four male workers who also fit. One is Lou Sullivan, the seasonal hire you saw with the box."

"Yes, the short blond guy. Winston said he ran out. Did he come back?"

Alex shook his head. "No. But Winston verified that Lou went back to his regular post. He was just here to drop off that box of supplies." So they could rule Lou out for now, since the strangler was no doubt still close by. And that narrowed it down to ten suspects—still way too many. "We have to trim this list."

"Well, we can't trim David Fowler," Leah insisted.

Alex knew where she was going with this. Fowler had also been in the hall when the body was discovered. His file was incomplete, because he'd only recently been hired. Recently as in the past week—or less. The assistant manager who'd hired him wasn't at the lodge and so far couldn't be reached to provide them with specific employment details, and Fowler was nowhere to be found. Maybe his absence was something as benign as the man finishing his shift and leaving. Or running out after seeing a dead body.

But Fowler could also be a serial killer.

Unlike Lou Sullivan, Fowler was unaccounted for, and that wouldn't do anything to get him off their suspect list.

"I didn't get any bad vibes from Fowler," Leah said. She drew in a hard, weary breath before she continued. "But I think we both know not to trust my instincts. After all, I walked in on an ambush."

Alex heard the unspoken garbage in that comment, and he nipped it in the bud. "Your instincts are just fine." It didn't come out exactly as he'd planned, because it was more of a snarl, so he made sure he softened his expression a bit when he looked at her.

Since she dodged his gaze, Alex put his fingers beneath her chin and lifted it to force eye contact. He'd had some good ideas in his life, but that wasn't one of them. Her vulnerability hit him hard, and before he could talk some sense into himself, he slipped his arms around her and pulled her to him again. Apparently, he hadn't learned his lesson about close contact with Leah.

"We can't leave," she whispered, her voice heavy with emotion.

"No," he agreed. Not that they could, anyway, at this point. The road leading to the main highway would soon be closed, if it wasn't already.

Plus Alex didn't want another dead body.

"He'll kill again," Leah added. Her voice cracked.

Alex stared at her, waited for her eyes to meet his. Their gazes collided. He didn't draw her any closer, but it didn't matter. The intimacy was there, and he could feel her deep in his arms, anyway.

Oh, man.

Would this ever end? *Ever?* He had a dozen things that should be occupying his thoughts. And they were critical. But Leah had a way of cutting through everything. A way of occupying his body below the belt.

Okay.

Maybe not just below. Other parts of him were in on

this, too. But that didn't make this close-quarters situation any easier.

Little by little her expression changed as she moved out of his embrace. She fought first a smile and then a scowl. "You dumped me, remember?"

He considered his answer. Considered ditching the conversation entirely, but when her scowl continued, he knew he had to set things straight—again. "*Dumped* isn't the right word. I ended things because the Bureau promoted me and made me your supervisor." He shrugged. "Besides, you said it was just sex between us."

She opened her mouth. Closed it. Opened it again, but then shook her head. "It was."

He froze, because he saw the slight dilation of her pupils. Heard the shift in her breathing.

Leah was lying.

Well, hell.

Had he missed those signs before? Or had he wanted to miss them, because a breakup was less complicated than having to work out a supervisor-subordinate relationship? Alex wasn't sure he wanted to know the answer. Not now, anyway. Not with a killer bearing down on them.

Because he was so caught up in thoughts that he shouldn't be having, the knock at the door nearly caused him to jump out of his skin.

Alex cursed. Great. Just great.

Losing focus was the best way to get them both killed.

He stepped in front of Leah, looked through the peephole and opened the door to the manager. Good. Winston was one of the few males there who didn't fit the profile. Plus, he'd been manager at the lodge for nearly fifteen years, and the serial strangler murders had happened miles away.

Well, except for Alisha Monroe.

"It took some doing, but I managed to get the sheriff on the CB," Winston said. He wasn't wheezing as much as he had earlier, but his breathing was still unsteady. "He can't get here because the avalanche closed the road between Graniteville and Ice Lake."

Even though it wasn't unexpected, the news was still bad. Without the sheriff's backup, Alex would have to involve Leah in a way he didn't want her involved.

"The sheriff seems to think you can handle this," Winston went on.

"We can," Leah assured him. "We've been working on this case for months. We did the profile, and we'll find this SOB."

Since that sounded a little like marking her territory, Alex intervened. "But we can still use your help," he explained to Winston.

The man nodded. "I did like you said. I typed up a note, telling the guests to stay in their rooms. We slipped it under all the doors and underlined that part about them making sure they were locked in." He checked his watch. "But it's nearly three-thirty. Soon, everyone's gonna start getting hungry. The restaurant opens at five."

Alex considered room service for all forty-two remaining guests and staff, but that wasn't without risks. After all, the strangler could use that as an excuse to get people to open their door to him.

"I'm about to start interviewing those who match the profile," Alex announced. They might get lucky, but he doubted it would happen before dinnertime. "It's best if we keep everyone together. Tell them to come to the restaurant at exactly six. Everyone at once."

It'd be harder for the strangler to pick someone off that way. *If* he was after anyone but Leah, that is. Now that the blizzard had trapped her here, the villain had exactly what he wanted. And that both infuriated and sickened Alex.

"Don't knock on the guests' doors alone," Alex reminded Winston.

"I won't. My brother's a handyman here, and he'll go around with me."

Alex mentally went over the employment records. Winston's brother was in his early fifties and didn't fit the profile, either. That was a plus. They didn't want the strangler using the cover of being a staff member to get to another victim.

Winston patted his pocket. "Besides, I've got my .38, and I know how to use it."

Good. Alex wasn't a fan of civilian help when deadly force was a possibility, but he had no choice. He waited until Winston had walked away before he turned to another civilian.

Leah.

"Here are the rules," Alex told her. "We're joined at the hip for this. We question all the suspects together, and you don't go out of my sight."

She paused. A long time. "Joined at the hip, huh?" she finally mumbled.

Alex followed her gaze and saw that she was staring at the lone bed in the room. "Yeah," he verified. "If we don't catch the strangler before exhaustion sets in, then we're sharing that bed."

It sounded a little like a threat, but it didn't feel that way. More like a torture session where Leah would be curled up close to him. Alex hoped he remembered that he was the boss and not some sex-starved teenager who couldn't control himself.

Good luck with that.

He opened his field bag, which he'd placed on the foot of her bed, and took out the Kevlar vest. He got a raised eyebrow from Leah when he handed it to her.

"Really?" she challenged. "Our guys aren't into bullets. So unless you've got Kevlar for my neck, I doubt this will do any good."

"Humor me," Alex insisted.

"Are you wearing one?" she demanded.

He shook his head. "There's only one in the bag. But I'm not their target."

She huffed, but then peeled off her sweater. For a moment he thought he might have to turn around or come face-to-face with her lacy pink bra, but she had a camisole top beneath. Also pink. She put the vest on over that and then topped it with the sweater.

"Satisfied?" she grumbled.

Not even close.

But Alex kept that to himself.

He shoved her key card into his pocket, picked up the guest list that had the names of their possible suspects highlighted, and turned to her.

"One more thing." Alex stared at her and made sure he had her full attention. "When we find him, I'll be the one to take him down."

Leah made Alex wait several seconds before she nodded.

It was a start, but he knew her assurance didn't mean much. She knew it, too. They weren't dealing with an idiot out-of-control killer here, and Alex had to anticipate that the strangler would try to draw them into a situation.

A deadly one.

One where he could get his hands—literally—on Leah.

CHAPTER FIVE

JOE TARKINGTON, number seven on their list, threw open his door just seconds after Leah knocked on it.

Alex introduced himself, then her, and proceeded to ask the questions that would help them eliminate this guy. He was the last of the possibilities from among the guests, though they still had the three employees to interview.

As she had done with the other six Alex had questioned, she watched and observed while making notes. So far, there hadn't been much to note—mostly just a group of guys who seemed worried they might be murdered or mistaken for a serial killer. Joe-number-seven seemed no different.

Until Leah noticed his right leg.

And the cast that was there.

"Ski accident," Tarkington volunteered, when he saw where her gaze had landed. "It happened two days ago, but since I prepaid for the room, I decided to stay. Figured I'd get my money's worth. Of course, that was before I heard there was a killer here."

Leah jotted down info as Alex continued with the questions, though the cast put some doubts on Tarkington being the strangler. He was thirty-two, and the home address he gave them matched the one he'd written on his lodge registration. Unlike suspect number six, who'd who said he'd been sleeping off a long night of drinking,

Tarkington had heard about the murder at the resort. He had also heard it was the work of the Big Sky Strangler.

"Does this strangler kill men, too?" Tarkington asked, and that brought Leah's attention from her notes to his eyes. A nondescript brown color.

"We're not sure," Alex answered honestly. "That's why we've asked everyone to stay in their rooms or to travel in pairs."

"That's a problem for me. I don't know anyone else here." He tipped his head to the memo on the foot of his bed. The one Winston had delivered, asking everyone to gather in the restaurant at 6:00 p.m.

Only fifteen minutes from now.

"Just wait until there are other guests in the hall and go with them," Alex instructed as he went to the door. "Head straight to the restaurant. No detours."

"Don't worry. I got no plans to do anything stupid," Tarkington assured him, and he closed the door once Leah and Alex were both back in the hall.

"We need to speed this up," Alex said after he blew out a long breath. "We'll have to do the rest of the interviews in the restaurant."

As they walked in that direction, Alex glanced at her notes. She saw the frustration on his face.

Felt it, too.

With all the interviews, they had been able to rule out only two possibilities. Number four, because his five-one, rail-thin stature didn't make him a likely candidate for manual strangulation. And number five, because the female guest in his bed had given him an alibi. Normally, Leah wouldn't have taken the alibi at face value, but everything in the room indicated the two had been at sexcapades for hours and hours. Maybe even days.

"That cast means Joe-number-seven has limited mobility," Leah pointed out. She paused.

"But?" Alex questioned.

"But I'm not ruling him out."

"Neither am I. The killer used a stun gun on the last victim. It wouldn't have taken much mobility to strangle someone who's incapacitated."

True. And they had to consider that the recently broken leg might be the reason he'd resorted to the stun gun. *If* this was their killer. It was a big if because with only two people ruled out, there were still eight possibilities.

At least.

"He might not even be on that list," Leah mumbled.

"Yeah." Alex scrubbed his hand over his face. "Maybe he didn't register. Could be just staying out of sight. Lurking. Watching."

That didn't help case the knot in Leah's stomach. She hoped it was her imagination working overtime, but she could feel the stranger watching her. Feel him waiting to have another go at killing her.

"I thought maybe I'd know him if I saw him," she said. "That I'd feel something in my gut."

"Don't give up on that yet," Alex mumbled. "If we don't get any solid leads soon, we'll reinterview everyone. We'll keep pushing until we get him."

It sounded like a promise, and Leah was going to hold Alex to it.

He stepped into the restaurant ahead of her. The waitstaff were there, all of them female. They were huddled together, their eyes wide, many of them whispering behind their hands. They were scared, and if they'd known as much about the case as Leah did, they would be terrified. Every female in the building was essentially in danger. Alex, too, since he would risk his life to save them.

Alex showed the workers his badge, and Leah and he took positions at the door where they could observe everyone who entered. She gave the room a sweeping glance, noting the location of the exits, windows and furniture. All rote for her. But it wasn't rote to give Alex another look. Her nervousness was no doubt showing because he touched her arm with his fingertips. Rubbed gently.

First Leah scowled at him, but there was no bite to it. "That's not helping me keep my mind on serial killers," she murmured.

"Good. You deserve a break for a second or two."

Leah shook her head, she didn't move away. "Sometimes I think I deserve to be dead. Maybe if the killers had stayed there in that house, trying to finish me off, you could have gotten there in time to catch them."

Alex cursed, then cursed some more. "I'll still catch them. But if you think there's any scenario where I'd want you dead, then think again."

The words were right, but there was something about his tone. It came off like a lover's confession, and it touched her deep in places it shouldn't.

She stepped slightly away, so his fingers were no longer on her. "I thought of you." That was all Leah said for several long seconds. "While he was choking me, my life flashed before my eyes. Yes, I know—it's a cliché. But it happened, and I saw…some things."

She instantly regretted saying that to him, and was sure he was about to ask for more details. But they heard footsteps and chatter, and spotted guests making their way to the restaurant. Right on time, and not alone. There was a group of five and another group of three behind them. Leading the pack was Winston, the lodge manager.

"Showtime," Leah whispered, and she got her notepad ready.

Alex stayed quiet a moment, probably filing away some questions about her near-death experience. Questions he'd ask later, and she would avoid answering.

"Joe-number-seven found some traveling buddies, after all," Alex pointed out.

He had. The supposed injured skier was in the second group. No viable suspects were in the first group—wrong gender or wrong age. But Tarkington was hobbling just a few yards ahead of someone who did match the profile.

Patrick Harper—number two on their list.

Both men stared at Alex and her as they filed into the restaurant. Leah tried to examine the two with an objective eye. She looked at their hands, their arms. They had the physical strength to choke the life out of a woman, but were they killers?

She didn't see it.

But then she reminded herself that the strangler had managed to blend in, and had charmed his way into some of his victims' homes.

He wouldn't look like a killer.

Wouldn't put out any vibes that would frighten women. Well, he wouldn't until he was ready to commit murder. Leah had experienced this strangler's true colors the hard way and knew he was calculating and smart. If he'd been anything else, he wouldn't have gotten her in such a vulnerable position.

Winston moved next to Alex and her. "I went through the payroll records." He kept his voice at a whisper. "And I checked them against the date of that murder in

Billings last week. Two of my guys were here working, so they couldn't have killed that woman. David Fowler is the only one left I haven't been able to rule out."

Fowler, the man who'd been in the hall after the discovery of the most recent victim. "Any sign of him yet?" Leah asked.

The hotel manager shook his head. "But I'll keep looking."

With two more workmen, their list was now down to six, and Leah realized five of those were in the restaurant. She studied each man again and wished one would make a move so she could put an end to this now. Of course, that wouldn't be wise in a room filled with innocent people.

Winston excused himself so he could talk with the food staff, but Alex stayed near the doorway with her. The waitresses dispersed to take orders, even though no one other than the handful of children looked hungry.

Leah figured many of the adults must be already thinking about how to get out of there. The storm would stop them for a while, of course. She hoped none of them got killed trying to get out of the path of the strangler.

"I'll start counting," she offered.

Another necessity. They had to make sure no one was skipping out on this little get-together dining experience. Leah did a headcount and came up with forty-two. It was exactly what it should be, minus Fowler.

"Should I start another round of questioning?" she asked Alex.

He glanced at the group and tipped his head toward their number-two suspect, Harper, who was seated alone. "You take him," he told her. And he strolled toward Joe Tarkington, who was also alone at a table.

Leah knew exactly why Alex had chosen Tarkington, and it didn't have anything to do with interrogation tactics or random selection. It was because she'd be close by and in his line of sight. Even though it wouldn't match the strangler's profile to grab a victim in such a public forum, Alex wanted to be ready for anything.

So did she.

Like their other suspects, Harper had brown hair and an average build. He was the kind of person you wouldn't notice in a crowd. And that meant he fit the profile to a T.

He spared Alex a glance before he turned his attention to Leah. "Looks like someone did a real number on you," he commented, and took a long sip from the glass of ice water he'd just been served.

It wasn't the opening Leah expected, and she made a mental note of it. They'd interviewed him just an hour earlier, and most people in that situation would have asked about the progress of the case and expressed some concern. After all, they were trapped in the building with a dead body and a serial killer. But Patrick had instead focused on her.

Interesting.

"I'm fine," she lied. She inched closer, knowing it would violate the man's personal space and hopefully make him uncomfortable. Uncomfortable people often spilled things they didn't intend to say.

"You come here often to Ice Lake?" she asked, already aware of the answer, since she'd studied the guest records.

"First visit. And last." He downed some more water. "I'm not exactly comfortable with what's happening, you know?" His gaze drifted to her cast. "Rumor has it the Big Sky Strangler nearly killed you."

Leah figured it was a good time to stay quiet, especially on that subject. She didn't have to wait long for Harper to continue. "Rumor also has it that you set this up. People are saying you lured the strangler here so you could get revenge. Not a smart move. Now our butts are all in a sling because of you."

Leah's training had taught her not to lose her cool—ever—but this guy was pushing hard. She considered moving him to the top of the suspect list, but didn't want to do that based solely on a hot button this moron had managed to push.

"I didn't bring the danger here," she stated, though she had to fight not to clench her teeth. "But I plan to stop this killer before he hurts anyone else."

"Oh, yeah? What if he gets you first?" The man didn't wait for an answer. "Wouldn't be much of a stretch if he did, since he's already done it once." He leaned in closer, violating *her* personal space. "What did it feel like to come that close to dying?"

Leah didn't back away, though she was certain she was more uncomfortable than Harper was. He seemed to be enjoying this. She wasn't.

"What do you think it felt like?" she countered.

He didn't smile, but she got the feeling that's what he wanted to do. "Like you'd lost control. Like you'd failed," he answered.

She didn't deny it, and just nodded. "And that's why I'll stop him. Because I know just how high the stakes are."

Leah geared up to add more, but there was a slight hissing sound.

That was all the warning she got.

The lights went out, plunging them into darkness.

CHAPTER SIX

ALEX AUTOMATICALLY DREW his gun, even though it was impossible to see anyone or anything in the pitch-black restaurant. However, he could hear gasps, whispers and other sounds of fear.

"Leah?" he called out.

"Here," she quickly answered.

He hurried toward the sound of her voice and nearly plowed into her. Alex felt her gun and was glad that she'd drawn it. This might be nothing. After all, power failure was common during a blizzard, but they were in the room with serial killer suspects, so he didn't want to take any chances.

"Hold tight, everyone," Winston called out. "The generator should kick in soon."

Alex hoped that "soon" would be soon enough. And prayed the killer wouldn't use the darkness to strike again. Just in case that was the strangler's plan, Alex kept shoulder to shoulder with Leah.

"Let's back toward the door," he whispered to her. That way, they could stop anyone trying to leave.

Or come in.

They had to watch for both, since one of the suspects, David Fowler, still hadn't made a repeat appearance.

Alex took short, slow steps, making sure Leah stayed right by his side. By the time they reached the doorway, his eyes had adjusted a little to the darkness. While he couldn't make out anyone, he could at least see shadows.

"Stay put!" he ordered when he heard footsteps and movement.

He cursed the fact that there was another exit, at the far end of the room. If Leah had been a hundred percent, he would have stationed her here so he could cover that exit. But it was too big a risk to take, since she was the strangler's primary target.

"Why hasn't the generator started?" she asked in a whisper.

Alex was wondering the same damn thing. Fear and panic were crawling through the room, and he didn't want people to start stampeding out of there. It would give the strangler a perfect opportunity to pick off Leah or someone else.

"Winston?" Alex called out.

"I'm on my way toward you," he answered promptly.

"Something's wrong," Leah said, taking the words right out of Alex's mouth.

Alex tried to pinpoint which of the footsteps belonged to the lodge manager, but it was impossible. Too many people were moving around, and worse, his own heartbeat was pounding in his ears. All of that, however, wasn't enough to drown out the sound.

The scream.

A woman's scream.

It sliced through the rest of the noise. Sliced straight through Alex. Because it wasn't the sound of someone merely frightened. This was terror.

Beside him, he felt Leah's arm tense, no doubt because her finger was now on the trigger. Alex's certainly was.

"The strangler's killing someone," she said. He could hear the fear in her voice.

"It didn't come from this room," he told her, though he figured she already knew that. The sound had come from the other side of the resort, where the guest rooms were. "Stay calm," he called out to the guests. Though he doubted that was possible. "And stay here."

Still no generator, but Alex couldn't ignore that scream. Leah was right; the strangler could be choking the life out of someone, and he had to stop it.

"Maybe there's a flashlight at the reception desk," he murmured. "Let's go."

Even though it was a risk to leave the guests unprotected, Alex had no choice. Leah and he raced out the doorway and made their way toward the desk. Not easily. Each step through the chilly darkness was a challenge, and it didn't help that every shadow looked like the strangler ready to pounce on Leah.

Alex was thankful when they reached the lobby fireplace. The logs had burned down to embers, but the meager light was better than nothing.

"I'll look behind the counter for a flashlight," she offered. But Alex went with her, keeping watch.

"Nothing," Leah said eventually.

At the exact moment, there was another scream, followed by the sound of someone running.

Hell. Alex would have preferred some light, but couldn't wait any longer. "Stay right behind me," he warned Leah, and they hurried forward. He already had one dead body on his hands and didn't want another.

The fireplace didn't provide illumination for long. As soon as they reached the hall, the scant light was gone. Alex paused for a second to get his bearings and to focus in on those footsteps.

At the end of the hall.

Of course. Where else? That meant taking Leah into

one of the most vulnerable points in the lodge. Since the guests were in the restaurant, all the rooms would be locked, and if the strangler was using this to lure them in, Leah and he could be trapped, with the only escape route behind them.

"Help me!" someone yelled.

A woman. Maybe the one who'd screamed. Maybe not. But whoever it was kept repeating it.

Alex kept his gun ready and started down the hall. He couldn't see his hand before his eyes, only the murky darkness. But the woman's call for help kept him moving and praying that Leah wouldn't get separated from him during this rescue.

With each step they took, his heartbeat revved up. So did the adrenaline, and by the time they reached the door, Alex was primed and ready for a fight.

Without warning, the lights flared on.

He did a quick check over his shoulder to make sure Leah was okay. She was, though her face was tight with pain no doubt because of her broken arm and the grip she had on her gun.

"I'm Special Agent McCade," he called out. No response, other than the woman's repeated plea.

Alex tested the doorknob. It was locked. With his gun ready, he kicked in the door and braced himself for an attack in progress.

But there was no attack.

The lights were on here, as well, so he had no trouble seeing that the room was empty. He did a quick check of the closet and bathroom. Nobody. He looked under the bed and spotted the source of the sounds.

A tape recorder.

It had speakers attached to it and was set at top

volume. It was also rigged with a timer. So, not an attack but a hoax.

"Is this some kind of trap?" Leah asked hoarsely.

Alex hurried back to her and pulled her into the room with him. He peered out into the hall.

Also empty.

That didn't make him breathe any easier. What the devil was going on?

"Maybe the strangler wanted us out of the restaurant so he could attack someone else," she suggested.

Maybe. But that didn't make sense. Leah was the one he wanted.

The recorded woman's plea for help continued, and even though it wasn't real, it rattled Alex's already raw nerves. He couldn't turn it off. It might disturb some trace evidence, or the recorder might be rigged in some kind of way.

Maybe with an explosive.

"Let's get out of here," he muttered.

They turned, ready to do just that, but the recorded calls for help suddenly stopped. The room went silent for several seconds, and then there was a new voice. A man's.

"Leah," he said.

There was nothing unique about the voice. No heavy accent or memorable tone. But just that one word made Alex's blood run cold. He instinctively knew it was the voice of the Big Sky Strangler.

"Ready for this to end?" the man asked. He paused. "If not, I can play with the woman in room 311. She has a cute kid that might make things interesting."

Alex cursed and wished he could reach through that recording and rip the monster to shreds.

"It's them or you," the man continued. "Your choice.

If you want them to live, then meet me *alone* in the storage room at 2:00 a.m. See you then, Leah."

He paused again.

"Oh, and Leah, this time only one of us will walk out of there alive."

CHAPTER SEVEN

Only one of us will walk out of there alive.

The words kept firing through Leah's head. She didn't try to shut them out, because she'd known it would come down to this. The trick was to make sure she was the one still standing when it was over.

"You're not meeting a killer in that storage room," Alex warned her as they walked back to her room. He didn't add more until they were inside and he'd shut the door. "In fact, you're not going *anywhere* alone."

Leah didn't argue, though sooner or later she would have to convince him that this had to happen. They couldn't let the strangler continue to have free rein in a lodge filled with potential victims. And the storm wasn't letting up so they could evacuate. No. This showdown was coming, and there was nothing Alex could do to stop it.

Of course, he wasn't ready to admit that yet.

"We'll have to find another way," Alex went on. He started to pace, a little maneuver that reminded her of a caged tiger looking for something to pounce on. The energy coming from him was dangerous and palatable. "A way that doesn't involve using you as a target."

"I'm already a target," she reminded him.

He shot her a glare that was blazing hot and ice-cold at the same time. "You're not meeting this bastard." Alex added more profanity. "The second you step into that storage room, he'd be on you, and with that broken wrist, you don't stand a chance of fighting back."

"But I can shoot." *Probably.* She mentally paused. And amended that to *maybe.* "I could appear to go in alone, but you could be nearby. Close enough to respond the moment he reveals himself."

Alex started shaking his head before she even finished that last sentence, but the argument stopped at the sound of a sharp knock on the door. He drew his gun, reholstering it when he'd looked through the peephole.

"It's Winston," he announced, and opened the door to the harried-faced manager, who was holding a large canvas bag.

It wasn't just Winston and the bag that snagged Leah's attention. It was the sound of a man's voice in the hall. She looked out and spotted Joe Tarkington limping toward them.

Alex drew his gun again.

Tarkington raised his left hand in surrender while holding on to the crutch with his other. "It's just me," he said, as if that would make Alex and her relax. It didn't. Tarkington was one of their three top suspects.

"What do you want?"

Alex asked the question at the same moment Winston said, "I told everyone to go to their rooms and stay put."

"I'm in pain, all right?" Tarkington snarled. "And I don't have any meds in my room. There's no one at the desk, so when I spotted you, I figured you'd be the person to ask."

Winston volleyed what-should-I-do? glances at Alex and her, and it was Alex who answered.

"Wait for Winston by the reception desk. He'll find you some meds."

"Wait for how long?" Tarkington pressed. His face twisted and he reached down to massage his leg.

It was a reasonable question, but Leah wasn't in a reasonable sort of mood. She was suspicious and tried to look at their suspect with a fresh eye. Was this some kind of ruse to find out what Alex and she were planning?

"You'll have to wait as long as it takes," Alex insisted.

But Tarkington didn't budge. Nor did he keep his attention on Winston, the man he was supposed to go wait for. No. Tarkington looked at her.

Unlike Patrick Harper, there was no cockiness in his expression, but he did comb his gaze over her bruises. Especially the ones on her throat. Leah put her hand over them before she could stop herself.

"The strangler did that to you?" Tarkington asked. Again, no cockiness. No accusation.

Leah didn't answer, but her silence was an answer in itself.

"You can leave now," Alex reminded him in a growl. He was clearly losing patience with the man.

Tarkington still didn't go. "If he could do that to you, a federal agent, imagine what he could do to the rest of us." He glanced back down at his cast. "I've got no way to fight off a guy like that." And he fixed his attention on her broken wrist.

"You won't have to fight him off if you stay in your room with the door locked," Winston barked.

Tarkington didn't even spare him a glance. He stared instead at Leah. "I need protection," he insisted. "A guard or something. It's not safe for me to be alone."

Alex stepped forward, blocking the man's view of her. That finally got his attention off Leah.

"Leave now," Alex repeated. And there was no doubt about it—it was a warning.

Tarkington clearly wasn't pleased with the dismissal, but after seeing Alex's drawn gun he mumbled something about Ice Lake being a hellhole and hobbled away.

Leah was glad to see him go. Not because she thought he was the strangler; she had no clear opinion about that. But she hadn't wanted Alex to get into a scuffle with a suspect. They had enough to do without escalating things in the hall.

Best to save that for the storage room.

"Please tell me there aren't any more dead bodies," Winston said the moment Tarkington was out of earshot.

"No," Leah answered. "Just screams and then a threatening message left on a tape recorder. We'll need protection for the female guest and her daughter in room 311."

The manager nodded. "I'll have my brother stay outside her door." He paused. "For how long?"

Now it was Leah's turn to pause. "Until 2:00 a.m. at least. The strangler wants me to meet him in the storage room then."

"That's not going to happen," Alex insisted, though she didn't know how he managed to speak with those iron-stiff jaw muscles.

Leah ignored him. "Where's the storage room?"

"In the basement," Winston replied. "We keep furniture and equipment down there. It doubles as the overflow laundry room."

She got a clear mental image of a room with lots of equipment and plenty of places for a murderer to hide. Which was probably why he'd chosen it. He would have picked a place to give him the best advantage. Of course, the best advantage of all was that she was desperate to stop the killings. She wouldn't sacrifice herself, but she couldn't just stand by and let the killings continue, either.

"How many exits are in the storage room?" she asked.

Winston shook his head. "Just one way in or out."

Alex's huff let her know that her argument was getting thinner.

"What about lighting?" she inquired. "Is there a way a person could cut the power to the hotel from inside that room?" Darkness would favor a killer, and it was possible the strangler had managed to cut the electricity flow earlier. It seemed too convenient that the blackout had happened only minutes before that tape recorder was triggered to play the woman's screams and then the threat.

"There's a light switch for the hall outside the storage room. It's by the stairs," the manger explained. "But even if someone turns off the overhead fluorescents, there are some floor lights that will kick on because they're on generator power. They're dim, but they'd help you see."

So it wouldn't be totally dark, even if that's what the strangler wanted. Of course, the darkness could also be an advantage for Alex and her.

If Alex allowed it to be, that is.

Winston reached into his canvas bag and brought out a laptop. "The internet link is still not working," he told them. "But the computer might come in handy. I've turned the two security cameras at angles to cover some of the halls." He put the computer on the desk, opened it, and a few seconds later Leah saw the feed on the split screen.

"Some of the halls" was indeed an accurate description. Two corridors, specifically, leaving two uncovered. Still, it was better than nothing.

"Any chance Tarkington or Harper saw you adjust the security cameras?" Alex asked.

Leah knew the reason for his question. If they had, and one of them was the strangler, he would just use a hall that wasn't monitored.

"I don't think they saw me," Winston answered. But then he shook his head. "But I can't be positive."

So Alex and she had to count on the strangler knowing how to avoid camera detection.

Well, maybe.

Leah stayed quiet a moment, studying the situation. "Could one of the cameras be taken down and moved to another part of the building—the storage room, for instance? Maybe place it somewhere out of sight?"

Winston frowned. "I guess. I'd have to see how they're wired in. But I could try."

"Please do," Leah insisted, ignoring Alex's glare.

Still, he couldn't argue with having some visual surveillance in the very area where the strangler had said he would be. As a minimum, they could capture his image, and then do something to lure him out. She wasn't yet sure what that something would be, but they had a little time to come up with a workable plan.

If Alex budged, that is.

"One more thing," Winston went on. "We've got an old intercom system that hasn't been used in years. There's this woman, a guest here, who's an electrician. She said she might be able to get it working. It could come in handy if this drags on."

Leah didn't see it dragging on much past 2:00 a.m. But the intercom was a good idea. At the very least, they could use it to remind everyone to stay in their rooms.

Alex obviously thought so, too, because he nodded. "Get her working on it."

Winston reached in the canvas bag again and took out a pair of walkie-talkies. "The maintenance staff uses them, but I thought they might do you some good."

"Thanks. They could." Alex deposited one next to the laptop, then he handed the second back to Winston. "Keep it with you in case I have to contact you." What he didn't say was that he had no plans to be apart from Leah.

Joined at the hip indeed.

The hotel manager started to leave, but then stopped. His face twisted a little, letting Leah know this wouldn't be good news.

"I nearly forgot to tell you. There are two master key cards missing from the maids' carts." Winston mumbled something, shook his head. "It's possible they're just lost. But..."

He didn't finish. He didn't have to. They all knew the strangler could have taken one or both of them. And if so, that meant he had access to every room in the building.

Oh, mercy.

Things had just gone from bad to worse.

"Most folks are scared spitless, so they'll already be using the arm latches on their doors," Winston declared. "But until we get the intercom working, I'll send around the cleaning staff—two at a time—to tell everybody to double latch their doors."

It was going to be a long night.

Only one of us will walk out of there alive.

That message sliced through Leah again, and she closed her eyes a moment to shut out the flashbacks of the other attack. When she opened them once more, she realized both Winston and Alex were staring at the laptop screen.

"Patrick Harper," Alex mumbled.

Yes, it was. Leah could see their suspect on the screen, surrounded by four other guests. There was no audio, but it was clear from the way he was moving his hands that he was agitated.

Winston glanced at Leah, then quickly looked away. "He's trying to stir up trouble about you. Keeps harping that you're to blame for this mess." The manager gave her a sympathetic look. "I'll get down there and have them all head back to their rooms."

"Tell Harper it's an order," Alex barked. "If he leaves his room again, I'll arrest him for interfering with a federal investigation."

Winston didn't smile but came close. "Oh, I'll gladly let him know that."

As soon as the manager left, Alex locked the door and aimed a fresh scowl at Leah. "You knew Harper was trying to pin the danger on you?"

She nodded. "He mentioned it when I questioned him in the restaurant. Right before the lights went out."

Alex looked back at the laptop and studied the man on screen. "He fits our profile."

"Yes. But so do others—David Fowler and Joe Tarkington. Patrick Harper could just be having a bad reaction to the fear and stress. There's no crime in being a cocky jerk."

"Or he could be a killer who thinks he can bait you into meeting him in the storage room."

Leah couldn't help it; she smiled. "You make it sound as if we have another option." She dropped the smile. "We don't."

"We do," he snapped. "When the intercom is working, I'll use it to broadcast a new plan—that you won't be going to the storage room. I will be."

Leah rolled her eyes. "You know the strangler won't agree to that. He wants me. Not you."

The muscles in Alex's jaw flexed, and his index finger landed against her chest. Or rather, the Kevlar vest. "He's not getting you, and that's the end of this discussion."

With that hanging in the air, Alex went back to studying the screen, where Winston had appeared, obviously to talk with Harper and the small group of people around him. It didn't take long, just a few seconds, before everyone dispersed but Harper. He continued to argue with Winston.

"We don't need a hothead like this," Alex mumbled.

No, they didn't. Fear would hold people in their rooms for only so long. Soon they would need to feel safe, and would want answers about how this strangler could be stopped. Frustrated at exactly how they might do that, Leah sank down onto the foot of the bed.

The mattress shifted a little and sent her suitcase and Alex's field bag sliding into her. She pushed them away, but not before she noticed the paper on top of the supplies in the field kit. Her eyes skittered across it before she could stop herself. What she saw caused her mouth to drop open.

"What the heck is this?" She snatched up the paper and repeated her question.

Alex whirled around, looking puzzled at first, until his gaze landed on the paper. He groaned softly. "You weren't supposed to see that yet. But I was going to tell you after...well, after this."

She tuned him out for a few seconds so she could read through the forms. "This is a request for a transfer of supervision, effective tomorrow." Leah got to her feet so she could look him in the eyes. "You no longer want to be my boss."

"I never wanted to be your boss," he quickly admitted. He groaned again and put his hands on his hips. "I thought I could make it work, but I can't. So I requested that Sanchez become your supervisor."

Martin Sanchez, an agent in their field office, he was someone Leah respected, but still…

"You worked hard for that promotion," she reminded him. "You deserve to be the team leader for everyone in the office, including me."

Alex stepped closer, reached out and ran his hand down the length of her arm. It was a gesture no doubt meant to calm her, but Leah didn't want to be calmed down. She wanted answers. Something like this could possibly hurt Alex's chances of promotion down the line. She didn't want him to risk what he loved most just because it was an uncomfortable situation.

"I can try harder," she suggested. "Maybe not mouth off to you as much."

He gave a weary sigh. "This isn't about you. It's about me. About what I didn't do."

Leah had to shake her head. Alex was a model agent. A model supervisor. "I can't imagine you not doing something required for the job."

"Imagine it," he mumbled. And that's all he said for several moments. "When I went running into that house and found you nearly dead, I wasn't thinking like an FBI agent. I reacted like your…friend. Your former lover."

She shook her head again, uncertain of what he was saying. "What did you do?"

"I didn't secure the scene," he blurted out. "Didn't check to see if the killers were still in the house. Hell,

I didn't even check on the other woman. I went to you and started CPR."

Leah swallowed hard. Some of the images of the attack were still a nightmarish blur, so this was the first she knew about how Alex had responded. One thing stood out loud and clear. "If you hadn't done CPR, I would have died."

"Yeah." He hesitated again. "But the point is, I quit being aware of my surroundings and focused only on you."

Despite what she'd said earlier about wishing the strangler had stayed in that house long enough for Alex to catch him, Leah was thankful to be alive.

She took a step closer to him. "If you think I'm sorry for the way you responded, I'm not."

"I'm not sorry, either," he stated, staring at her. "But if the stranglers had still been there in the house, they could have killed both of us."

When she started to object, Alex touched his fingers to her mouth. "Yes, our personal relationship is over, but too many things have gone on between us for me to be objective when it comes to you."

Leah didn't know who was more surprised by that revelation—Alex or her. Judging from the way his forehead bunched up, he hadn't intended to tell her about this. Not tonight, anyway. And she knew how much it cost him to give up what he loved most—that promotion. Even if it was only a small part of his power and position. Alex was married to the badge, and it was a huge concession for him to do anything that would affect his job.

"I'm sorry," she said. And she meant it.

She leaned in to brush a kiss on his cheek. A mistake,

she quickly realized. There was too much energy zinging between them for that kind of personal contact.

Alex cursed, slid his arm around her waist and pulled her to him.

Before Leah could tell him what a bad idea it was, his mouth was on hers. Kissing her senseless. Kissing her until she forgot all about the massive mistake they were making.

Leah lifted her arms, wrapped them around Alex and melted into the kiss.

CHAPTER EIGHT

ALEX FELT THAT FAMILIAR punch of heat. He should have been immune to it by now, or at least aware enough to know that he should resist it. He was still technically her boss, and they had other things they should be doing.

But he didn't resist.

One touch of his mouth to Leah's, and the taste of her slammed through him.

He dragged her closer until she was plastered against him and tangled in his arms. In the back of his mind, he knew he was being too rough. Too stupid. But even that didn't stop him. Alex shifted them, placing her against the door and deepened the kiss.

Yeah.

Another huge mistake.

Leah made that little eager sound of pleasure. Another familiar punch that was like lighting another fuse that shouldn't be lit. It was the sound she'd often made just seconds before he hauled her to bed. And with every passing moment, bed was feeling like more of a possibility.

She lifted a leg, sliding it along the outside of his. Making the contact in the midsections of their bodies even more intense. Because he was already too deep in that zone, Alex helped her. He dropped his hands to her butt, lifting her so that her sex aligned with his.

Good.

But not good.

It only made him think of sex that couldn't happen.

Still, Alex didn't stop kissing her. And he sure as hell didn't back away when they started to grabble for position and fight to get even closer to each other. Being closer while still clothed wasn't possible, of course, but that didn't stop them from trying.

He slipped his hand between them to cup her right breast, pausing at the barrier of the Kevlar vest—if only she was naked so he could taste her there. Of course, that wasn't the only reason he wished their clothes would vanish, but it was a start. He slid his hand lower, to her stomach.

Then lower.

Alex put his hand at the juncture of her thighs. The one spot that would make them even crazier. It worked. Yeah, they still had the clothes barrier, but his fingers were now where another part of him wanted to be. *Bad.* Since that couldn't happen, he settled for touching her. All in all, it was a paltry substitute, even though Leah was clearly enjoying it. That meant Alex was enjoying it, too. He loved seeing her soar.

She made that sound again, the let's-have-sex-now sound. She pushed her hips toward him, getting the most from his touch. But soon even that wasn't enough. She wanted more. So did Alex. But she was the one who did something about it. She started maneuvering him toward the bed, one step at a time, without breaking their intimate contact.

And that's when Alex knew this sweet torture had to stop.

He caught her shoulders, anchoring her in place against the edge of the mattress, and backed away from her. Not easily. It took every ounce of his willpower, but Alex finally managed to put a few inches between them.

Leah's breath was gusting and her face was flushed. Except for that bruise. And it was the bruise that caused Alex to realize just how big of a mistake he'd just made. He opened his mouth to tell her how sorry he was, but she clapped her fingers over his lips.

"Don't," she rasped, still panting. "We both know it shouldn't have happened."

Yeah, they did. But Alex eased her hand away. "I could have hurt you."

She gave him a flat look. "Trust me, I wasn't hurting." Her gaze dropped to the front of his pants. "And neither were you."

No pain then, but he was damned uncomfortable now. And probably couldn't walk, thanks to the erection that kept urging him to go back to Leah for another round. A round that would lead to sex.

No. Make that *great* sex.

Alex cursed, stepped back even farther.

Leah stayed put, still trying to level her breathing. "We've always had this thing for each other. It's apparently still there, whether we want it to be or not."

"This thing" was lust. According to Leah that's what it had been. It had always felt a little more than that to Alex.

"We should get back to the case," she mumbled. "Two in the morning will be here before we know it."

Alex knew she was right, but he didn't want to go there just yet. Yes, catching the strangler was important. However, Leah was, too. And maybe, just maybe, this had all been more than lust.

"What did you see when your life flashed before your eyes?" he asked.

She blinked. Shook her head. "Best not to answer that when we're still burning from that kiss."

Leah brushed past him and went to the laptop Winston had delivered. "The job," she reminded him. Maybe she was reminding herself, too, because she repeated it.

"You can avoid this conversation," he said, "but not forever."

She made a sound of disagreement. Alex copied it, causing her gaze to swing back to him. He saw the debate in her eyes. The argument. But then she lifted a shoulder.

"Not forever," she finally agreed. "But for now."

Alex huffed, knowing she was right, and they had no choice. A killer was bearing down on them. It was that thought alone that kept him from pulling Leah back into his arms and demanding answers about what that kiss had really meant. He couldn't save her by kissing her or having sex with her. So he turned toward the laptop and focused on what Leah was watching.

The right side of the screen showed a man on a ladder taking down a security camera—one of the lodge workers. Thankfully, no one was around to see what he was doing. At least no one else within camera view. It was possible the strangler was in another hall, watching. And waiting for 2:00 a.m.

A moment later, that side of the laptop screen went blank. The worker had disconnected the camera.

"Maybe he'll be able to move it closer to the storage room," Leah remarked.

Yeah, maybe. Alex knew where she was going with this, but she wasn't spelling out the bottom line. "A camera won't stop an attack."

"And dodging the strangler's request won't stop him."

She met Alex's scowl with one of her own. "You know he'll just find another target if he can't get to me."

Alex did know that. And here's where he had a conflict of interest the size of Montana. If Leah were any other agent, he would have already seriously considered using her as bait to stop a serial killer. But he kept going back to that cast on her broken wrist, to those bruises.

To the psych test she'd failed.

It was an easy evaluation to pass, if you were careful about how you answered.

Or if you lied.

Most agents did one of the two rather than risk being placed on leave. But Leah had let it slip to the shrink that she wasn't sure how she would react in another situation like that.

She might freeze, she'd confessed.

The comment had been the kiss of death. And it literally could mean her death, if she froze at the wrong time.

Such as during another attack by the strangler, in that storage room.

"What?" she pressed, her scowl turning to a concerned stare.

Alex went through several things he could say, but there was an obvious answer: that they had to stop this SOB from killing again. And for that to happen, he had to risk Leah.

Hell.

He met her concerned look with one of his own, and repeated the key question on the psych eval. "What will you do if the strangler manages to get his hands on you again?"

Her chin came up. She made direct eye contact. "I'll do what I've been trained to do."

That was the right answer.

It was also a lie.

In the depths of those green eyes, he could see her split-second hesitation. A second that could get her killed.

"Let's consider our best-case scenario." Leah tossed out the suggestion before Alex could voice his obvious concern. "Winston gets the camera set up, and we're able to see the strangler sneak into the storage room. I go to meet him—with you right behind me," she quickly added.

"What if he shoots you when you walk in?" Alex asked.

She tapped her chest. "I'm wearing Kevlar, remember?"

Alex gave her a flat look. "Yeah, but if he goes for a head shot, you're dead."

She mimicked his skeptical look. "Nothing about his profile says he'll go for a head shot, or any other kind, for that matter. He kills with his hands. Face-to-face. That's what gets him off. And that's what he'll want to do to me. He didn't follow me all the way out here to Ice Lake just so he could end things quickly with a bullet."

"Is this supposed to reassure me in some way?" Alex pointed to her throat. "Hell's bells, Leah, I can still see his handprint on you."

"No, it's not meant to reassure you." Her voice softened. So did her expression. "But if he wants his hands on me, he'll have to get close enough to me to do that. You'll be there to stop him."

Alex went through that so-called plan and saw an immediate flaw. "What if he has his partner in there, waiting?"

Without taking her gaze away, she walked closer.

"There's no indication whatsoever that his partner is here. The threats have all been from one source. The dominant guy. But if I'm wrong, then we stop them both."

Alex was about to point out that the strangler could be the one who did the stopping, when he saw something flash on the laptop screen: the image of the hall just outside what appeared to be the storage room. It wasn't a clear shot, because there seemed to a red object obscuring part of the screen. However, a moment later, Winston moved in front of the camera and gave a thumbs-up. He had managed to relocate the camera, and it was working.

"Step one's a success," Leah concluded. She stared at Alex. Waited. And he knew exactly what she was waiting for. She wanted him to approve this plan.

While he didn't want to approve anything that put Leah in even more danger, he knew he had no choice. So he nodded.

"Good," she mumbled. But there was no celebration in her tone or expression. She knew they could be walking into a death trap.

To minimize the danger, Alex made a quick mental list of what he needed to do. "I have to question Patrick Harper and Joe Tarkington again," he told her. "I'll also search their rooms, and if I come across anything out of the ordinary—*anything*—I will find some place in the lodge that we can use as a containment area."

"You're going to arrest them?" she challenged.

In a heartbeat. Even if it might be stretching the law, that didn't matter to him. "If they're contained, we can keep watch over them, and if our strangler doesn't show, then we'll have a pretty good idea that either Tarkington or Harper is our killer."

She nodded. “All right.”

Alex reached for the security latch, but before he could open it, someone knocked on the door. Probably Winston. However, when Alex checked, he saw it wasn’t the hotel manager, but someone else he definitely wanted to talk to.

He made sure Leah was behind him, and just in case this was about to turn ugly, he drew his gun.

“What the heck is going on?” she asked. She drew her gun, as well.

Alex flipped the latch, opened the door and came face-to-face with the lodge’s missing employee.

David Fowler.

CHAPTER NINE

OF ALL THE PEOPLE Leah might have expected to see at the door, David Fowler wasn't one of them. She figured if he was the strangler, he would have stayed in hiding—until 2:00 a.m., anyway. And if he was an innocent bystander in all this, then he would have been long gone.

Yet here he was, knocking on their door.

"I heard you wanted to see me," Fowler announced. He flicked his gaze around, as if he expected someone to jump out and grab him. And maybe he did. After all, he'd seen the dead woman in the room just across the hall.

"We do," Leah verified. "Where have you been?"

He glanced around again, this time toward the room where the body had been. "I'll answer all your questions, but first I want to come in. I'm not exactly comfortable standing out here in the open."

"And I'm not exactly comfortable having you in here with us," Alex snapped. Clearly, he was not pleased that Fowler had pulled a disappearing act and was just now showing up.

"Then maybe you can talk fast," he suggested. "Because I don't want to be the killer's next victim."

"Funny, I thought maybe you *were* the killer." Alex aimed one of his hard glares at the man.

Fowler's eyes widened and he tapped his chest. "You think *I* killed that woman? No way would I do something like that! I just happened to be in the hall when the maid opened the door and found her."

"Yeah, and then you disappeared," Leah reminded him. "Pretty suspicious, if you ask me."

"Because I was scared!" the man practically yelled. He mumbled something under his breath, then shook his head. "Look, when I was seven, I came home from school and found my mom dead. She'd committed suicide. Seeing that woman brought the memories flooding back. I couldn't stay. I couldn't stand to see her another second."

Despite the chilly temperature in the hall, sweat popped out above Fowler's upper lip. He certainly had the signs of a man on edge, but Leah knew serial killers could be deadly chameleons. The Big Sky Strangler fit that bill, and she was glad that Alex hadn't let this guy in with them.

"You saw the woman's body hours ago. Where have you been since then?" Alex asked, in his best special-agent tone. He definitely wasn't reacting sympathetically to what Fowler had just told them about being traumatized over his dead mother.

The man volleyed glances at both of them. "You really think I killed her?"

"We really think it's a possibility," Leah informed him. "And that possibility is getting bigger because you seem to be dodging my partner's question. Where have you been in the last few hours?"

That didn't help his sweaty lip or his nerves. It seemed as if he changed his mind a dozen times about what to say before he finally looked at her. Direct eye contact this time. However, Leah knew from experience that serial killers were often excellent liars.

"There are some empty guest rooms on the second

floor," Fowler finally said. "I let myself in one so I could calm down and get some rest."

"And take a shower," Leah observed, noticing his damp hair and the scent of the resort's shampoo.

There went the eye contact and his brief episode of relative calm. He propped hands on his hips. "Yeah, I took a shower. So what?"

"It could be a big so-what," Alex commented. "You could have done that to wash away any evidence of the crime."

"I didn't commit a crime." It wasn't a shout, but there was so much emotion on his face and in his voice that it might as well have been.

"Then why shower?" Leah pressed.

His eyes narrowed and his breathing speeded up. "I figured the hot water would help me relax. It was either that or have a panic attack."

If he was telling the truth about all this, Leah would apologize later. Right now, she just had to be sure that he wasn't a killer playing some kind of mind game. Because every one of his physical responses could be faked.

"How did you get in the guest room?" she demanded.

Fowler reacted as if she'd slugged him. His shoulders went back, and there was a look of panic in his eyes. "I took the passkey from the maid's cart."

"Just one key?" Alex asked.

Fowler gave them a funny look. "Of course just one. Why would I take more than that? The passkey works with all the rooms."

Alex and Leah exchanged glances. If the man had taken two, then it would be good news, maybe. That could mean the killer wouldn't have access to the rooms and new victims. Unless Fowler *was* the killer. Or was lying about the missing extra key.

"I'll give the key back," Fowler added, after another glance up and down the hall. "Can I go now?"

Alex shook his head. "You can wait in Winston Cooper's office until I've checked out a few things."

And Leah knew what those few things were: Patrick Harper's and Joe Tarkington's rooms. Plus they had to find a place to contain the two men, and possibly Fowler, if Alex and she came across anything they could use to hold them. Heck, even if they couldn't find anything, she hoped Alex would lock them up. Yes, it would create possible problems. Might even result in a lawsuit. But no one else would die today.

Unless the killer was someone else entirely.

Leah couldn't help but go back to that. The Big Sky Stranglers knew how to fit in, how to hide in plain sight, but that didn't mean that's what they were doing now. No. They literally could be hiding, and if so, there were few precautions that Alex and she could take to stave off a surprise attack.

"Go straight to Winston's office," Alex warned the man. "And don't leave until you've heard from me."

For a moment she thought Fowler might argue, but he mumbled a terse "Thanks for nothing," and headed back down the hall.

Leah waited until he was no longer within earshot. "You think he'll really go to the office?"

Alex lifted a shoulder. "If he doesn't, then he moves to the top of our list of suspects."

Yes, and they'd just let him walk away. But what choice did they have? Too many suspects and no place to put them all. Not yet, anyway. Alex and she would have to remedy that situation soon.

They watched Fowler walk to the end of the hall, but then Leah saw someone else heading in their direction. Winston. The manager stopped for a few seconds to chat with Fowler, and then continued on.

"Fowler said you ordered him to stay put in my office," he said, even before he reached them.

Alex nodded. "I need to search Harper's and Tarkington's rooms, and then I can deal with Fowler. Any idea where I can keep them contained? Separately, that is? If one of them is the killer, I don't want to lock two innocent men in there with him."

Winston paused, considering. "We have linen closets on all three floors, and each one has a lock on the outside of the door."

"That'll do." Alex didn't sound totally convinced, and Leah figured that was because those kinds of locks weren't meant to keep a determined serial killer inside.

Still, there weren't a lot of choices here, and maybe she and Alex could reinforce the locks in some way. If worse came to worst, they could drag furniture in front of the doors and then pray there wasn't a fire, trapping an innocent man inside.

Winston glanced into the room, toward at the laptop on the desk. "Is the camera outside the storage room working all right?"

"Yes, thanks," Leah answered.

"No problem. I hid it on the side of the fire extinguisher, so maybe no one will notice it."

No one as in the killer. Leah checked the time. Less than four hours until what could be the final showdown. If the strangler hadn't seen Winston plant the camera, then he might go through with his plan.

To kill her.

Leah couldn't completely eliminate the fear that

stirred inside her, but she tried to tamp it down. Fear wouldn't get her through this. And there was no other option—she had to stop the strangler once and for all. This was the only do-over she was likely to get, and if she failed...

She stopped herself from going there, and focused instead on what she could control. "What about the intercom?" she asked Winston.

"Still working on it. In the meantime, you want me to have staff patrol the halls, to make sure people are staying put in their rooms?"

Alex nodded again. "Armed patrols, if possible. People with a clear head, who aren't likely to panic if something goes wrong."

"I got a few of those," Winston stated. But then he looked past them, at the laptop screen, and shook his head. "I told him to get to his room."

It was Patrick Harper. He was definitely not in his room, but rather near the lobby, where the camera was recording his every move.

But what the heck was he doing?

He seemed agitated—or maybe that was his natural state. And he appeared to be talking to someone, Or maybe to himself. Leah hoped the man hadn't gone off the deep end. It could happen in situations like these, but Alex and she didn't have time to babysit anyone.

"I'll speak to him," Winston grumbled, and headed in that direction. However, the manager had barely made it to the end of the hall when Harper disappeared, moving out of camera range.

"It's probably too much to hope that he went back to his room," Leah commented.

"Let's pay him a visit," Alex said, glancing at Leah's notes to confirm the room number.

"Harper is wrong, by the way," she told him. "I didn't lure the stranglers to Ice Lake. I had no idea one of them would come here after me."

"I know." Alex slid his hand the length of her arm, and it sent a shiver through her. A good shiver. Well, maybe a bad one, since it was a distraction neither of them needed right now.

"We'll talk to Harper first, search his room," Alex said. "Then Tarkington."

"And if we don't find anything in their rooms that we can use to hold them?" she asked.

The muscles in Alex's tightened jaw stirred. "Then we hold them anyway, and deal with the fallout later."

Since their lives were on the proverbial line here, Leah couldn't argue with that, but in the back of her mind, she wondered if this would put a serious dent in both their careers.

Later, *much* later, she'd worry about that.

"By the way, that question you asked me earlier..." She hesitated, but decided what the heck. The moment felt a little fatalistic and called for some soul-clearing. "When the strangler was choking me and my life flashed before my eyes, I saw—

Alex's hand flew up to stop her. "Why are you telling me this now?"

It was her turn to stare. Leah wasn't about to admit that she wanted him to know, in case she didn't make it out of this alive. "Because you'd asked about it." She frowned when she realized that sounded more like a question than an answer.

He nodded. "I did ask." Then he paused. "I just thought maybe it would come out at a better time. Like when it doesn't sound like a goodbye confession."

Leah shrugged. "Maybe I need to get goodbye off my

chest." Goodbye, and other things. She wanted to tell him that she missed him. Not just the kisses and the sex.

She missed *him*.

But Alex shook his head. "Later," he stated.

Later, as in when they weren't trying to track down a killer. Leah couldn't agree more, but she only hoped there *was* a "later" for both of them.

"I don't have to remind you to stay behind me," he warned. His tone left no room for personal confessions and goodbyes. "And just in case we rattle one of our suspects enough that he panics, I don't want you in the line of attack," he added. "If things go wrong, get out of there."

"Of course."

She met Alex's intense glare as he studied her eyes. He cursed, no doubt because he knew she'd just lied to him. There was no way she would leave him under fire in order to save herself.

Alex touched his fingers to her face and gently brushed his thumb over the bruise on her cheekbone. It was clear he had something on his mind. Maybe something to do with that steamy kiss that was still clouding her judgment. Or maybe this was about her almost near-death confession. Something darted through his eyes—regret, maybe—and then he shook his head.

Had he been about to tell her that he cared for her? Or—she swallowed hard—that he felt more than that?

Was Alex about to use the *l*-word?

Leah was surprised that she wanted to hear that word from him. Even when he shouldn't be saying it. But she couldn't help herself. Being with Alex in such close proximity, and having him kiss her blind, only reminded her of how much she'd lost when he had broken off things with her.

She tried to push her feelings for him aside again. And she failed. Lately, the failures in that particular area were greatly exceeding the successes. Worse, she wanted to fail. She wanted to move those thoughts and feelings off the back burner. Except the timing really sucked.

"We'll deal with this after we have the strangler in custody," Alex whispered, as if he knew exactly what she was thinking.

And to complicate the heck out of things, he brushed a kiss on her mouth.

Once again, Leah had to tell her body to cool down.

They turned to leave, but something on the computer screen caught her eye. Not movement from the camera near the lobby, but the other one.

A man was walking down the hall, directly toward the camera outside the storage room.

Leah automatically moved closer to the screen to get a better look. So did Alex. And a moment later, they both muttered a curse.

What the heck was *he* doing there?

CHAPTER TEN

ALEX WATCHED AS Patrick Harper glanced up and down the hall. It wasn't an ordinary, casual sort of look, but the look of a man who was making sure he wasn't being followed. Seconds later, he ducked into the storage room and closed the door.

"He's the strangler," Leah whispered. Her voice was thin and breathy, and Alex figured that reaction was just the tip of the iceberg. Underneath, she was no doubt doing a heck of a lot more than breathing hard.

"Maybe," Alex answered. "If he is, then he's way ahead of schedule." Four hours ahead.

Of course, that could be the strangler's plan. Get there early. Find the best place to launch an attack. And then wait for Leah to show up, so she would be an easy kill.

But Alex rethought that.

Certainly, the strangler was aware that Leah wasn't alone. Even if he was someone not on their suspect list, he had to have been watching. He had to know that Alex wasn't just going to let Leah be strangled to death.

So what did this bastard have planned to neutralize him?

Whatever it was, Alex had to be ready for it. And so did Leah. Because he doubted there would be anything straightforward about this planned attack.

He glanced at her to see how she was handling the situation, and found he'd been right about her body language and expression. She had her chin up and was trying her best to look rock-hard, but he knew her well enough to see the fear that was cutting her to shreds. He hated the SOB for putting her through this again.

"Maybe Harper is just scoping out the place," Leah suggested.

That was possible, too, but Alex was betting the strangler had already done a thorough search of the storage room before he'd named it as their meeting place.

Leah sank down into the chair and stared at the laptop screen. "I couldn't tell if Harper was carrying a gun."

"Neither could I. But it would have been easy to conceal a weapon under that bulky sweater he's wearing. We have to go in assuming he's armed."

And dangerous.

"So, do we wait until 2:00 a.m.?" she asked.

"No." Alex didn't even have to think about that. "The sooner we go in, the better. I don't want to give him time to put himself in a better position to attack."

Leah pulled in a long breath, got to her feet. "All right. Let's do this."

Alex grasped her arm. "Since we know he's already inside, here's how this is going to work. We'll make our way to the storage room, and I'll go in. Just *me,*" he emphasized. "You'll wait in the hall in case his partner shows up. And you'll yell for help if anything goes wrong."

She glanced at him. "You'll yell for me if something goes wrong inside the room?"

Alex looked her straight in the eyes. "Sure." And they both knew that was yet another lie.

He was going into that room with one thought in mind—anticipate anything the strangler had planned to neutralize him, and then end the danger. If that meant killing Harper, then that's what would happen. And he would do that with Leah safely outside in the hall.

Well, as safe as she could be with a murderer around.

Alex pressed the communication button on the walkie-talkie, and thankfully, Winston answered right away.

"We got the intercom working," the manager said. "I was about to call you to see if it was okay to test it."

"Wait a little while," Alex answered. He didn't want to spook Harper and send him running. "Do you have a way to view the surveillance feed from the camera outside the storage room?"

"Sure. I could if I go back to my office."

"Do it, please. *Now.* And put Fowler somewhere else." Not just because the man might be dangerous to Winston, but also because Alex didn't want him seeing what was going on. "We just spotted Harper going into the storage room, and we're about to head there now. We need you to tell us if he leaves. Or if anyone else goes in there with him."

"Harper's the strangler?" Winston cried.

"It looks that way," Alex answered. "I doubt it's a coincidence that he's at the very place where the strangler demanded a meeting."

But it could be. They couldn't discount that.

Alex could practically feel the manager's concern. "I'll see what I can do to keep everyone else in the lodge far away from that storage room and the basement."

Good. Because Alex couldn't guarantee that shots wouldn't be fired. Just because the strangler hadn't shot victims in the past didn't mean he wouldn't this time.

Alex clicked the button to end the conversation, and turned to Leah to make sure she understood that she would take a backseat in this operation. Oh, she knew all right. Her face was tight with anger and fear, and Alex knew it wouldn't help if he kissed her.

But he did it anyway.

He brushed his lips over hers and hated that it made the stakes feel even higher. If that were possible. They were already as high as they could get.

Leah drew her weapon, adjusting it so it would fit in her hand despite the cast. Alex didn't want to think about just how bad her aim would be. Maybe, just maybe, she wouldn't have to fire or respond. This was one scenario where he hoped the only thing she would be doing was waiting in the hall for him.

He took out his own gun, and shoved the walkie-talkie into Leah's pocket. If something went wrong, maybe she'd be able to call Winston for backup. After all, the manager was armed. Plus this way he could contact them if Harper left the storage room before they got there.

"Let's go," Alex said, and they didn't waste any more time.

By now, hopefully Winston had made it back to his office to keep watch on the computer. And perhaps Harper hadn't yet had time to set up everything he'd planned in the storage room. Alex just needed the man to be one step off. That was all. It would be enough to take him down.

Thankfully, the halls and the stairs were clear. No guests. They should all be tucked away in their rooms with the doors locked.

Leah and Alex took the stairs to the basement, trying to keep their footsteps light so Harper wouldn't hear them coming. When they reached the bottom, Alex paused to look around. Listen.

And to get his bearings.

The hall was empty, but that didn't put him at ease. After all, he'd expected it to be that way. The danger was inside the storage room.

It was colder here than in the rest of the lodge. Probably not a high priority area for heating, since they were still on generator power. Alex saw Leah shiver, and he wished they'd worn coats.

Reaching the wall switch, he turned off the overhead lights. As Winston had told them, auxiliary lights on the baseboards lit up, though they didn't provide much illumination. Just enough for them to see where they were walking.

So that meant Alex had a decision to make.

When he opened the door to the storage room, the near darkness might not immediately alert Harper. That could buy Alex some time. But he didn't want that little advantage if it meant putting Leah at greater risk.

"I don't want you in the dark," he whispered. "In case someone else comes down here."

"I can see just fine," she whispered back.

Alex let his eyes adjust, and realized that was true for him, as well. He could see. Well, shadows, anyway. Maybe that would be enough.

With Leah right behind him, he crept toward the storage room door. The only door in the entire hallway, thank God. That meant if Harper's accomplice or someone else came down to the basement, they'd have to use the stairs, and Leah would be able to see them.

"Stay put," Alex mouthed to her, praying she would obey. He didn't want to have to watch out for her while he was dealing with the devil.

"Be careful," she whispered back. Though it wasn't

necessary. He had to be careful, because the stakes were too high for him to take a risk.

Alex pulled in a deep breath to steady his nerves, and got his gun aimed and ready. Staying low, he slowly turned the knob, trying not to make a sound. The door was heavy, and Alex pulled it open just enough so he could slip inside.

Like the hall, the storage room was dimly lit, but humming with sounds from the generator and other equipment. The place was a tangle of industrial-size washers and dryers and wheeled laundry bins overflowing with bedding. There were plenty of places for a killer to hide. And be trapped. Plenty of places for an ambush, too.

Alex let the door ease shut behind him.

He waited, on high alert, trying to pick through the mechanical sounds to find if he could pinpoint Harper.

Nothing.

Bracing his right hand with his left wrist, Alex took a step, his gaze slashing from one side of the massive room to the other. Harper was somewhere inside. Alex was sure of that. But where?

The question had no sooner crossed his mind than he heard a scuffling sound. Next to one of the dryers. He didn't actually see the person, but sensed he was there.

Alex went closer.

He thought of Leah. Of her standing guard in the hall. She'd be terrified, and probably was having the mother lode of hellish flashbacks. She'd never admit that, of course. One reason why Alex wanted to end this as quickly as possible and get back to her.

Another sound reached him.

Alex still couldn't make out who or what was causing it, but he eased closer, making sure no one sneaked up behind him.

Then he saw the source of the sounds: Patrick Harper.

But the man wasn't ready to attack.

Instead, Harper was on the floor, his hands and feet tied together. There was a gag in his mouth, but he was frantically shaking his head.

What the hell?

Alex braced himself for anything, but the sound still came as a shock.

A hiss.

A split second later, before Alex had time to react, a blast tore through the room. And through him.

The force of the explosion slammed into Alex and threw him into one of the filled laundry vats. Somehow, he managed to hang on to his gun, but it knocked the breath from him. He fought for air. Fought to get back on his feet. He finally managed it.

Until there was a second blast.

This one was louder than the first, and came with a flash of blinding light. Alex automatically sheltered his eyes. And then he heard it.

The door opening and then closing.

His stomach dropped to his feet.

The strangler had left the storage room and was in the hall with Leah. This couldn't be happening! But Alex reined in his fear and tried to think like an agent.

He raced toward the door, grabbed the knob and turned it, he pushed hard, but the door didn't open. No! Someone had blocked it so he couldn't get out.

Alex tried harder, ramming his shoulder into the metal panel, hoping he could dislodge it. It gave way, just a little, but not enough for him to get through.

Outside the door, he heard a sound that turned his blood to ice.

Leah screaming.

CHAPTER ELEVEN

GOD, NO. PLEASE.

Those three words rifled through Leah's head when she saw the man rushing toward her. For a split second, she'd thought it was Alex escaping the explosion, that's why she hadn't fired right away.

And the delay turned out to be a mistake.

A mistake that might cost her big time.

Because it wasn't Alex. Nor Patrick Harper.

It was Joe Tarkington, moving like a man bent on murder.

He rushed from the room, kicking the door shut. No cast on his leg. And he certainly wasn't limping—the injury must have been a ruse.

Tarkington planted his weight against the door, and in the same motion, latched on to her, dragging her against him so that her back was glued to his chest.

Leah managed a scream. Barely.

And then he had her by the throat. Not face-to-face like the last time, in the dead woman's house. He was behind her now, his beefy right arm across her throat. But the new position was just as effective, just as deadly.

He was squeezing the life out of her.

Leah tried to rip his arm away, but he yanked her head back. The pain was instant, blinding—hard pressure against old bruises and wounds. He didn't stop there. He slammed his left fist against her hand, just below the cast and her broken wrist.

Pain shot through her. Too much pain. And he kept on punching her, trying to dislodge the weapon.

He succeeded.

Even though Leah tried to hang on, she couldn't. Her gun clattered to the floor, and he squeezed harder. And harder.

She fought for air. Fought him, too. But he was a lot stronger than she was, and the kicks she landed against his legs had no effect.

Behind them, she could hear Alex shouting and banging on the door. He was trying to get out so he could save her, but Tarkington wasn't budging. He'd wedged his body in place, anchoring the door shut while he murdered her.

So, this was how she would die?

That question managed to make it through the unbearable pain and the fear. It cut through everything she was feeling and doing. Or rather *not* doing. And then her question had an easy answer.

No.

She would not die without a fight.

Leah had to act fast. A gray light was closing in, and she knew she had just a few moments of consciousness before she would pass out. Then she'd be an easy kill.

She gathered what little strength he hadn't managed to choke out of her, and forced herself to react. Tarkington was a lot bigger and stronger than she was. And he was fueled by a killer's adrenaline.

But Leah let her own adrenaline surge through her.

She dug her fingernails into his arm, clawing at him, kicking harder. Doing anything she could to break his grip. She drew back her right arm and slammed the cast into the side of his ribs. Pain jolted through her again and threatened to rob her of what little breath she had left but she persisted.

Finally, she got a reaction.

He cursed and staggered to one side. Just enough that he was forced to ease up on his grip.

Leah punched him again, and again. She battered his ribs with the hard plaster, and when he staggered again, she threw her weight against him.

Both of them slammed to the floor.

Just as Alex crashed through the door.

He had his gun aimed and ready, and even in the dim light, she saw the fear and the determination on his face. But Leah also saw that Alex didn't have what they needed most.

A clear shot.

Tarkington and she sprawled in a tangle, and despite her pain and lack of breath, she tried to scramble away from him so that Alex would be able to shoot him. But Tarkington grabbed her and managed to get his arm around her throat again. He then snatched her gun off the floor.

And fired.

At Alex.

Leah hadn't thought she could be more terrified, but she was wrong.

Oh, God.

Not Alex.

The strangler couldn't kill him.

Alex dived to the side, but she couldn't tell if he'd been hit. Or worse, if the bullet had been fatal.

The flashbacks came. Slamming into her. Leah had to battle the fear all over again, but she had more motivation than ever when Tarkington took another shot at Alex.

"I'm coming to help," she heard someone call out. Winston. But he wasn't nearby. His voice boomed over the intercom.

The sound of it caused Tarkington to freeze for just a second—not enough time for Leah to get away. Tarkington dragged her in front of him, using her as a shield. He got her in a choke hold again.

He hadn't given up his plan to murder her.

No surprise there. It was reasonable, in a twisted-killer sort of way. After all, they knew who he was. And he couldn't possibly get away, with the blizzard raging outside. Which told her that he was willing to make this a suicide mission just so he could finish her off.

That riled her to the core.

And made her fight even harder.

It wasn't a tactic she'd thought she would ever use, but Leah bit into his arm and didn't hold anything back. She dug her teeth into his flesh while she bashed her cast against any part of him she could reach.

Tarkington cursed her, calling her a vile name.

He fired again.

Leah couldn't see where the bullet landed, but it went in Alex's direction. She didn't give up. Couldn't. She kept fighting. Kept biting and hitting at him. But he didn't give up, either. He was hell-bent on murdering her tonight.

She heard a feral sound, and it took her a moment to realize it had come from Alex. Leah tried to shout for him to stay down, but it was too late.

Alex came rushing at them.

Tarkington pulled the trigger again, the loud blast echoing in the narrow hall. But Alex still kept coming.

He dived, crashing into them, so they all landed in a heap on the floor, arms and legs interlaced. But the danger was still there, since Tarkington had hold of the gun.

Alex latched on to the man's right arm. He drew back his own weapon and bashed it against Tarkington's forehead. There was a sickening thud of gunmetal against flesh and bone, but their attacker still didn't give up, or release Leah.

She knew that as long as she was in the mix, Alex wouldn't have a clean shot. She had to get out of the tangle. But how? She didn't have many options. Since her right arm was numb from the pain, she rammed her left fist against Tarkington and finally wriggled free from the choke hold. She scrambled to the side, finally as far from the fray as she could get.

Which wasn't far.

Trapped against the wall, she was less than two feet from Alex and Tarkington, but she got a much clearer picture of their situation. Both men were battered, bloodied and bruised. Alex was possibly shot, since there was a fair amount of blood on him. But that didn't stop them from fighting. They were in a life-and-death struggle, and Leah had to do something to help.

She looked around and spotted the fire extinguisher that Winston had used to hide the camera. It was a challenge to move, a challenge to reach for it, but Leah managed to rise to her feet and pull it from the wall.

"Get down!" Alex yelled.

It took her a split second to realize he was yelling at her. She turned to face him, only to see Tarkington swing the gun in her direction—and point it directly at her.

Despite Alex's desperate clawing at him, Tarkington pulled the trigger.

Leah saw horror register on Alex's face, just before the bullet slammed into her chest.

The pain was instant. Searing. Blinding. Leah felt as if a keg of dynamite had exploded in her chest, and she couldn't breathe.

Her legs turned to rubber and, with no other choice, she dropped the fire extinguisher and sank to the floor, unable to move. Unable to do anything except watch. And feel.

Oh, mercy.

She *could* feel. Not just the pain in her body, but the pain in her heart. It was tearing at her, and she wasn't sure she could take it much longer.

Everything started to swirl around her. Not the flashbacks or the fear. But Alex. Just Alex.

She'd tried to keep her feelings for him locked away. Well, that wasn't working. The lock was off, and everything she felt for him flooded through her.

He was risking his life for her. Ready to die for her. And yet she'd never told him that he'd been more than just her lover.

He was the man she *loved.*

Alex dropped his gun so he could use both hands and all his strength to grip Tarkington's shooting arm. He rammed it and the man's weapon against the wall, over and over again. Still, the gun didn't fall. Tarkington's face was twisted. Sick. And he laughed.

Leah could only watch as Tarkington took aim. Not at her, but at Alex.

Until that moment, she hadn't known if she could move. But somehow she did. She pushed aside the pain and lurched forward to pick up the gun Alex had dropped. All her training and instincts became focused on the man who was about to kill Alex.

She took aim.

Fired.

The recoil sent another jolt of pain through her broken wrist and her burning chest, but Leah didn't take her eyes off the Big Sky Strangler. She held her aim steady in case she had to fire again.

But it wasn't necessary.

The gun slid from the madman's hand, and his head flopped back, bashing against the wall. His oily smile was still in place, though. Frozen on his face, as his lifeless eyes gaped up at the ceiling.

Alex got to his feet and stood over Tarkington, looking very much like the agent he was. He was ready to act, but there was nothing left to do. The shot Leah had fired had gone directly into the strangler's heart and put an end to his worthless life.

"The Kevlar," Alex grunted. He came toward her and started loosening her top. "You're okay," he said, though he didn't sound certain of that at all.

Leah wasn't, either.

Alex fumbled at her clothes, peeling off her top and then the vest beneath. With the release of pressure, the burning stopped almost instantly. But not the pain. It was still there, throbbing in the center of her chest.

Leah looked down, terrified of what she might see. There was no blood. Maybe it was the adrenaline or the aftermath of the attack, but it took a moment for that to sink in. The vest had stopped the bullet Tarkington fired at her. Alex had insisted that she put the vest on, and because of his insistence, she was alive.

She looked at him. No wounds there, either. Yes,

there was blood, but it didn't appear to be his. It had likely come from Tarkington during the fight.

"You're okay," Alex repeated in a hoarse whisper. And this time, Leah believed him.

"It's over," she managed to say, just as he gathered her into his arms.

CHAPTER TWELVE

ALEX HEARD LEAH MOVING around in the bathtub, and he waited. While waiting, he paced, something he'd been doing a lot of since the start of her marathon bath session. He could do something else, but couldn't quite figure out what.

It had been only a few hours since Leah had killed a man and nearly been killed herself. He wasn't sure how fragile she would be when she stepped from the bath and came back into her room.

He certainly wasn't faring well.

His body was a tangle of nerves and spent adrenaline, and he was battling bad flashbacks. The strangler had nearly succeeded in finishing Leah off this time. If Alex and she had done one thing differently, one tiny thing, Leah might not be bathing in the next room, and he might be grieving her death. As it was, he was grieving all the pain she'd gone through, not once but twice, so they could nail this bastard.

But by God, they had nailed him.

The Big Sky Strangler would never kill again.

Burney Novak, not Joe Tarkington, was the SOB's real name. Alex had learned that when he'd done a search of the man's room and found his driver's license, plus a master key card that had obviously gained him entry to the dead woman's room and the room where he'd left the tape recorder. Alex had also learned the cast was a fake, since Novak hadn't been wearing it when he'd attacked Leah.

Alex wondered how many lifetimes it would take to get the images of Novak's last murder attempt out of his head.

Apparently not too many, he decided when Leah appeared in the bathroom doorway wearing just a resort bathrobe that hit her about midthigh.

Her hair was damp and pushed away from her face, and she looked a lot more relaxed than when she'd stepped into the bathroom. Of course, the bruises were still there—both the old and the new. But Alex saw past the bruises and looked at *her*. She was and always would be a knockout, and tonight she was a knockout that he was thankful to have alive.

Oh, man.

He was toast.

Even though his brain was telling him to keep some space between them, Alex went to her and drew her into his arms. He brushed a kiss on her cheek—just a quick peck. But the reaction he felt echoed through him.

Yeah, he was toast, all right.

"It's okay," she whispered. Her breath was warm against his neck. "I won't fall apart." But she didn't move out of his arms. "Any luck getting through to anyone in the Bureau?"

"Some." Alex forced his mind back to the case—after he kissed her cheek again. "Winston managed to contact the sheriff on his CB. The sheriff will get word to the office in Billings."

No one could get to Ice Lake to retrieve the strangler's body, so Winston had had it moved to the cold storage room, with that of the woman that the strangler had murdered.

In a day or two, as soon as the roads were cleared, other agents would arrive, and the investigation and paperwork would officially start. For now, Alex was thankful for the reprieve that the blizzard was giving Leah and him.

Soon, reality would set in, and they'd have to resume the search for the strangler's partner. One thing was for certain—whoever he was, he wasn't at the lodge. There was no hint of anyone else staying in Novak's room, and if he'd been nearby, he would have almost certainly helped out Novak with his planned attack on them.

"Winston's making arrangements for us to move to one of the cabins not too far from here," Alex explained. "It has its own generator and is stocked with plenty of food. The roads aren't passable, but the cabin isn't far, and we can use a snowmobile to get there."

Leah looked at him in surprise. "A cabin?"

"Any place away from here. I didn't think you'd get much sleep here, what with everything that's gone on in the lodge."

She didn't argue. Good thing, too. Because Alex wouldn't have gotten much sleep here, either.

"Anyway, Winston will let us know when we can go," he added.

She nodded. "How's Patrick Harper?"

"Fine." More or less. The man was certainly shaken up. "Harper said Novak lured him to the storage room with a note that he thought was from us. It said we had something important to show him."

"Important," Leah repeated, her voice weary. "Novak probably figured once he'd killed us, he'd kill Harper, too, and then set him up to take the blame."

That was Alex's guess, as well. There's no way Novak would have let a witness live.

Leah made a shivery sound with her breath, and Alex feared this was it—the meltdown. Heaven knew, if anyone deserved a good meltdown, it was Leah.

"Guess you know this means you passed your psych eval," Alex offered.

Yeah, it was a bad joke. But there was plenty of truth to it. Leah hadn't frozen in the worst of circumstances. Her aim had been dead-on.

She pulled back just slightly, met his gaze. She smiled, but it didn't last. Pursing her lips, she kissed his cheek.

Another punch of heat burned through him, followed by a lot of inappropriate thoughts. This wasn't the time for kissing. Or sex. But that brainless part of him below the belt said otherwise.

"Does this mean I get back my badge and gun?" she asked.

Alex nodded, and wished he had them with him so he could do the deed now. It would give his hands something else to do rather than caress her back and inch her closer.

"When I do the paperwork for the case, I'll recommend to Sanchez that he reinstate you immediately." Alex looked down at the cast, after he'd glanced at her breasts. "Desk duty, though, until that's off."

"Believe it or not, I'm looking forward to desk duty. For a little while," she added. She lifted her left arm and slipped it around his neck. "Since Sanchez will do the reinstating, does that mean he's my boss now?"

Alex checked his watch. "Yeah. As of about two hours ago."

The air instantly changed between them. Alex felt it. Leah, too. He could see it in the depths of her cool green eyes.

Being her supervisor was just one obstacle in the way of a possible relationship.

"You said it was just sex," he reminded her.

She moved closer, her body brushing against his. "I lied."

Alex smiled, and knew this should probably be the start of one of those conversations. A good air clearing. But he ditched that idea and kissed Leah instead. He didn't bother to keep it sweet and gentle. Neither did she.

He was mindful of the cast. Of her bruises, including the new one on her chest from the Kevlar-protected shot. But he was just as mindful of the searing heat between them. It had always been there, just below the surface. But now it was a full blaze, and they'd simply kissed.

He did something about that "simply kissed" part next, running his hand between them and into her bathrobe, to find her breasts. No pink bra. Just a warm, naked woman who fired up every inch of him.

"If you're going to say no…" he began.

Leah gave him a split-second glance. "Why the heck would I say no?"

"Just checking," he mumbled, bending to press a kiss on her right breast.

Leah made a sound. That sound—part moan, part gasp, all pleasure. It hurried things along, and Alex backed her toward the bed. She helped, latching on to his shirt and starting to undress him. Together, they tumbled onto the mattress.

The kisses continued, fiery hot. Alex pulled open her robe so he could kiss her all over, and the taste of her slammed through him. So familiar. Yet tasting Leah always felt new, as if this was their first time.

He dropped some kisses on her stomach, then lower. To the juncture of her thighs. Her little yearning sounds got louder, and she fought with his clothes as if she'd declared war on them. He finally stopped the kissing session so he could help her. Alex peeled off his shirt. His boots. His pants. At which point Leah latched on to him and pulled him back to the bed.

On top of her.

All in all, not a bad place to be. It felt right. Like coming home for the holidays and his birthday, all rolled into one. And while he would have liked to take his time and go for another round of body kisses, Leah was ready.

Her green eyes weren't so cool now; there was heat in them. Her face was flushed. And everything about her begged him to take what she was offering.

So Alex took.

He tried to enter her gently. Failed at that, too. Because she lifted her hips off the bed, wrapped her legs around him and dissolved any chance of gentleness. That was okay. The fire was already too hot to contain.

They moved into a rhythm that was as old as time. Faster, harder, deeper. Until the fire was unbearable. Until there was only one place that either of them could go. Alex thrust into her one last time, pushing her over the edge. In that moment, at the second of her fall, her eyes met his and she said just one word.

The only word necessary.

"Alex."

That was his trigger. Always had been. Alex kissed her and let her finish him off.

It took him a while to come back to earth. A while, too, to regain his breath. He lost it again when Leah laughed and maneuvered her body to give him a nice after jolt.

"You'll be ready again in a half hour," she teased.

"Less," he joked back, but it was too close to the truth for him to laugh. He always wanted Leah, even when he'd just had her.

He gently pushed her hair from her face and looked at her. It was time for that heart-to-heart talk. The one they'd been avoiding. Then he could coax her into getting ready so they could leave for the cabin.

Alex rolled off her and sat up so he could look at her.

"It wasn't just sex this time, either," she stated, before he could even start the conversation. She sat up and pulled the sheet over her. "It's never been just sex with you."

Alex opened his mouth, but realized that's exactly what he'd planned to say to her.

"You've asked what I saw when my life flashed before my eyes," she continued. "Well, I saw you. *Us,*" she corrected. "Our first kiss."

And it had been a memorable one. They'd just collared a drug dealer, and Alex was dropping her off at her place. In the rain. Both of them soaked to the bone. Cold, too. Well, cold until they'd shared the hottest kiss on record.

Ten minutes later, after they'd nearly broken down her door, they'd landed on her sofa. With Leah and him, sex had always seemed a life-or-death matter.

Still felt that way.

"So here we are," Leah whispered, a naughty little smile lifting the corners of her mouth. "Alone. Pretty soon we'll be alone in a cabin with no phone. No work to do. No one to bother us." She glanced out the window. "With this storm, we might be shut in for days. Just me, you…and a bed."

He moved in closer until his mouth was right against hers. "What will we do to pass all that time?" he teased.

But he wasn't looking for an answer. He knew how this would play out. Alex hauled Leah back to him and started a whole new set of memories with a sizzling kiss.

* * * * *

STONE COLD

Julie Miller

Thanks to B.J. Daniels and Delores Fossen.

I appreciate all the creative energy
and support you shared
as we put this anthology together.

Besides, you're just fun to hang out with!

CHAPTER ONE

"I FOUND HER."

Daniel Stone turned his face to the wind and braced against the crystals of snow biting into his skin.

This storm was going to be a bad one. The certainty came from the years he'd spent growing up on this mountain, as much as from the weather warnings that were shutting down this region of the northern Rockies in Montana. The blizzard was almost here. He could read it in the rising wind speed and in the moisture that turned the dry snow, so perfect for skiing, into icy shards that meant trouble for all but the most experienced of mountain survivalists like himself. He knew Mount Atlas the way mamas knew their babies, the way a shaman knew the earth itself. And he knew that in the next few days—in the next few hours, even—everything around him would change. The storm would bring whiteout conditions, windchills, closed roads and buried landmarks.

But nothing Mother Nature could throw at him would be as treacherous as what the dead woman in the snow at his feet had faced.

"Home base to Eagle One. Daniel? Report." The voice of his boss and best friend, Kent Webber, cut through the static crackling over the walkie-talkie. The main lodge at Ice Lake, where Kent was located, sounded miles away. Must be the utter isolation Daniel was feeling up here near the top of the main ski run that quadrupled the distance between him and headquarters.

Only, he wasn't alone.

"She fits the description of Stacy Beecham. Early twenties, blond hair." Daniel looked down at the woman with the vacant, staring eyes, and swallowed the bile that crept into his throat. Despite the skintight suit and boots she wore, this was no skiing accident. And the damn storm hadn't gotten her, either. His gaze settled on the angry marks around her neck. Judging by the gash in her scalp and the ripped, bloodied fingernails on the hand that was missing a glove, she'd put up one hell of a fight against whoever had hidden her here inside the edge of the tree line. "It's not good. She's been strangled."

"How the hell…?" Kent cursed as Daniel breathed in a lungful of fragrant pines and frigid air to clear the tragic image from his head. "That's impossible. We're practically in lockdown here at the main lodge with these weather conditions."

Yet the woman was dead. Once the Big Sky Strangler had been eliminated, all the guests had been allowed to leave the safety of their rooms in the early-morning hours to congregate in the lobby and dining area of the Ice Lake Lodge, to conserve the heat and electricity the generators had to make. Stacy's roommate said they had been determined to get in one last ski run before their vacation was over, even though the conditions weren't the best, to say the least. But when Stacy failed to show up at the bottom of the hill, her friend had reported her missing, and Daniel and the rest of Kent's Ice Lake ski patrol team had been dispatched to search for her.

Someone had gotten Stacy away from the roundhouse at the top of Mount Atlas, or diverted her off the course on her way down, and murdered her. Daniel was no cop, but he'd seen more than enough death and violence in his time. He guessed the struggle had happened right here. The lower, dead branches on a pair of Douglas firs had been snapped off, the scrub at the base of the trees had been crushed, and there were enough ripples and dents in the area around the body to create a gross facsimile of a snow angel.

Daniel had followed a faint set of ski tracks into the trees, but found no sign of an exit. Either the killer had been skilled enough to retrace the victim's path exactly, or he was lucky enough to have the wind and extra layers of snow mask whatever evidence he'd left behind.

"So why didn't you come back to the lodge with your friends?" Daniel mused aloud as he looked at the lifeless body of the young woman. A romantic rendezvous? Some kind of emergency? Her skis had been ripped from her boots and only one pole was still looped to her wrist, making it impossible to tell whether or not she'd had some sort of equipment malfunction. Maybe she'd been a rookie on too challenging a slope, and she'd panicked and veered off the course into the shelter of the trees when the wind and snow conditions had proved too much for her. If that was the scenario, then she'd probably been eager to greet the false Good Samaritan who'd stopped to help.

Something or someone had to have lured her here after the warning had gone out to clear the mountain and return to the safety of the lodge. But whatever or whoever that had been was long gone or long buried by the snow.

A break in the static brought his attention back to the radio again. "Any idea how long she's been there?" Kent asked.

"It's hard to tell, as cold as it is." Daniel forced himself to stoop down and pull off his own glove to touch the woman's icy fingers. Stiff as a board. From rigor mortis? Or the dropping temps? He quickly snatched his fingers away, remembering another cold hand he'd once cradled in his. He pulled his glove back on as he straightened, and spoke into the radio clipped to his reflective orange coat. "It can't have been too long," he said, trusting his knowledge of the mountain more than his expertise with casualties. "She's sheltered some by the trees, but with the way this wind is blowing, she'd have a lot more snow on top of her if she'd been here for more than a couple of hours."

"Impossible." Kent was swearing again. "We've got that murdering bastard on ice down here. How can the Big Sky Strangler kill another woman when he's already dead?"

Daniel didn't have an answer for that one. They were barely keeping a lid on the panic that the storm and missing skier were causing among the lodge's guests. There had already been enough suspect interviews for them to know that two FBI agents had tracked a serial killer to Ice Lake. But they'd ID'd Burney Novak and shot him in a deadly confrontation during the blackout they'd suffered early that morning. Learning that a second killer had struck in this winter retreat…?

"Everything I've seen on the news about the Big Sky Stranglers indicated authorities were looking for duo serial killers. You've got only one in the freezer, Kent."

"Yeah, but the agents said the one they got was the actual killer—that it was a dominant-submissive thing, and that his partner who abducted his victims for him, his sidekick, was long gone."

"Apparently, they were wrong." A submissive who'd

been trained to abduct victims for his master would have the skills to lure a woman off a ski trail. Hell, he could have been here days, if not weeks, ahead of Novak, setting up potential victims in the area. Maybe this woman had even met the guy, and hadn't realized the danger she was in until it was too late. He must be a hell of a charmer to gain a woman's trust like that.

Kent did his thinking out loud. "The FBI thought this guy had run out once their search zeroed in on Novak. But I can see how someone who'd been a part of that kind of sick symbiotic relationship might want to come back to save his partner. Or avenge him."

Made sense to Daniel. This wasn't Burney Novak's work—he'd heard about the woman Novak had killed at the lodge hours before his own death. Her murder had been neat. Calculated. Precise. But there was nothing clean or controlled about the violence of this murder scene.

They had another killer on the mountain.

Daniel masked a curse of his own and turned his mouth to his radio again. "What are your orders, Kent? You want me to bring her in?"

"Negative. I wish we were still in contact with Special Agent McCade. We need to call the cops."

Daniel could hear the frustration coloring his friend's voice. Once the man they'd dubbed the Big Sky Strangler had been identified and killed, the two FBI agents had made their way to one of the resort cabins closer to town, to try and get phone service to report in to their superiors in Billings. But, like everyone else in the area, they'd gotten cut off by the blizzard. "Although how we're going to get anyone else here with the road closings and avalanche warnings… I just don't know. Let me talk to Winston and I'll get back to you in a couple of minutes."

"Roger that. Eagle One out."

Winston Cooper, the manager of Ice Lake Resort, where Daniel worked, would probably have a heart attack at the news of his gruesome discovery of the missing skier. But Winston was his boss's boss, and as a man who'd served eight years in the United States Marine Corps, Daniel understood the chain of command. Keeping his eyes peeled for any sign of movement among the trees and snow, he settled in for a cold, lonely wait.

His team had already gone up to the roundhouse and the supply sheds spaced along Atlas's three ski runs in search of Stacy Beecham, and were on their way back to their base office at the lodge. Daniel hadn't seen signs of anyone else up here. With the dead woman lying beyond the tips of his skis, that meant he was the last man on the mountain.

The irony of being the last, lonely soul wasn't lost on him.

He tugged off his wraparound sunglasses and pulled his binoculars from one of the zippered pockets of his parka. He wore an Ice Lake Patrol stocking cap low around his ears and forehead, and a dusting of beard stubble over his jaw to insulate against the freezing weather.

Yet he was a man who craved the cold and wet, and clean, bracing air. A shiver meant he was still alive. A wincing blink against the wind meant he could still feel. Coming home to a Montana winter was a much needed change from the sand and heat and death of his last tour of duty in the Middle East.

But coming home to a murdered woman and an

AWOL serial killer wasn't the healing respite he'd been looking for.

Dormant skills that had served him well on the front lines of a war awoke inside him with the same painful tingling of a frostbitten foot coming back to life. He surveyed as far as he could see up and down the slope, but his vision was limited. He spotted the orange forms of the last two search-and-rescue teammates through the curtain of falling snow, and heard their blades chopping and crunching against the hardening snowpack before they disappeared from sight.

He was alone, for now.

Daniel stashed his binoculars and adjusted his glasses back over his eyes. Normally, he relished his isolation up here on the mountain. But something was different today. An unsettled feeling nagged at him, a certain wariness. If he believed in premonitions, he might think that death was stalking him—that there was danger just beyond the trees lining the ski run, that something evil skulked behind the granite outcroppings of the rugged mountain, that the ghosts from his past were chasing him through every swirl of snow blanketing the world around him.

Maybe it was the blizzard that was gaining strength and altering the rocky landscape. Maybe it was the murdered woman. Maybe it was just his guilty, screwed-up head that was messing with him.

"G.I. Joe?"

"No, kid. Captain Stone to you."

Daniel remembered the feel of soft black silk beneath his fingers as he'd ruffled the hair on the little tagalong his unit had picked up while checking bombed-out buildings in the village a week earlier. Tariq had been smart, happy—and no more than ten years old.

Daniel braced for the inevitable detour of his thoughts.

"Captain G.I. Joe. Look what my mother—"

A sniper's bullet meant for Daniel had taken out Tariq midsentence, spattering blood over the freshly baked flatbread he held, before it and the boy both crumbled to the sand at his feet. He picked the boy up in his arms. He weighed nothing. He tried to help, tried to breathe life back into a lifeless body. But he couldn't save him. A barrage of mortar shells at nearly the same instant drove his unit to ground, taking three good men before the team could eliminate the insurgent threat.

Daniel unzipped his parka to the middle of his chest and clawed at the neckline of the insulated sweater he wore underneath. He was suddenly burning up. The snow was falling all around him, weighing down the trees, clinging to his coat and gloves. Yet he felt feverish.

His gaze strayed to the spruce and firs that climbed up the mountain. Every instinct in him told him that the unseen threat that had taken this woman's life was still in the area. One killer had been dealt with. But there was someone else on the mountain with him, trapped by the blizzard—someone intent on destroying him and the things he cared about. More innocents were about to die. On his watch.

"Captain G.I. Joe." Tariq's laughter was drowned out by the sound of a single gunshot, by the roar of mortar fire.

"Stop it," Daniel muttered.

This was his mountain. His world.

Mentally shaking the haunting images from his head, he reached down and grabbed a handful of snow to rub across his hot face. The chapping cold cooled his thoughts, centered him.

Mount Atlas. Ice Lake. Montana.

Not sand and heat and death.

Daniel scooped up another handful of snow and packed it into a firm snowball, testing the weight of it before tossing it against the trunk of a tree twenty yards away.

He'd better get his brain back in Montana. There was a lot of moisture in the snow now. That meant snowpack and extra weight on the tree branches and drifting overhangs on the edge of every rock face. Which meant the risk of avalanche.

Daniel zipped his parka back up beneath his neck and got on the radio again. "Eagle One to home base. Come in home base. Kent, I need an answer."

Static crackled on the walkie-talkie and the line cleared. "This is Ice Lake home base. Sorry to make you wait, Daniel." Kent's heavy pause warned him the news wasn't good. "We can't reach Special Agent McCade or his partner—phone lines are out. And the sheriff says there's no way he can get here from town. Cover the body and mark where she is, then get back down here as soon as you can."

"This storm is going to run another eight to twelve hours, Kent. That's plenty of time for this guy to strike again," Daniel pointed out. "We're in survival mode already. We're not equipped to deal with a murder investigation."

"No. But I know someone who is. And she's on this side of the avalanche blocking the highway to Graniteville." The apology he heard in Kent's tone put Daniel instantly on guard.

"No." It was a dangerous idea. "Don't call Kylie. Do *not* call your sister."

Daniel's breath whooshed out on a sigh, blinding him in a cloud of regret. Kylie Webber. Hair like a short cap of soft, sable fur. Eyes as clear and blue as the mountain lake that gave the ski resort its name. Legs like… No, he wouldn't go there. He couldn't even think about the forbidden fantasies Kylie's long, lean body had given him since their first meeting in high school—not with her big brother on the radio with him. Kylie had been stolen kisses, all-night conversations, and a lot of frustrated hormones before he'd gone off to college and the Marine Corps, leaving her behind to finish growing up.

There was no mistaking that the innocent teenager who'd had a crush on him a decade ago was all woman now. She'd written several heartfelt letters that had kept him going while stationed overseas—treasured letters he'd never failed to answer, until that afternoon patrol and the death of Tariq and his men.

He was the problem now. *He* was the reason a relationship between them could no longer work. Daniel Stone was a different man than the Semper Fi superhero he'd once been. He was far older than the three years that separated him and Kylie. He didn't want to love and lose anybody else. His soul was weary, beaten, used up. No matter that she was still the only woman who could ignite his frozen desires, he wouldn't subject her good heart to the nightmares and cynicism and guilt that were a part of him now.

Daniel glanced down at Stacy Beecham's fractured body and flinched. He could replace her blond hair with dark brown, her green eyes with blue. This could be Kylie.

And he couldn't handle another death like that. He just damn well couldn't handle it.

He didn't want Kylie Webber here. Her presence would not only put her life in jeopardy, but having Kylie around would also endanger the fragile grip he had on his self-control.

But you didn't know a guy all through middle and high school without him knowing your secrets and fears—and Kent knew Daniel's. "My baby sister stopped being a kid a long time ago, Daniel. She wears a gun and a badge now. She grew up on this mountain just like you and me, and she knows how to work a crime scene. You do your job, and we'll let Kylie do hers."

"Do you know where she is?"

"We're snowed in, buddy—you can't avoid her." Kent's wisdom turned into teasing. "Are you worried she'll try to scratch your eyes out for letting her go? Or kiss you because she knows you're dealing with stuff and it's not your fault the two of you didn't work out?"

Damn mind reader. But his screwed-up emotions weren't the priority here. Daniel's thoughts had taken a much darker turn. "Do you know her location?"

"Sheriff Quick said she called in a vehicle accident about a mile north of here on Route 6."

"Is she alone?"

"I didn't ask. I take it the sheriff's department is spread pretty thin. But she's tough. She can handle herself."

Bless Kent's soul that he wasn't so jaded and distrustful of the world that he couldn't see the worst-case scenario here like Daniel could. Standing over a murdered woman, Daniel had trouble picturing anything *but*.

Still, Kent Webber was smart enough to be able to read the inflection in Daniel's tone—and the meaning in his silences. "Daniel?" His voice was sharp, commanding now.

Daniel pulled a Mylar blanket and neon marking flag from his search-and-rescue pack and knelt down beside Stacy Beecham.

"Daniel! I know what you're thinking. You report back here to base right now."

Scooping up handfuls of snow, Daniel anchored the blanket around the body and preserved as much of the area nearby it as possible.

"Daniel Stone! I've got dead bodies and a blizzard on my hands. I need you here for backup."

Daniel thrust the flag into the snow and stood. He turned his mouth to his radio and calmly asked, "What if someone in that car accident Kylie's working is the killer trying to escape?"

"Ah, hell." A string of curses followed, and Daniel nodded his head, adjusted the pack on his back and kicked the excess snow off his skis, knowing what Kent's next order would be. "You go find my sister and make sure she gets here in one piece."

"Roger that."

"Watch yourself. I don't want to lose either one of you. Not to a killer, and not to this storm."

Daniel crosshatched his skis and stepped into the clearing beneath the ski lift before turning toward the bottom of the hill. "This is my mountain. Nobody knows it like I do. I'll be there to back you up within the hour."

Unless a run-in with Kylie Webber killed him first.

THE MAN SAT BEHIND THE wheel of his car, picking at the blood caked beneath his fingernails and staining the cuffs of his jacket. He idly noted that he needed to change his clothes.

The rage and grief-fueled adrenaline that had pumped through his system was fading, leaving him feeling weak and disoriented. He'd done what he was supposed to do, what he had always done, just the way he'd been taught—just the way he had always done for his partner. Scout out the territory. Take days, weeks, even months, if necessary, to find the right woman—the perfect victim. Then call his partner to let him know the stage had been set. That was the prize. Make his partner happy. Prove they were the perfect team. Nothing. No one. No woman could ever come between them.

He'd found the perfect victim, more than one, in fact, right here in the Ice Lake area. He'd done what he was supposed to do. His partner had come as soon as he'd called. His partner would take care of him.

Ah, hell. He caught a glimpse of his reflection in the rearview mirror. He had blood on his neck, too. He lightly touched his fingers to the wound before turning the mirror away in disgust.

He should be feeling better than this. He'd played his part perfectly. That woman on Mount Atlas had been so concerned about helping an injured skier. She hadn't hesitated one whit to come to his aid.

Burney would be proud of him.

But this time was different. Something in him had snapped, making it difficult to think.

What am I supposed to do now? He curled his fingers into fists and leaned back in the seat. The wind buffeted the vehicle like the emotions roiling through his system buffeted him. The snow was burying him. But not any more than the confusion and loss that paralyzed him.

He stared so hard into the hypnotic flakes of white in front of him that his eyes began to water. Or maybe those were tears. His best friend was dead. His partner was gone. His soul mate had been taken from him. And a woman was responsible for his death—that lady FBI agent who should have just kept her mouth shut and died instead of hiding from them. The irony only compounded the loss. "Damn woman."

They'd caused him nothing but trouble his whole life.

He had to get to his friend. He had to reach him soon. Now.

He hadn't been alone for ten years. Burney Novak had always been there to protect him, guide him, support him. Through all the abuse, through the loneliness, Burney had been there. Since that fateful night when their foster mother, Donna the truck driver, had come after him with her belt for not having her dinner ready, and Burney had knocked her out with a two-by-four and then wrapped that same belt around her neck to free them from their torturous existence, Burney Novak had been everything to him.

Burney was strength. He had guts. Burney didn't take crap off anybody, especially no woman. Women were for bedding and serving and dying.

He'd never been the man his partner was…the man he needed to be now. He'd been weak, but the blood on his hands proved he was weak no more.

His spine straightened against the back of his seat and he adjusted the mirror to meet his determined gaze head-on. He needed to be more like Burney. He needed to *become* Burney Novak. It was the only way he knew how to survive.

He'd need a new partner. Their best success had always come as a team. He'd been in the area long enough to know that pickings were slim. But there had to be someone else who could help him out, someone who needed rescuing the way he had. And he'd need a plan. The weather was working against him—he was basically trapped here in Montana, limited in resources. But Burney would have been able to come up with a plan even with the odds stacked against them like this.

He would come up with that plan now.

He'd be creative. He'd be smart, patient, as ruthless as he needed to be.

Feeling a stirring of warmth inside him, he reached across the seat and picked up the ski pole that had snapped in two when he'd cracked it over that woman's head. A hungry need lit in his blood, clearing his thoughts and making him feel powerful. These hands could kill—he knew that now. They could do everything Burney had done.

Rolling down the window, he tossed the broken pole down the embankment, where it disappeared into a well of snow. He shrugged out of his winter jacket and tossed it out the window, too, letting the storm hide the evidence of his deed.

A woman had taken Burney from him. And she would pay. They would all pay.

It was the only way.

CHAPTER TWO

DEPUTY KYLIE WEBBER, blizzard tamer. Rescuer of idiots.

Tipping her head into stinging gusts of wind and snow, Kylie squinted beneath her sunglasses. "Seriously?" she bemoaned to the afternoon's gray light.

She'd already worked two accidents today, one minor and one that had required the department helicopter to airlift the driver to the nearest trauma hospital in Bozeman. Who knew how many other serious accidents or missing tourists or stranded locals truly needed her help? And she'd been sent to deal with Bozo 1 and Bozo 2.

The Graniteville sheriff's office didn't pay her enough money for this. She scanned over the shoulder of the road to where two drunken twentysomethings had slid their car down the embankment and wedged it between two tree trunks in a ten-foot snowdrift. Then, instead of staying in the warmth of their car, they thought it would be a good idea to climb onto the roof and dive into the snowbank. Half-dressed.

"Okay, boys." She called to them again, her voice louder and sterner to cut through the wind and their tipsy senses. "Graniteville County Sheriff's Office," she announced. "Come on up to the road. I've got a nice warm vehicle for you to sit in. Don't—!"

With a kowabunga yell, the one in jeans, an undershirt and a tie knotted around his bare neck dived head-first into the drift. He disappeared to his waist, and his muffled shriek of pain pulled Kylie a couple steps farther from her SUV to the edge of the road. "You okay?"

"Dude!" The second one, wearing athletic shorts and snow boots with his turtleneck, plunged in after him, oblivious to the dangers of tree trunks and rocks that could be buried in the drift.

Kylie curled her gloved fingers into fists at her sides, curbing her frustration. Give her a dog any day. Even a mutt would have the sense to come in out of the cold. "Boys?"

Bozo 1 slowly backed out of the drift and landed on his rump in the snow. Judging by his groans and the way he cradled his wrist, he'd hurt himself.

Okay. Time to take charge.

Retreating to her sheriff's department SUV, Kylie opened the back door and pulled out an emergency blanket and first aid kit. If the bozos wouldn't come to her, then she was going to have to haul them in for their own protection.

"Don't move," she ordered, plunging up to the knees of her lined khaki slacks into the snow—half sliding, half climbing down to the injured man. The booze had probably numbed him to the onset of frostbite and hypothermia with those wet, insufficient clothes. But the pain of an injured wrist was quickly bringing him back to the reality of his situation. "Easy."

Kylie wrapped the blanket around his shoulders and knelt beside him to inspect his swelling wrist. Holding it gingerly, she urged him to wiggle his fingers.

"What happened?" the young man asked, blinking snowflakes from his lashes, perhaps trying to bring Kylie's face into focus. "Did we wreck the car? Where's my shirt?"

With his injury, she wasn't going to stop and give him a Breathalyzer test, but she could guess that he had enough alcohol in his system to impair his body's ability to retain its needed heat. Wherever these two had come from—possibly older college students on their holiday break, or simply a pair of travelers who'd gotten stuck in the area when the storm hit, and had alleviated their boredom with a six-pack, or two, or six—it would be her responsibility to get them back in one piece.

Resting his wrist in the snow beside him, she packed more snow around it, creating a cold compress to stop the swelling. Kylie summoned up her patience and a reassuring smile. "What's your name?" she asked, wanting him to focus on her and provide some lucid answers while she wrapped his wrist and the snow pack in plastic and a bandage. "I'm Deputy Webber."

"I'm Tony." His words began to slur. From drink? Or the onset of hypothermia? "You're awful pretty to be a badge. To wear a badge, I mean."

"Can you stand up, Tony?" she asked, growing more concerned than irritated now. His partner, his legs flailing out of the snowbank like a fish stuck in the mud, would be of no help. "Did you say something, Tony?"

"I think I might be sick," the man groaned, doubling over.

That wasn't what she'd heard. For a moment, she'd imagined someone shouting in the distance. But it must be a trick of the wind bending the branches in the forest behind her. Or maybe just Bozo 2 trying to say something with his mouth and face full of snow. They were too far below the road to see if another vehicle had pulled up, and a 360-degree squint into the flying snow made her think the word she'd heard had been just her imagination.

"No, you don't." This was the time for practicality and efficiency, not fanciful imaginings about the wind whispering her name. She needed to get Tony up the slope and into the SUV while he could still move under his own power, or else she'd have to rig up a wench to pull him there. She slid her hands under his elbow and tugged. "Stand up, Tony. Come on." Despite his wobbly balance and chilled skin, he managed to get his feet under him without puking. Kylie kept his arm elevated while she pushed him into step ahead of her. "That's it. One foot in front of the other. I've got a thermos of coffee and a nice warm place where you can rest for a few minutes."

"Coffee sounds good."

Kylie.

A pair of boots thumped on the snow behind her. "Hey, honey. I'm talkin' to you."

Honey must have been what she'd heard, not *Kylie*. She checked back to see Bozo 2 advancing on her in a lurching gait. "Go back to your car and wait inside, sir."

"You arresting Tony?" Great. Bozo 2 had decided he wanted to be a part of things, after all. "You plan to take us both, honey?"

"Get in the car," she repeated, catching Tony as he stumbled, forcing her to take her eyes off the second man.

Bozo 2 didn't sound nearly as weak and docile as Tony. Nor was he paying attention to her command. "We ain't hurtin' anybody."

"Back it up, pal," she warned, getting her legs solidly beneath her in case he forced her to take physical action to stop his advance.

"We're here on vacation between s'mesters. What happened to Western hospitality?"

When she felt his long fingers clamp on to her elbow, Kylie whirled around. But she never had the chance to pinch his hand and twist free.

"Kylie!"

She hadn't imagined her name.

A blur of bright orange slid down the embankment.

The thick orange arms of a parka closed around the man's chest, breaking his grip, slinging him to the ground.

"Get your hands off her. Now."

"SERIOUSLY?" Kylie glared at the tall, rangy mountain man looming over the half-dressed fool sprawled in the snow. His sunglasses dangled from the lanyard around his neck, and his hands were clenched into fists at his sides. He'd swapped out his skis for a pair of snowshoes and his shoulders heaved up and down as if he'd just crossed the finish line in a cross-country race. "Daniel, you could have hurt him."

"Dude, what the…? What the hell's happening to me?"

But the man on the ground was ignored. Daniel Stone peered over his shoulder at Kylie, his breath forming multiple white clouds in the air. "He was sneaking up behind you while you were working with that drunk. You wanted me to let him hurt you?"

"I wasn't gonna hurt her."

"Of all the presumptuous…" Kylie propped Tony up with one hand and pulled open the front of her coat to remind Daniel of the badge clipped over her Kevlar, and all that it represented. "I don't need to be rescued." She'd been doing this job since she'd graduated college four years earlier. She was hardly a rookie anymore. She was far stronger and more self-sufficient than this version of Daniel—who was more volatile and mysterious than the one she'd seen off to the Middle East two years ago—seemed to believe. Or maybe Daniel's strike first and ask questions later assault stemmed from another source. "Did Kent send you to find me?"

A silent warning from those gray-green eyes kept the man in the shorts on the ground. Their striking intensity didn't soften any when he looked back at her. "It was a joint decision."

She stretched out an arm to help the shivering man up out of the snow. "Well, you may take orders from my brother when it comes to search and rescue. But this is a traffic accident and a pair of drunks *I* need to get off the road, for their sakes as well as everybody else's. It has nothing to do with Ice Lake Search and Rescue." She tucked the blanket more securely around Tony and nudged him toward the embankment. "When it comes to this kind of job, *I'm* in charge."

The gentle brush of Daniel's hand at her hip surprised her more than his sharp words of a moment ago. "We need to talk."

She narrowed her gaze in response to the hushed intimacy of his gravelly tone, but let the unspoken question slide. Just because every jigger of heat in her body had rushed to the unexpected yet well-remembered touch of Daniel's hand, that didn't lessen her responsibility or change the reason why she was here. "Not until we get these two safely inside my Suburban and get his wrist checked out."

Daniel pulled his hand away, his answering sigh clouding the air between them, obscuring his lean face for a moment.

"What is going on with you?" Kylie prodded. Lately, he'd kept to himself and had avoided her like a bad case of frostbite whenever she visited Ice Lake. And now he was in her face with this whole Marine-to-the-rescue routine? Resentment quickly turned to worry. "Has something happened to Kent?"

"No."

"Winston Cooper?" The lodge manager had been under a great deal of stress the past few days, taking in refugees from the blizzard as well as dealing with the FBI and the serial killer they'd tracked to Ice Lake. None of which was good for Winston's heart condition. But Sheriff Quick's last briefing this morning had issued an all clear on the statewide manhunt. A man named Burney Novak had been identified as the murderer they'd sought, and he'd been taken out by the FBI. "Is he coping with everything okay?"

"Winston's fine."

Frustrating man. Relief at hearing that her brother and her friend were safe never really registered. "Is there some other kind of trouble I need to know about?"

"No electricity at the lodge? No phone lines or radios that'll reach the outside world? A dead killer locked up in the freezer? Isn't that trouble enough?"

Tony staggered to a halt. "Did you say killer? Are we safe?"

"You are, buddy." His nod seemed enough to reassure the injured man and get him moving again. Yet Daniel's gaze slipped over to Kylie, sending a very different message. *She* wasn't?

Suspicion bristled inside her. Daniel's cryptic mood swing left her believing the *talk* he wanted to have couldn't wait, after all. "Is it police business?"

He wound his gloved finger into a curl that strayed onto her cheek, and tucked it up under the sheepskin lining her cap. Despite the cool contact of the snow-dusted fingertip, the tenderness of the gesture warmed her skin. Yet she recognized the regretful caress for the stall tactic it was. "Like you said. Let's take care of them first, and then I'll fill you in."

Very frustrating man.

"All right." She could agree to that truce. For now.

"Let me get my kit and I'll check your guy out." He grabbed Bozo 1 by the neck of his sweater and pulled him beyond Kylie's grasp. "If that one makes any move he shouldn't...don't be nice about putting him in his place."

Choosing to work with her for the time being, Daniel half pulled, half carried Tony up the incline. Relying on a little more finesse rather than Daniel's brute strength, Kylie got the second man to the car and seated inside, as well. While Daniel tended to Tony's sprained wrist, Kylie pulled another blanket from the back of the Suburban to wrap around Tony's friend.

With a little coaxing and a promise not to let Daniel put his hands on him again, the second man identified himself as Mike Osterman. He and Tony had driven the rental car out of Graniteville, where they'd spent most of the night at one of the local bars. Once the prospects for a one-night stand had thinned out to nothing, they'd set out—against official warnings—for Ice Lake Resort and the abundant snow bunnies they'd hoped to find there. And Kylie let them know that, no, she wasn't a prospect that either one of them needed to be flirting with right now or ever.

Neither man had a driver's license on him, but instead of sending anyone back out into the snow, Kylie wrote down the plate number from the car. It wasn't going anywhere. Once the blizzard had blown over, she could come back and get the insurance and registration numbers, as well as their billfolds.

When their work was done, she climbed in behind the steering wheel and cranked the heater to warm up the men, who were now locked in behind the steel mesh screen that separated the front seat from the back. While Daniel stowed his gear in the rear of the Suburban, Kylie tried calling the sheriff's office over her CB.

"This is Deputy Webber to Granite County One, over." A crackle of static and the piercing screech of a radio desperately trying to tune itself was her only reply. "Deputy Webber to Granite County One. Sheriff Quick, can you read me?"

More static. Then dead air.

Then Daniel was climbing into the passenger seat across from her. As soon as he shut the door, blocking out the worst of the wind and cold, the space inside the roomy vehicle seemed to shrink.

"Any luck?" he asked, sliding off his gloves and flexing his long fingers in front of the blast from the heating vents.

Kylie shook her head. "They were cutting out when I first called in the wreck. I've got nothing now."

Prophetic words. She shifted in her seat, feeling curiously uncomfortable and embarrassingly vulnerable as the familiar scents of musky man and the outdoor freshness that clung to Daniel's clothes filled her nose. The man she once thought she'd marry had made it perfectly clear that he wasn't interested in rekindling a relationship with her now that he was out of the Corps. And though it crushed her heart to see him hurting and broken inside, she'd respected his need to isolate himself from her and the feelings they'd once shared, while he healed. If he could.

If friendship was all Daniel wanted, then that was what he'd get from her. Although even that strained relationship was more about being acquaintances who ran into each other from time to time because of her brother. But if distance was what he needed in order to cope with his demons, then she had to make it clear to him that charging in to protect her was not only unnecessary, but unacceptable. She needed him to understand that the distance between them had to go both ways, or else her confused heart would never give up hope and get over him.

But having that conversation in the middle of a blizzard with the roads to town blocked off and two drunks eavesdropping from the backseat didn't seem like a wise move at the moment.

Deciding it was better to concentrate on the situation at hand rather than relive the past and mourn the loss of what could have been between them, Kylie forced her attention to the radio again. She twisted the CB knob through all the different channels, but couldn't raise anything more than static from the sheriff's station. She didn't bother trying her mobile phone, since the town's cell tower had been toppled in a gust of wind and no repair crew could even get to it until the snow stopped and the roads were cleared.

Having Daniel here complicated her efforts to do her job. Wondering why he'd braved the storm because he needed to "talk" piqued her curiosity and provided an untimely distraction. But a glance in the rearview mirror at the two bozos shivering in her backseat reminded her that she shouldn't be thinking of herself—or Daniel, even—right now.

"Do you have any kind of communication at the lodge?" she asked, hanging up the radio receiver. "I can't get these guys to the hospital in Graniteville, so your EMT's are the next best thing."

"Short-range radio is all that Kent's been able to keep up and running," Daniel answered. "I lost contact with HQ once I got about a half mile beyond the entrance to the resort. I take it you haven't heard from him, either?"

Kylie shook her head. "Tell me what's going on. Is this about the Big Sky Strang—"

"Shh." Daniel reached across the center console and squeezed her hand. With a slight nod to the two men in the back, he released her. "Later."

No. Now. "Give me something so I have an idea of what I'm dealing with."

He leaned closer and dropped his voice to a whisper. "I found another DB on patrol about an hour ago. A woman about your age. It wasn't an accident."

Another dead body? But Burney Novak was no longer a threat.

An odd mix of icy trepidation and fiery adrenaline surged through Kylie's system. She was the only law enforcement between Ice Lake and the snow slide that cut them off from backup in town. This would be her case. Her responsibility. She needed to know everything Daniel did so she'd know exactly what she was up against. "Same MO?"

"Similar enough." He moved back to his side of the car, ignoring her unspoken plea for more information. The tilt of his head reminded her they had extra ears in this conversation. "Get your car moving. We've got cots set up at the lodge, where these two can sleep it off and we can monitor their body temps. We'll be there in fifteen minutes unless we run into another roadblock. I'll brief you then."

Guessing that whatever details Daniel had to share

about the dead woman made him suspicious of the men locked up behind them, she nodded and shifted the SUV into gear. She could wait. For the time it took to get them to the lodge safely, she could wait.

She was used to waiting for the right moment with Daniel Stone.

CHAPTER THREE

EVEN WITH THE WINDSHIELD wipers working double-time, Kylie could barely see beyond the hood of her SUV as she pulled up beneath the rock archway in front of the Ice Lake Resort's lodge's tall glass doors. Her fingers ached as she eased her grip on the steering wheel, and her eyes burned from the focus it had required to keep the Suburban on the road.

"All right, let's move out," Daniel ordered. He spared a glance across the seat to Kylie before opening his door. "I'll get Tony inside first and have Kent double-check his vitals and that wrist. Will you be okay in here for a few minutes?"

"Go. I'll be right in."

"I'll be back to help you escort this yahoo inside."

"No, you won't." So they were back to save-the-pretty-little-lady mode? That was one thing she *didn't* need from Daniel. "I'll catch up with you in the patrol office."

Yeah. She could do the stubborn glare thing, too.

With a muffled curse, Daniel relented. "Winston has gathered all the guests in the lobby area. He told them it was to conserve the generators instead of trying to heat each of the rooms. But he's worried about someone else straying from the herd and..."

Winding up dead? Kylie could read the foreboding that narrowed Daniel's eyes. She didn't need him to finish the sentence. Whatever he had seen on that mountain had been messed up enough to resurrect all his warrior-mode defenses. Maybe the murder scene had tapped into his PTSD, and his over-the-top protectiveness was more about him dealing with something inside than with any doubts about her abilities to take care of herself.

"Just so you know," he continued. "There's a crowd in there."

Kylie tilted her chin toward the double front doors, keeping her words equally cryptic to ensure the privacy of their conversation. "Do any of them know about it?"

"About what?" Mike piped up from the backseat.

At the interruption, Daniel's hand fisted. But instead of giving in to the impulse to vent his frustration, he scrubbed his fingers through his short golden hair, leaving a trail of rumpled spikes in their wake. "Just Winston, Kent and me. And..."

The killer.

Kylie's own fingers itched with the urge to straighten his hair, to soothe his temper, to offer a tender reassurance that she was going to be safe and that she could handle a murder investigation. It had been a long time since she'd stroked her palms against the soft, ticklish texture. And it would be longer still. She wrapped her traitorous hands back around the steering wheel and breathed a deep sigh. Daniel didn't want affection from her. As far as she could tell, he only wanted her to follow his orders. And since he wasn't her commanding officer, that wasn't going to happen.

"Does she have any family here?"

Daniel shook his head. "A roommate. Barb Hughes. Kent's got her sedated in the infirmary. She doesn't know exactly what happened yet. If anyone else here is missing her, they haven't said—"

"Whoa. Someone's missing?" Mike Osterman's fingers curled through the grate between the seats as he invited himself into the conversation. "First you're being all hush-hush about a killer. And now you can't find somebody?" It could have been the cold, or perhaps it was genuine concern that made his voice shake. "Just what the hell kind of place have you brought Tony and me to? We have rights."

Kylie jumped in before Daniel snapped the fool's head off. "You're lucky I didn't leave you on the side of the road to freeze to death."

Mike pulled his fingers back and huddled inside his blanket. "Coming here for our vacation was a bad idea, right, Tone?"

Tony just stared at his friend through droopy eyelids and groaned.

Kylie unhooked her seat belt. "Let's get our patients straight to the infirmary." *Before they spread rumors and suspicion among the guests inside,* she added to herself. "Gentlemen?"

With a lingering look that could have been impatience or regret, Daniel pulled his patrol cap back over his head and got out to open the back of the SUV. Once he and Tony had disappeared through the lobby's doors, Kylie blinked to give herself a moment of respite from whiteout conditions and dueling wills.

If a woman had been murdered on the Mount Atlas ski run, it wasn't too soon to start taking stock of her surroundings. A cornered killer could be desperate, unpredictable—especially if he was used to having a partner telling him what to do. She needed to act quickly before he panicked and lashed out at another innocent victim.

But there was still too much snow flying for Kylie to be able to detect whether anything seemed out of place around the main lodge, the parking lot or any of the outbuildings and craggy, forested landscape surrounding them. She inhaled a deep, steadying breath to counteract the responsibility weighing down her shoulders, before turning to her passenger in the backseat.

As she peered through the side window, a gust of wind cleared her line of sight for a split second and she spotted the orange vest of a snowsuit over by the snowmobile shed. Who would be out in this mess?

Just as quickly, the man was swallowed up by the snow. But her pulse had already given a little lurch of recognition. Was that her brother? Another member of the search and rescue team?

Or something else entirely?

She made a mental note to prioritize her investigation list. First thing on the agenda was to get an accounting of every guest and staff person currently taking refuge at the resort. It would be far easier to find the man who *didn't* belong if she knew the names and faces of everyone who did.

"Okay, Mike. Let's move it." The cold and wet slapped her in the face as soon as she climbed out of the SUV. Bending her head slightly to take on the wind, she opened the back door, bracing her hip against it to anchor it in place while she helped the man out.

"This is a mighty fancy hospital." Mike Osterman's breathy tone indicated that he was dealing the effects of his needless exposure to the elements. "A little out of my budget. No one's going to charge me for this, right?"

"The hospitality is free during the storm." The citations and fines he'd be receiving later, for his reckless behavior and a possible DUI, were all on him.

The flash of orange caught her eye again, and Kylie instinctively turned to see who was approaching her. The man hurrying toward her car was too short to be her brother. And he was moving with a purpose that put her on guard. When the next wave of snow hid him from view again, she squeezed Mike's arm. "Time to move."

The wind howled through the archway and smacked the car door against her hip. It knocked her off balance and she tumbled into Mike. But before the two of them crashed to the ground, an unexpected hand caught her arm and righted her.

"Deputy Webber?"

Kylie spun around. A glint of light from inside the lodge reflected off the shorter man's round glasses, and she exhaled an embarrassing sigh of relief at recognizing her savior.

Louis Sullivan was one of Ice Lake's seasonal hires who'd been around for a couple of months now, doing odd jobs and handyman work. He released her to close the SUV's door. "Wh-wh-what are you doing here?"

Although she guessed him to be about thirty, Lou's wiry frame and soft-voiced stutter often made her think she was talking to a shy teen. "You gave me a start there, Lou. But thanks for the help." She eyed the snow shovel in his free hand as he hurried around them to open the first of the lodge's double glass doors. "Looks like you're fighting a losing battle."

"We have to k-keep the drive in front of the shed doors clear, in case there's an emergency. I'm doing it by hand to save the gas for the g-g-generators. Is every…th-thing all right?"

"Dude. You need to—"

Kylie could hear the remark about Lou's speech impediment forming on Mike's lips, so she pushed him on through the second set of doors for a time-out in the lobby. "I can't get back into town with this weather, so I brought two stranded travelers here for shelter and medical attention. Looks like we're going to be snowed in with you guys until the storm breaks and the roads are cleared."

Simply getting out of the wind between the doors warmed her enough to unzip her coat. But the sudden difference in temperatures fogged up Lou's glasses, and with thickly gloved fingers, he pulled them off to wipe the lenses on a bandanna he drew from his pocket. "You want me to park your car in the g-garage for you?"

"Thanks, but—" she nodded to the Suburban outside "—I'm afraid I can't give a civilian access to my car. Would you make sure the garage is unlocked for me, though? I'll move it in in a few minutes. As soon as I get my passengers the medical attention they need."

"G-g-glad to. I s'pose you heard about the k-killings. It isn't safe for a woman…." His cheeks flushed and he glanced away to put his glasses back on and compose himself. His eyes lingered at her waist before he looked at her again. "Even with a g-gun, it isn't safe."

She reached out to give his shoulder a friendly pat. "I appreciate you looking out for me, Lou. But it's my job. I'm not afraid."

"Of c-course." Was it her imagination, or did Lou's chin sink lower into the folds of the thick wool scarf he'd tucked into his insulated coveralls? "I wasn't s-saying that you were."

Under the circumstances, perhaps it would be wise to play down the badge and body armor angle just a bit. Anyone gathered around the fireplace in the lobby had a clear view of her khaki uniform and the Kevlar she wore under her coat. If the Big Sky Strangler's partner was here, then she'd just put a big target on her back. Time to tone down the tough chick attitude she relied on when she had to handle drunken idiots like Mike and Tony, and let a little demure female come out.

She pulled off her sunglasses and winked at Lou. "I wouldn't mind a thorough scrape down on all my windows, though. Since you're already bundled up?"

His chin lifted and an instant smile was his answer. "S-s-sure. No problem, Deputy."

It was easy to make her smile match his eagerness to please. "It's Kylie, Lou. If you're going to be working with Kent and my friends here at Ice Lake, then we're going to be friends, too. There's no need to be so formal."

"Right. Thanks, K-Kylie. S-stay warm."

"You, too. Thanks, Lou. I'll be back out in ten." While he hurried off to the snowmobile shed to exchange the shovel for a broom and an ice scraper, Kylie stepped into the lobby.

She was instantly met with a wall of heat and dozens of curious glances. The warmth emanating from the circular fire pit at the center of the lobby opened the pores of her skin and thawed her tensed muscles like a good massage. But the looks she was getting from the guests gathered around the fire kept her from relaxing her guard. Mike had stopped to hold his hands up to the crackly, pine-scented blaze, and was more interested in scoping out the young women in the room than in noticing her.

But everyone else seemed to have taken note of the lodge's newest arrival. A few of the men and women must have felt relief at seeing a cop on the premises, and returned to their books and knitting and roasting marshmallows. Others seemed to take her arrival as a sign that the danger they'd endured for the past forty-eight hours wasn't over, and quickly bowed heads and closed ranks to speculate as to what Kylie's presence might mean. No one stuck out as being overly curious or nervous about her pulling the front of her coat back, past her holster and handcuffs, and sliding her chilly fingers into the pockets of her slacks.

Good to know. If the Big Sky Strangler's missing partner was here, then he was a damn fine actor who blended in with the other guests. Other than the fact they were using candles and kerosene lanterns instead of electricity to add more light to the meager sunshine seeping through the windows, it could pass for any afternoon at the resort lodge during the height of ski season. Weeding him out of the crowd without arousing his suspicion wouldn't be an easy task.

If he wasn't one of the fifty or so people wrapped in blankets or sipping something steamy by the fire pit or in the nearby seating areas, then that meant he was hiding out somewhere. That could prove to be an equally difficult challenge. As long as the blizzard raged and the lodge's guests were all gathered here, he'd have plenty of empty rooms and mountain cabins where he could stay out of sight.

And if he had any kind of outdoor survival training? He'd have the whole mountain to hide on.

As the lone officer on site until backup could get through, Kylie knew she had a daunting challenge ahead of her. Tracking down a man who'd evaded the FBI's detection for weeks, maybe even months, was a tall order for one woman to accomplish. But it wasn't impossible, so long as she kept her head and relied on her training.

"Let's go." She tugged off her gloves and cap and combed her fingers through her hair to help the short waves fall into place as she guided Mike toward the front desk, and the hallway beyond it where the staff quarters and ski patrol offices were housed.

"Kylie?" Victoria Cooper closed the book she'd been reading by flashlight and hurried to the edge of the counter. "What are you doing here?" She squinched up her plump cheeks. "Did you hear about the…bodies… in the freezer?"

"I heard." Kylie stopped to squeeze the college student's hand. "How are you holding up?"

"Fine. I guess. I'd relax a little more if Dad wasn't so stressed out about everything. We've never had one death here, much less two."

Good. So word about the woman Daniel had found on the mountain hadn't gotten out yet. Kylie intended to keep it that way for as long as possible. "We'll be okay. I'm here now to keep an eye on things." She gave the younger woman a wink. "The biggest thing you and your dad need to worry about right now is not running out of marshmallows and firewood for the guests."

The tension eased and Victoria relaxed. "I'll be sure to tell him."

"Hey, darlin'." Unfortunately, Mike wasn't shivering so hard that he couldn't lean in and flirt with the petite redhead. "You got a bed for me? I need some warming up."

Kylie turned him away from the desk. "Ignore him."

"Kylie!" Her brother's deep-pitched voice boomed from the hallway. Before she could answer, he swooped around the corner and gathered her up in a big bear hug that lifted her onto her toes. "Daniel told me the kind of trouble you were having." She was flat on her feet now as he pulled back to inspect her from head to toe. “Are you okay?”

“I’m fine.”

The once-over he gave Mike Osterman wasn’t nearly as friendly.

Taking Mike by the arm, Kent positioned himself between the man and Kylie, then led them down the wood-paneled hall into the ski patrol office. As soon as they were through the door, Kent summoned another EMT to take Mike into the adjoining infirmary and get an examination started. Alone with her for the moment, big brother propped his hands on his hips and frowned down at her. “I don’t know what to do here. We need your help but…I don’t want this to be your responsibility.”

“But it is. I’ll do my job and you do yours. Your team needs to keep everyone here alive and healthy. Get them safely through this blizzard.”

“The weather I can handle.” He rested his hands on her shoulders for a moment, then turned her around to pull off her coat. “But you’ve always been a handful. The Big Sky Strangler and his partner targeted strong women—women they perceived as having power or authority over them.” When she turned back, he dropped the coat into her arms and flicked his finger against her badge. “Hello.”

Indulging the instinct she hadn’t been able to with Daniel, she reached up and brushed a strand of dark hair away from the worry lines on her brother’s forehead. Then she deftly changed the subject. “So, how’s my other snow-diving buddy? Anything broken?”

Understanding her stubbornness better than anyone on the planet, Kent let the conversation drop. He took her to his desk and pulled out a chair for her to sit.

Knowing she was with someone she could completely trust, Kylie relaxed and let him fuss over her for a few minutes. He poured her some hot coffee with a slug of milk in it, the way she liked, and handed her the mug. "It's not like I've got an X-ray machine here I can use, but I'm not even sure it's a sprain. He scraped a chunk of skin off, so I'm guessing he knocked it against a tree root or trunk and hyperextended it. Good field wrap, by the way. The swelling was almost nil."

Kylie savored the heat of the mug between her hands and inhaled the pungent aroma before taking a sip. "If Tony wasn't seriously hurt, then why was he moaning and groaning so much?"

"Hangover? A touch of hypothermia and he's thawing out?" Kent poured himself a cup and then settled his hip on the corner of his desk, facing her. "He seems a little groggy to me. Maybe he's on something and it hasn't worn off yet. We're getting him some dry clothes and hot soup to bring his temp back to normal. Then I'll have a better idea of what's going on. We'll do the same for the other one."

"Thanks. I knew I could count on you."

He drank another swallow before clearing his throat in a way that reminded her of their father. "I don't know what you intend to do, but be smart about it. Be safe. You know you don't have any backup here."

"Yeah, she does." Daniel Stone strolled in from the infirmary. The gravelly promise—or was that a warning?—in his voice danced across Kylie's eardrums and seeped into her blood.

He'd shed his coat to reveal a form-fitting sweater and waffle-weave undershirt that hugged his shoulders and every ripple of muscle along his lean frame. While he poured himself a cup of coffee, Kylie slipped her guard back into place, stiffening her spine even as that innate awareness of his masculinity softened her resolve to remain immune to him. She'd do better standing on her feet and meeting him face-to-face rather than having him tower over her and make pronouncements like that. "What are you talking about?"

"We're partners again, babe." He turned and raised his mug in a parody of a toast. "I'm not letting you out of my sight until this guy is caught."

THE MAN SHIVERED.

He was cold. He was alone. The clothes he was wearing itched against the scrapes and scratches on his skin.

His foster mother used to beat him until the skin broke. He remembered her telling him that that was how she knew he really felt the pain, really understood whatever the lesson was she wanted him to learn—do her bidding, guess what she wanted before she had to order him to do it, never guess wrong.

He pulled the Ice Lake Resort stationery from his pocket and warmed the pen between his hands so the ink would flow.

He'd kept house for truck driver Donna. Cooked her meals. Folded her laundry. Woman's work. She'd always given *him* the woman's jobs, emasculated him, treated him like he was too weak to ever fight back.

He had been too weak.

But he'd been a boy then.

Now he was a man.

Now he was the one in control.

Taking extra care not to disturb anyone in the room, he moved silently to finish his work. The woman in the room was of no consequence. She posed no threat.

But that lady deputy was another story. That one would put up a fight.

Kylie Webber had legs like a fine racehorse. And she was pretty when she smiled. A part of him recognized her as an attractive woman. That part had wanted to impress her, tame her, earn one of those smiles for himself.

But another part knew she was trouble. Nothing to him but trouble. She was here because of the dead woman. Here for him. Flashing that badge as though it put her in charge. Making sure everyone could see that gun strapped to her waist. Giving *him* orders. It didn't matter if it was couched in one of those pretty smiles—it was just a ploy, a trick she used to get him to do her bidding. He had no doubt she would have drawn that gun on him to get her way if he hadn't done what she asked.

False power. Female power.

He would take it from her.

No woman would ever make him feel like that helpless little boy again.

He cursed his shaking fingers as he hurried to complete his task without being seen. His fingers had shaken earlier, too, when he'd had them around that stupid blonde's throat. She should have listened, shouldn't have rebuffed his advances the night before—shouldn't have thought she was doing him a favor when she'd come over to the trees to rescue him.

When she'd thought he was injured, weaker than her, she'd been all smiles and help and saving the day. She'd been so confused when he didn't need her help, after all. Then she got angry, talked down to him as if he was a little boy again. *"I don't have time for this. Get on your feet and follow me down the mountain. The ski patrol ordered all of us down to the lodge before the blizzard hits."*

Another order?

He'd grabbed her ski pole when she'd tried to leave him.

She had no smile for him then. She'd cut him deep with one of her fingernails. She'd broken the skin.

The rage had swelled inside him. And then he'd showed her who was weak.

The rush of power, the satisfaction of knowing he had bested her, despite her smiles and tricks and threats, had flowed through his veins, canceling out the cold, giving him strength.

Standing up, he spread his fingers in front of his face and forced them to stop shaking. They were battle-scarred now. But they were powerful hands, a true man's hands.

Oh, yes, he wanted to put these hands on Kylie Webber.

He wanted to wrap his hands around her neck and squeeze until there was no more fight left in her.

CHAPTER FOUR

SOMEHOW DANIEL HAD imagined that keeping Kylie safe while she investigated Stacy Beecham's murder and tracked down the missing half of a pair of serial killers involved her being locked in a windowless room with him standing guard. And while the rational part of his brain knew Kylie would never allow such a thing, he hadn't really expected that the first words out of her mouth in her brother's office would be, "Show me the body."

So now they were being buffeted by forty-mile-an-hour winds on the face of Mount Atlas and digging an extra foot of snow off the Mylar blanket he'd covered the body with only a few hours earlier.

Even with his glare-resistant sun goggles, he was getting a headache from keeping a vigilant eye on the weather, signs of unwanted company on the deserted slope, and on the tautly rounded backside of Deputy Kylie Webber as she knelt down beside the reflective marking flag that was half buried in the snow.

At least one enemy was giving up the fight. Although the temps outside were nothing to mess with, the wind was settling down from those sixty-five-mile-an-hour gusts. And if he used his imagination, the sky had a shade more color through the treetops than the white-out conditions of even a half hour earlier. The storm was waning. But it would be nightfall before it finished. And then the real threat of avalanche, plus the digging out and making Mount Atlas habitable for humans again, would really begin.

The conditions were still too treacherous for the skis strapped to their survival packs, so they'd suited up in snowshoes and trekked almost a mile up into the trees to dig out Stacy Beecham's frozen body and find out if the killer had left any clues behind.

"I've got it." Kylie set aside the portable shovel as a corner of shiny silver Mylar peeped through the snow.

Daniel pulled his gaze from the unknown secrets lurking in the shadows among the trees, and squatted down beside her to help brush away the last of the snow by hand. Kylie worked quickly, quietly, while every bump of a boot or knee or face that was revealed pushing through the material as they removed the snow took him to a darker, more dangerous place inside himself.

"All right." She handed him one corner of the blanket and stepped across to the other. "The snow is packed in pretty hard and deep around her, but when I lift this, I'll need you to hold it up to keep the wind from blowing more in."

"Yes, ma'am."

Kylie arched an eyebrow above the rim of her sunglasses at his response, but was all business as they peeled the Mylar away from the body. First the blond hair. Then the dark, matted gash in Stacy's scalp. Then the eyes.

Daniel's stomach clenched and the cold fingers of an awful memory clawed at his soul. Her eyes were still open. Staring. Afraid. He had to look away.

Another innocent, gone. Someone who trusted men like him to keep them safe was dead.

Daniel fought off the clawing fingers, and reached

over to take hold of the blanket, to create a wind block so Kylie could examine the scene. He'd lost a young boy and a group of men who'd been good Marines and friends. Two women, murdered by different men, had died in the past two days here at Ice Lake.

He wouldn't lose Kylie, too.

She pulled off her insulated gloves and swapped them out for plastic ones she pulled from her coat pocket.

"Work fast," he warned. If she showed any signs of exposure or frostbite, he'd get her off this mountain just as quickly as he intended to if he spotted anyone who could be the Big Sky Strangler's missing partner.

With a nod, she flexed her fingers and snapped some photos with the camera she'd looped around her neck. After tucking it back inside her coat, she blew on her fingers and rubbed them together.

"Put your gloves on," he cautioned.

"I'm not done yet." Ignoring the practicality of covering her extremities in the windy, chilled air, and unaware of the knot twisting in his stomach, she brushed a clump of blood-streaked hair off the victim's bruised face.

Daniel wanted to look away, but refused to. Not that he was much help in the forensic department, but he didn't want Kylie to deal with the gruesome scene alone. Hell, he didn't want her to deal with it, period.

He'd seen limbs ripped from bodies, heard the cries of dying men on the battlefield, watched a little boy…

"Definitely signs of petechial hemorrhaging around the eyes." Kylie's curt analysis forced him back to this place and time. "She was strangled." He wondered at the trembling in Kylie's fingers. Was she feeling the cold? Or the enormity of the task at hand? She unzipped the top of the woman's ski suit and touched her fingers to the bruise marks around her neck. "I'm no CSI, but this looks like the guy did it with his hands. With the Big Sky Strangler dead, I'd say this is his partner's work. We've definitely got another killer out here."

"That's a comfort." If she was looking for Daniel to hold up his end of a conversation, sarcasm was all he could manage.

Perhaps she was finally understanding why having her take charge of this investigation was scaring the life out of him. That could be her on the ground with bruised eyes and a crushed throat, with only a pair of strangers and Mother Nature to mourn her violent passing. Kylie tilted her face up to him and smiled. It was a serene picture of beauty and reassurance. "I'm done."

He nodded, willing it to be true.

She rezipped Stacy's outfit, helped him tuck the Mylar back into place, and then pushed herself to her feet. Daniel reached for the shovel and quickly reanchored the covering, while Kylie peeled off her plastic gloves and walked a wide circle from tree to tree around the body. "This scene reads like a blitz attack. I'm guessing she realized she was in trouble about as soon as he lured her away from the ski slope. She tried to get away, put up a fight. He had to subdue her with the blow to the head before he could get his hands around her throat."

Daniel tossed another scoop of snow over the blanket. "How do you know that?"

"All the blood." Kylie shoved her hands into the pockets of her sheepskin-lined coat. "It's hard to tell how much of it has soaked into the snow and ground beneath her, but she lost a lot of it from that head wound before she died."

He couldn't stop imagining Kylie lying under that

blanket. Daniel squeezed his eyes shut against the haunting image that filled his head. His breath shuddered through his chest.

A firm hand squeezed his forearm, dragging him out of the darkness that consumed him. Daniel's eyes popped open and zeroed in on the pale fingers resting against the bright sleeve of his jacket. Kylie's soft voice whispered beside his shoulder. "I'm sorry you had to see this."

He pushed his goggles up onto the cuff of his stocking cap and angled his eyes to hers. "I've been in a war. I've seen bodies."

"There are things you expect to see in a war zone that you don't expect to find in your own backyard. Handling something like this without losing your lunch or cursing or crying or going nuts—it's a mental game."

His laugh was a wry sound that held no humor. "Tell me about it."

"Daniel..." Those deep blue eyes captured his and held on tight. A frown of confusion, of sorrow, perhaps, marred her smooth features. She pried the shovel from his unresisting grip and dropped it in the snow as she circled in front of him. And then his bold, brave Kylie reached up to capture his face between her hands. Even through the dusting of his beard, her bare fingers were ice-cold against his skin. But they were a cool balm to the feverish memories—a gentle reminder that she was real and alive, and the ghosts that haunted him had no power here in this moment. With this woman. "What happened to you on that last deployment? It must have been something terrible to make you withdraw from me like you have. I think it's a defense you've thrown up between us. Help me understand. You know I'm a good listener. It's hard to shock me. And nobody cares about how you're hurting more than I do."

He was quickly learning that nothing about Kylie Webber could surprise him—except for her unflinching loyalty to him and what they'd once meant to each other. And the idea that she hadn't moved on to someone who was safer, saner and a lot less complicated than the man he'd become. Part of him was touched by that undeserved devotion to their past, and part of him felt more guilty than ever at seeing the sexy, sassy brunette unattached and alone and worried about him, when she could have kids and a career and a man who loved her the way she deserved to be loved.

Although her familiar touch soothed something inside him, Daniel pulled her stiff fingers from his face. He rubbed her cold hands between his, lifted them to his lips and blew his warm breath over them. He wasn't sure he could have this conversation yet. But for her, he'd try.

He focused on her fingers instead of the compassionate curiosity in her eyes. "I lost…too much. I can't…find my way back to…normal. And I don't want…" *to dump on you the way I'm doing right now.*

His hands stilled around hers. He raised his gaze to her upturned face and took in the dark wisps of hair peeking from beneath her cap and dancing against her skin. He noted the parted invitation of her full pink lips. He saw the undeserved patience and caring shining from the depths of those beautiful blue eyes. But she couldn't fix him. She shouldn't have to. He was paranoid and suspicious, and too damn afraid to attach himself to anyone or anything he might lose or destroy.

But they had history, and, oh, she made it so tempting to go back to that idyllic innocence they'd once shared. Giving in to one moment of the fantasy, he cupped his hands on either side of her jaw, bent his head and covered her mouth in a kiss.

Long-denied needs and remembered passions flared inside him, and he slipped his tongue between her lips and claimed a deep taste of her. If she'd protested or gasped with surprise, he would have stopped. But Kylie rose up onto her toes, curled her fingers into the front of his coat and demanded he concede to the bond that still burned between them.

Her lips softened, warmed, beckoned. She tasted of coffee and woman and happier times.

And the moment she leaned into him and he braced his feet apart, the demons got inside his head and he pushed her away. This was what he could lose. This generous, beautiful woman was the one thing he refused to tarnish.

Planting a quick kiss of apology on her lips, he released her entirely. "I can't do this. I'm sorry."

A dark brow arched above that perceptive gaze. "Sorry about almost opening up to me? Or reminding me that you're the man who taught me how to kiss?"

Dead body? Killer in the wind? Blizzard? He wasn't going to let old feelings or his own screwed-up needs get in the way of protecting Kylie.

"Are we good to go now?" He plucked her gloves from her pocket and handed them to her. "We're pretty exposed to the elements out here. Better put those on."

"All right. Small steps it is. For now." The smile she offered never reached her eyes, but at least she wasn't pressing him to keep talking, or rubbing in the fact that he was the one who'd started that kiss, when he'd been insisting for months that they could never again be more than friends. She pulled on her gloves and fixed her sunglasses back over her eyes. "I've got what I need. Any more details will have to come from a CSI and an autopsy."

While Daniel packed their gear, Kylie tried her radio again. "This is Deputy Webber to Granite County One. Over? Come in, Granite County One."

She rotated between channels, getting a mix of static and silence. But no sheriff's office.

"Do you really think you're going to raise anyone up here?"

"A girl can always hope." There was no missing the double entendre she tossed over her shoulder at him.

But false hope was worse than no hope. And until this killer was found, and Daniel could get his head screwed on straight, he wouldn't give her either one. "Let's get back to the lodge, warm up and get some dinner in us."

"Warm sounds pretty good." Apparently willing, for the moment, to ignore that kiss and concentrate on the business at hand, Kylie bent down to strap her snowshoes back onto her boots.

Daniel seized the opportunity to pull out his binoculars and point them to the top of the mountain. There were no signs that the killer had returned to the scene of the crime or followed the ski lift up to the roundhouse to hide out. Of course, by this time of the late afternoon, all but the most recent of footprints would have been wiped out by the blizzard. But he was also checking for signs of snow disturbance. Was the snow drifting deeply against the roundhouse's door? Or had someone cleared a path to get inside?

Plenty deep. The entrance to the nearby supply cabin remained blocked with snow, too.

"You think he went up that way?" Kylie asked, shrugging her pack onto her back.

But Daniel had shifted his binoculars to the perilous

overhang of snow growing over the edge of the granite outcropping above the edge of the tree line.

"Daniel?"

He handed her binoculars and pointed out his concern. "Check that out. About thirty yards north of the roundhouse."

"Do you think the snow will hold?" She returned the binoculars, the frown line between her eyes indicating she understood the danger he'd pointed out. "If that gives, do you think the avalanche will hit the lodge? Should we call Kent?"

Daniel was already turning to the radio clipped to his coat. "I'll report it. Although I'm guessing at that angle, it'll hit through the trees, probably take out this half of the ski run. It'll bury Stacy's body for sure."

"Then we need to get moving. We need to find this guy before the mountain wipes out every last trace of him."

Daniel called in the avalanche warning, and promised Kent he'd get his sister off the mountain before the ridge of snow came crashing down on them. Kent said he'd see about boarding up the big windows facing the slope, and move the guests to the far side of the lodge as a precaution. Depending on the size of the slide and how firmly packed the snow was, it might not even reach the lodge. But it would definitely hit the shelters nestled in the trees on this side of Ice Lake.

"I'll send a couple of men out to make sure we don't have any homeless stragglers taking refuge in the lake cabins."

The cabins. There were ones farther north on the mountain, already evacuated, that were cut off from any sort of transportation. But the lake cabins were still accessible on foot. Daniel swung his binoculars down through the trees. Instincts and training that had served him well as a Marine were kicking in, sharpening his senses, quickening his thinking time. Spotting the places where the killer might hide on the mountain wasn't all that different from knowing where the enemy lay hidden in a remote desert village. "Keep your men there," he told Kent. "We'll check them out on our way down."

"What are you thinking?" Kylie asked after he signed off.

Daniel turned her around to untie her ski poles from her pack. While the snowshoes gave them surer footing, they'd make better time if they took a more challenging route straight down through the trees. "That there are a lot of places away from the lodge that bastard could hide. If he had a heat source and a few emergency supplies, he could wait out the storm. If he's got the right kind of gear and a good sense of direction, he could hike out of here in a day or two and we'd never see him again."

"We're checking out the cabins by the lake?" She returned the favor and handed him his ski poles.

He assessed the color on her cheeks to see if she was up to this. "Can you still feel all your fingers and toes?"

Kylie nodded.

"Then let's take the scenic route back to the lodge." Daniel studied the spacing of the trees, the lay of the rocks and size of the drifts around them before setting out on the steep descent. The last thing he needed was for one of them to take a tumble down the mountain or fall into a snow well. "Follow my path. We can circle down by the lake and check the buildings there without going too far out of our way."

"I'm right behind you."

KYLIE SWALLOWED a spoonful of spicy tomato soup and let the soothing warmth of it slide all the way down her throat before answering her brother's question.

"We found some signs of activity around two of the cabins on the uphill side of the lake." She bit into her grilled cheese sandwich and checked the ski patrol office again to make sure the doors to the infirmary and hallway were still closed, and that no one was eavesdropping. "Old footprints covered by snow. It looks like someone tried to break into the first cabin, but couldn't get the door to budge. The lock had been forced on the other one."

Daniel picked up his second sandwich. "Someone may have been inside at some point during the storm, but no one is in any of those cabins now."

Kent let them eat a little more before saying, "Last I heard from those two FBI agents who took out the Big Sky Strangler, they'd gotten cut off by the snow trying to get back to Graniteville, and are outside of communication. I gave them directions to one of the remote shelters before we lost radio contact. If they'd been able to make it as far as the lake, I'm guessing they would have come on to the lodge."

"I agree." Kylie took another sip of her soup. "If they knew one of their suspects was still here on the mountain, I think the elements are the only thing that would stop them from coming back to search for him."

Kent nodded. "Did you think anything looked out of place at the cabins?"

Daniel swallowed another bite before answering. "There was food in the cabinets of the one that had been broken into, along with some ice fishing equipment. But those could have been left behind by the paying tenants when we evacuated them to the lodge."

"I'll find out who was in that unit and see if they can account for their belongings." Kent paused to throw another log into the woodstove near where he'd seated Kylie and Daniel to thaw out from their trip up the mountain, and share a meal away from the others taking their dinner in the dining room. Kylie was glad for the privacy, so they could discuss her investigation without being overheard by any potential suspects.

"Could your killer be stockpiling a hideaway?" her brother added.

She'd considered that. But it was an odd assortment of items for a man running from the law—both men and women's clothes, bait and tackle, a cabinet full of pudding mix and cereal, soured milk in the powerless refrigerator, and a pair of neatly made cots with tucked in sheets and blankets. "If that's his idea of survival gear, then he won't last very long."

"Did you see any signs of tracks leading away from the place? Maybe around the lake and down to the highway?"

Daniel popped the last of his sandwich into his mouth and shook his head. "The only recent tracks were between cabins and between there and the lodge."

"Do you think that means the killer is here?"

Kylie finished off her soup and dabbed her lips with a paper napkin. "No way to prove it. Yes, someone broke into that cabin, which is suspicious, but it could have been a guest who forgot a key, or someone who got lost in the storm and tried to get into the wrong unit."

"You mean they broke into one when their key didn't work, realized it wasn't theirs, then found their way to the right place?"

"It's something I intend to ask about. If no one will admit to the broken lock, then maybe it was an attempt at escape," she conceded. "But unless the Feds were mistaken and Burney Novak's partner is long gone, then I'm guessing he's one of those guests in the dining room or lobby. Hiding in plain sight."

"That's a comforting thought," Daniel groused.

"It's just a matter of identifying him." Kylie traded her paper plate for Daniel's empty cup and carried both mugs to the sink in the counter next to the coffee station. While she rinsed them out, he tossed the trash into the bin beside the desk.

Kent came to her side and draped his arm around her shoulders. "Any idea how you're going to do *that,* Sherlock? The list Winston gave me has the names of forty-two guests and itinerants who were stranded here when the storm hit. Plus, you've got twelve of us on the lodge and support staff."

Kylie shrugged beneath his supportive hug. "Well, I'm eliminating the women, since they don't fit the profile. And I think I can trust that neither you nor Daniel murdered Stacy Beecham."

"Glad we didn't make the suspect list," he teased.

A scoffing noise drew her attention to the golden-haired man holding the curtain aside to peer through the window. "Don't forget to look for someone with blood on his clothes," Daniel said.

Kylie curled her toes into the dry wool socks she'd borrowed from her brother, battling the urge to go to Daniel to ease the acid in his tone. Something about the gore and violence of Stacy Beecham's murder had gotten inside his head. She knew there were people who couldn't stomach the sight of a lot of blood, but she had a feeling that wasn't the case here. Daniel was dealing with flashbacks to the nightmare in the Middle East that had changed him.

She understood his cold shoulder toward her a little better now. For a few miraculous moments on the mountain, he'd shared a part of himself with her. Needs were exposed. Fears were revealed. Hearts had touched.

That kiss had told her more than six months of mood swings and avoidance had. Daniel still cared for her, wanted her. But he was raw and confused and waging a war inside himself that he needed to win before he could handle any kind of relationship. And as much as she wanted him to admit he still cared, she would never force him into anything that might damage the fragile healing going on inside him.

So Kylie stayed with her brother and focused on the investigation. "You're right. We should expand our search to look for bloody clothes or a recent injury. Stacy put up a fight. There's no way her killer walked away from that scene without a mark on him."

Daniel closed the curtain and strolled across the room. "The wind's dying. The snow should be done by daybreak." His eyes darkened in ominous warning at every step. "That's a full night, and however long it takes us to dig out over the next couple of days, in close quarters with a man who knows you're looking for him. He's got the advantage here, Kylie. Not you."

"Tell me something I don't know, Mr. Gloom and Doom." She picked up her Kevlar vest from the chair beside the stove and checked it to see if the cover was dry. Time to gear up again and go back to work. "I just have to stay sharp. He'll make a mistake. He'll give us a clue soon enough. And then where's he going to run?"

She pulled the vest on over her khaki uniform shirt, but Daniel's fingers were there to fasten the Velcro securely beneath each arm. She gasped as he cinched it a bit too tightly. "It's that point when he's cornered and has nowhere to run that I'm worried about. Think of how a wild animal reacts when it's trapped."

Batting Daniel's helping hands away, she ripped apart the strap and refastened the vest in a snug, but more comfortable fit. "Let's just hope I'm smarter than a wild—"

"Kylie?" The hallway door swung open with a bang against the wall and Daniel pushed Kylie behind him, putting himself between her and the man charging in unannounced. "Is she here?" The first question was to Kent. And then Winston Cooper spotted her nudging Daniel aside. "Kylie? Thank God." The big, overweight lodge manager huffed and puffed his way across the room. His pudgy cheeks were flushed with color. "I thought I'd find you here. Good."

She eased her right hand off her weapon, where it had instinctively gone to defend herself, and raised her left, urging him to slow down and catch his breath. "Take it easy, Winston. You okay?"

He inhaled a shallow gasp of air, but nodded. "There's something you need to see. Victoria found it. Damn fool girl—trying to impress a boy."

Kent rested a calming hand on the frazzled man's shoulder. "Take a deep breath, Winston. Is Victoria all right?"

"Yes." He watched Kent's eyes, mimicked his slower breathing as the EMT subtly kept the manager from hyperventilating. "I mean, she's freaked out. I sent her to the front desk and told that Mike fella to get back in the lobby with the other guests."

What now? "Mike Osterman?"

"I didn't ask his last name."

"Is Victoria all right?" Kylie echoed in a firmer tone. If the bozos were up to no good again...

Winston swung his gaze back to her. Something had clearly rattled him. *Please, God, not another dead body.* "Just come."

The door to the infirmary opened and Barb Hughes peeked out. The older man's noisy entrance must have awakened her from her drug-induced sleep. "Is it Stacy? Did you find her?"

"Barb?" Kent hurried over to the slim blonde and slid an arm behind her waist to steady her on her feet. "Remember? We talked about Stacy."

"We did?" She squeezed her eyes shut with a sob of lucidity and she leaned into Kent. "What am I going to tell her mom?"

Winston glanced Barb's way, flashing the friendly smile with which he normally greeted guests. But just as quickly, the panic was back and he turned to Kylie again. "Please. Before anyone else sees it."

"Go. I'll take care of her." Kent shifted his glance to Daniel. "You've got them?"

With a nod, Daniel slipped his hand beneath Winston's elbow. The older man was already backing toward the hallway. "I need you to come and look at something," he said.

A few minutes later Kylie and Daniel were standing in the kitchen's walk-in freezer. A dedicated generator had kept the room at a frosty temperature to preserve and isolate the first strangulation victim's body, along with that of her killer, Burney Novak.

"Son of a bitch." A warm puff of air formed a cloud when Daniel cursed.

"Your daughter and Mike found the room like this?" Kylie asked.

"That's what she said." Winston pulled a handkerchief from his pocket to wipe away the perspiration freezing on his forehead. "She was talking to that boy about the Big Sky Strangler, and he dared her to prove he was here. Something like that. She ran straight to me when she saw it."

Ignoring the woman's body, Kylie quickly moved across the concrete floor and knelt beside the stocky form of Burney Novak. The plastic tarp he'd been wrapped in had been pulled open. Spatter from the bullet wound that had killed him stained his shirt.

But she was more interested in what was curiously out of place. The right front pocket of his pants had been turned inside out. Overlooking the protocol of donning plastic gloves, she quickly felt the rest of his pockets. "His billfold is missing."

What was that about? Why rob a dead man when there was no place to spend his money? The dead man's credit cards would be no good, either. She wouldn't put a sick prank past Mike Osterman, but this was about more than a stolen wallet.

Behind her, Winston wheezed. "This is really bad, isn't it?"

"Yeah." Kylie braced her hands on her knees and pushed herself to her feet. "Our guy has discovered a taste for killing."

Just like his partner.

Her eyes focused on the handwritten note that had been taped to Novak's forehead: "You can't get rid of me this easily. This is prime hunting ground. I'm coming for you."

CHAPTER FIVE

I'M COMING FOR YOU.

Vague enough to make Kylie believe every woman at this lodge was in danger. Sinister enough to make the threat feel very personal.

And the man who'd sent that message was in this room.

"Gather around so you can see," Kylie urged the people in the lobby, fixing a smile on her face, although she knew there was little to smile about tonight. "We need to fit everyone in here. That's right. Sit if you want, or stand. We just need to make sure we're all here and that you can hear Mr. Cooper and Mr. Webber at the front desk."

Shining her flashlight into the guests and staff crowded into the lodge's lobby, Kylie looked for two things—any man boldly making eye contact with the only woman wearing a gun and a badge in the room, and any man making an effort to mask his face or some other part of his body that might have a cut, scratch or scrape that looked as if it had been earned in a brawl on the mountain.

She nodded to one gentleman. Too old to fit the profile. She tucked a blanket more securely around a woman. Wrong gender. Ah, yes. Her dear friends Mike and Tony. Mike looked right at her from his seat beside the fire pit. *Make a note.* With a flick of the flashlight, she directed his attention to her brother and the lodge manager climbing up onto the knotty pine check-in counter.

Tony stood behind Mike's chair, his face turned toward the fire. He'd worn a silly necktie when she'd first run across him in the ditch. And now he'd put on a borrowed turtleneck that went clear up to his chin. This morning he'd seemed too blitzed to be a threat to anyone but himself. But could that have been an act? She jotted a second mental note to look beneath that neckline for any scratches, or ask Kent if his staff had treated any injuries beyond Tony's wrist.

She tilted her chin, searching out Daniel, who was on the far side of the gathering, making a similar inspection of the guests. A glance with her eyes alerted him to her suspicions about Mike and Tony, and he answered with a subtle nod. Then he angled his head toward the staff members lined up in front of the picture window at the rear of the lobby.

Kylie began moving in that direction. What had caught his attention back there? The kitchen staff still wore their aprons, along with sweaters and gloves. Did he think one of them might be hiding an injury? The two maids were female. And the rest of them she knew from their work with Kent. Ski patrol. Lodge maintenance. Front staff. Having just come in from working outside, Lou Sullivan and the maintenance guys were brushing snow off their outdoor gear. Sure, a scarf or glove or coat sleeve could hide a mark from her.

But Daniel was part of the lodge team, too. Did he really suspect one of the men he worked with was a killer? Was paranoia a symptom of PTSD?

Frowning at the thought, Kylie turned her attention back to the two men speaking at the front of the room.

This gathering had been her idea. With nightfall looming and the blizzard waning, depleted fuel supplies for the generators, and new dangers that could result if anyone thought it was safe to leave once the snow stopped, they had a perfectly legitimate reason for holding a public meeting and making a few announcements.

Only she, Daniel, Kent and Winston—and possibly the killer himself—knew there was an ulterior motive behind getting everyone into one place at one time.

"If we could have your attention. Ladies and gentlemen, please," Winston called out again, his thick chest rising and falling with the effort of climbing onto his perch. One by one, side conversations quieted and he spoke again. "I can't thank you all enough for your cooperation and the spirit of camaraderie that we've shared throughout the storm. But for everyone's safety and survival, I must ask your indulgence for a little while longer."

"Are we running out of food?" someone shouted.

"We've got enough to get us through another week, if you don't mind canned supplies instead of a gourmet menu."

"We're going to be here another week?" someone else asked.

"We'll freeze to death by then," a voice complained.

Another guest chimed in, "I'm freezing now."

Winston patted the air with placating hands to quiet the stirrings of unrest. "No. No. We'll be fine. We'll all be fine. But the chief of the Mount Atlas ski patrol—my friend Kent Webber—has a couple of things you need to be aware of for your safety." Looking enormously relieved to be turning the meeting over to Kylie's brother, Winston gestured to the tall man standing beside him. "Kent?"

"Thanks, Winston." Kent stepped forward. "First, I want to assure all of you that we are perfectly safe here inside the lodge. However, based on my team's patrols and my experience with this mountain, I need to issue an avalanche warning, and tell you we need to stay put for another twenty-four hours. At least."

Kylie scanned the crowd again, face by face, as a buzz of complaints and concerns cropped up—travel plans, missing work, no way to notify worried family back home. But no one blipped across her radar as someone who seemed particularly upset or angered by the announcement.

Before he could be bombarded with questions, Kent hushed the crowd again. "I've asked the maintenance staff to put plywood over the north-facing windows, so please avoid that area. The main part of the lodge is literally rock-solid and we'll be safe here. But the wood-framed wings of the hotel and the lake cabins, along with the glass facing the mountain, obviously, aren't as sturdy. And absolutely do *not* venture outside for any reason."

"Are we going to die?" a woman asked.

Kylie swept the crowd for signs that anyone else understood the innocent double entendre of her question. Nothing. Either this guy was good—or she wasn't good enough.

And she damn well wasn't going to concede to that.

"We'll be just fine," Kent reassured her. "As long as we're smart about things, and you do as I say."

While his confidence seemed to calm the young woman, he darted his gaze to Kylie. *Did I stall long enough, sis?* he seemed to ask.

With the slightest of nods, she signaled him to go on to the next phase of her plan. She'd seen all the faces and had a short list of suspects. Now she needed to find out if Mike or Tony, or one of the other twenty-to-thirtyish, brown-haired, average-built men she'd spotted would reveal a clue that could help her determine who had violated Burney Novak's corpse and killed Stacy Beecham.

Kent jumped off the counter and asked everyone to form an orderly line. Then he pointed to Winston and Victoria Cooper and the lists of names they held up. "Since the computers are down, we have no other way to verify who is here. Whether you're a registered guest or not, even if you're staff, we need you to sign beside your name so we have a record of everyone we'd have to account, for should some unforeseen catastrophe hit us. Like I said, I don't believe we're in any immediate danger inside the lodge. But it's my job to be prepared ahead of time. Thank you."

Despite a few grumblings, there was more praise for Kent's proactive safety measures, and sighs of relief from the people lining up. Kylie and Daniel worked their way to the front of the room, encouraging those who signed the sheet to move on out of the way.

Mike Osterman winked at Victoria as he signed his name, and the young redhead giggled. "You've got a pretty laugh." Kylie got no wink, though, when he faced her. Maybe it had something to do with Daniel Stone lurking over her shoulder. "Deputy. Mountain man," he said in greeting.

Daniel encouraged him to move on by stepping right behind him. "You're holding up the line, Osterman."

"Like I said, this Western hospitality sucks. I'm movin'."

The sleeve of Tony's oversize sweater came down to his knuckles, but he made no effort to pull the knit out of his way to write.

"What is your last name, anyway, Tony?" Kylie asked. "We didn't know what to put on the sheet."

"Are you asking as a deputy so you can arrest me?"

"Just friendly curiosity."

He shook his head and signed. "I don't know what Mike told you, but I wasn't driving that car. He was giving me a lift from Graniteville after my vehicle broke down. I'd never even met him before that night at the bar. If I'd known he was as drunk as I was, I'd have never gotten into the car with him. You think about that when you're writin' up your tickets."

Interesting. Very interesting. So neither of the bozos could alibi each other for more than a few hours before she'd picked them up off the side of the road. Either one could have had the opportunity to kill Stacy Beecham, and then thumb a ride or pick up a hitchhiker once he'd discovered the highway couldn't get him out of town.

"Your last name?" Kylie asked.

"Marchek. Ma'am."

She watched him filter into the crowd and disappear into one of the seating areas overlooking the lake—on the opposite side of the lobby from Mike.

As the end of the line neared, Lou Sullivan joked with her. "You're hoping one of us is someone famous and you're g-going to sell our auto…g-graph for a fortune online, aren't you?"

Kylie grinned. "You're on to me, Lou. A cop's salary doesn't pay enough, so I'm looking for the big bucks. Who knows, maybe I can get a dollar for your autograph."

Lou chuckled, then saluted her with a gloved hand. "Maybe you c-can."

She was smiling as he moved on and the next person stepped up to sign. Twenty minutes later, Kent thanked them all for their cooperation, rolled up the papers and carried them back to the ski patrol rooms. Meanwhile Winston Cooper summoned the maintenance team and gave them assignments on boarding up the windows, digging out the sheds and warming up the engines of the snowplows so they could clear the parking lot, sidewalks and driveway outside.

The crew had a long night ahead of them, but not any longer than the one Kylie was anticipating for herself. She had twenty-four hours left to solve this murder and capture a killer. Once the roads were cleared and the avalanche warning was rescinded, she'd have no legal reason for keeping all these people here. Burney Novak's partner could drive away and never be seen again.

With Daniel at her back, making sure that no one was overly interested in their quick departure, Kylie hurried down the hall to Kent's office. She found her brother crumpling the corner of one paper in his hand and cursing. "Kent?"

With a nod to Daniel to close the door, he handed the paper across his desk to her. "Look at that last name on the list."

Kylie scrolled down, the handwriting samples she'd wanted for a comparison barely registering. Her breath rushed out of her lungs and her blood ran cold.

Daniel plucked the paper from her fingers. "What is it?"

"At the bottom."

"What kind of sick joke…?" Daniel's eyes darkened to a stormy mix of gray and green as they swept over her face. Was that anger? Concern? Some kind of told-you-so? "You need to stop this investigation right now."

As if retreating now would stop events that had already been set into motion.

Kylie sought out the strength stamped on Daniel's grim features, wishing for a moment that she wasn't quite so independent and he wasn't so tormented. Because she wanted nothing more than to walk into his arms right now and have him hold her, love her, make her believe their future would be all right, the way he once had.

"You know I can't," she answered grimly.

Someone was definitely sending her a message. Taunting her. Daring her to figure this out before another woman died. Reminding her that she was the ultimate prize on the killer's list.

She pulled the paper from his fingers and read the last entry again. "Burney Novak."

"WHAT DOES THAT MEAN?" Kent asked. "Novak's dead."

Daniel watched Kylie retrieve her camera from her coat hanging on a peg beside the door. Was it his imagination, or were her fingers trembling as she pulled up the photo she'd taken of the note taped to Burney's corpse?

Ah, hell. Tender, protective feelings that had nothing to do with keeping her alive, and everything to do with getting her chin back the stubborn, confident tilt that made her Kylie Webber, sneaked out from the recesses of his frozen soul and seeped into his blood.

"It means that Kylie was right." Before he understood the urge himself, Daniel slipped his hand beneath the short fringe of sable hair at her nape. She stiffened in surprise at the initial contact, but his fingers remembered the simple intimacies of touch and comfort that his heart had tried to forget. They worked their way underneath her stiff uniform collar and soothed the tight cords of tension there. Daniel rubbed away her resistance to his caress, until he heard her whisper a sigh, and she relaxed. Something in his own chest eased in that moment as well, and he couldn't quite bring himself to end the contact with her skin. "Our killer is here. And he knows Kylie's on to him."

"The handwriting matches," Kylie said in a throaty tone that let him know the simple massage was affecting her in unforeseen ways, too. "The man who left that note on Novak's body wrote this. Neither of you saw who was the last guy to sign?"

"It was someone on my team," Kent answered. "But he signed beside his name on the first page. Maybe Winston or Victoria had that sheet. I don't know."

Finally, Kylie shrugged and moved away, breaking contact. "Ooh, I wish we had enough electricity to run the security cameras. We could have caught him on tape."

The disconnect snapped Daniel out of the intimate haze of remembered touches and feelings. He needed to regroup, refocus. He'd built emotional barriers for a reason. He'd separated himself from Kylie on purpose, so he wouldn't hurt so much—so he could survive—if, God forbid, something should happen to her.

"If we had that kind of power to spare, then we wouldn't be trapped in a fishbowl with a killer," he pointed out.

The glare she shot him after putting away her camera indicated her fire and strength were returning, anyway. "I'm no closer to finding him than when we started." She clenched her fists in frustration and paced across the room. "How could we miss that signature? We were supposed to keep an eye on everyone."

Kent made the mistake of trying to reason with his sister. "The three of us couldn't watch sixty-plus people every single second we were there. And remember, this guy doesn't want to get caught."

Kylie spun around, snapping her fingers. "Yes, he does."

"Huh?"

"Why else would he sign Burney's name?"

"I don't get it."

"I need a couple of minutes to think this through." She linked her arm through Kent's and flashed a smile that could almost get even Daniel to do her bidding. "Would you do me a big favor and track down Winston and Victoria? Ask if they can remember who signed at the bottom of the page."

"And be discreet about it, I'm assuming?"

She opened the door for him. "I'll owe you one."

Kent paused long enough to look over the top of her head to Daniel. "I don't know what she's up to yet, but keep an eye on this one, will you?"

"You know I will," he promised. He folded his arms across his chest and met her eyes straight on after she closed the door. "Kent might not get the way your mind is working, but I do. You're going to play that perp's game. You know what the ultimate outcome will be, don't you?"

At least she had the good sense not to sugarcoat the truth. She tipped her gaze up to his. "He'll try to kill me."

"And the idea of retreating a couple of steps and waiting until we can get the sheriff or those FBI agents—some kind of backup—here to Ice Lake never occurred to you?"

"I'm not going to let him kill anyone else because I sat on the sidelines waiting for help to arrive. *I'm* the help. *I'm* the one who has to protect these people."

"Do you even hear yourself? These are murders we're talking about, not some high school football game. We may not know who he is yet, but he knows who you are." Daniel slid his fingers along the side of her neck to cup her jaw, needing the feel of her cool skin against his to stop the burning memories of waste and pain kindling inside him, forgetting his resolve of only a moment ago to distance himself emotionally from this woman. A harsh whisper was all he could manage. "Do you think I want to lose anyone else?"

She closed her eyes and rubbed her cheek against his palm. Another simple intimacy they'd once shared. "I'm sorry, Daniel. I don't want to hurt you." She turned to press a soft, quick kiss into his palm. "But I have to do this. It's my job."

And then she pulled away and scooted around Kent's desk to study the signatures again. She was back to her logical, legal, crusading self before Daniel could regain control of the walls that were breaking down inside him.

"There has to be some way to figure out this guy's identity." A frown of frustration creased the skin between her eyes and she set down the papers.

"Does anyone else's handwriting match the note and Novak's signature?" he asked.

She shook her head. "He wouldn't make it that easy."

"Why sign a dead man's name? Just to tease you?"

"I think it's more than that." And while Daniel spiraled down into the darkness inside, Kylie's eyes lit up like sapphires. She paced the room from window to door and back while she worked out her theory. "The FBI profiled the Big Sky Stranglers as a pair of serial killers. One partner was dominant, the other a submissive. Now that Novak is dead, the partner has no one to follow. He's been doing Novak's bidding for more than ten years. He can't think for himself. Toss in an unexpected cop, this blizzard and being trapped at Ice Lake, and the world he knows is spinning out of control."

Daniel perched on the corner of the desk, letting the alternating view of long legs walking toward him, and curvy bottom walking away, distract him from the gruesome images of war and murder, with Kylie in the middle of all of it, trying to get into his head. "So he fixes his problems by killing women?"

"He fixed his problem by becoming Burney Novak. I'm the enemy here. As a submissive, he's not powerful enough to take me down. But he believes Burney could."

"So he's assumed Burney's identity." That could explain the missing billfold. "Complete with a driver's license and an aversion to female authority figures."

"Exactly. He's trying to be the same deviant, conniving, powerful man Novak was."

"And he sees you as the only thing standing between him and getting away with murder?" Daniel snagged her wrist and pulled her to a stop before she passed him again. "Damn it, Kylie, you never should have come here."

"I was trapped on this side of the closed roads, just like you. It's not as if I had a choice." Her other hand came to rest on his knee, and other memories, more sensual images of sunshine and fresh air and a scratchy blanket spread amid a field of yellow glacier lilies, flooded his mind. "If I wasn't here, this guy would be going after someone else. At least I'm able to fight him, to know he's out there. Stacy Beecham didn't have that advantage. And I do have backup. I have you."

Daniel covered her hand with his, capturing it against his leg, holding on as the memory of bruised dead eyes tried to cancel out the lightness of what Kylie had once meant to him. "I may not be the best help you could ask for."

"I will always believe in you, Daniel," she vowed in a husky voice. "No one, not even you, will ever convince me that you're not a good man—that you're not someone worthy of being loved, that...you wouldn't be there for me if I really needed you."

Daniel shook his head. "What I want to do, and what I think I can, aren't—"

"Shh." She pressed her fingers against his lips to hush his protest. As if sensing the struggle inside him, Kylie nudged his knee to the side and boldly moved between his legs to close the distance still separating them. She cradled his jaw between her hands, gently stroking the tight line of his mouth, silently asking him to meet her questioning gaze. "Up on the mountain, you mentioned losing something...someone...? In the war? More than just your men, I take it. Someone special. Someone who shouldn't have died?"

Gritty tears burned beneath Daniel's eyelids at the thought of an innocent little boy. But he refused to cry. He traced the bottom edge of Kylie's thick belt and holster, settling his hands at her hips, anchoring them to crisp canvas and the warm curves beneath. "We're not talking about me."

"Then let's talk about me." She reached up and brushed a stray spike of hair off his forehead. Once. Twice. And judging by the pressure on the inside of his thighs and the heat arcing between them, she was drifting closer. She was petting him, soothing him, preparing him to hear her next words. "I may not be able to understand the depths of what you've gone through, with the post-traumatic stress and the counseling. But Daniel, think. I bet you can understand what *I'm* going through.

I'm fighting a war here at Ice Lake. I've got a lobby full of potential casualties and an enemy we can't yet see. I'm the first, last and only line of defense those people have. Do you honestly believe I want any one of their deaths to happen on my watch? Do you think I want that on my conscience?" Her hands stilled their gentle work. The tears he couldn't shed glistened in the corners of her eyes. "Look at how it's eating you up inside. I…I don't think I could stand that."

"Ah, hell." He wiped away a tear with the pad of his thumb. "You do not want to end up where I am. I never want that for you, babe. You need to save them." Dragging in a deep breath, he leaned forward and captured her mouth with his.

Her lips parted, welcomed, filled him with heat. Every cell in his body leaped to make contact with hers. As Kylie wound her arms around his neck and pulled herself into the embrace, the unforgiving wall of Kevlar she wore pressed against his chest. It was a symbolic barrier he was crashing through, whether he was ready for it or not. He slid one hand around to squeeze her lush bottom, tunneled the other into the soft velvet of her hair to hold her mouth against his and drink up her heat and healing.

Passion pounded through his veins with every tilt of her lush mouth, every foray of her tongue. Her grasping fingers—on his face, in his hair, inside the neckline of his shirt, skimming across the bare skin beneath—infused him with strength. The needy hums of desperation and delight in her throat fueled his own need.

Doors that had been locked inside him burst open and crumbled into sawdust. He wanted to feel her, taste her, inhale her. God, he wanted to be inside her. His feelings had been shut off from the world for too long and now were raging through every system of his body. It was a painful reawakening, an acknowledgment inside his head and heart that had to be made.

To become whole again, he needed Kylie. And she needed him to keep her world from falling apart.

She was his humanity. His hope. His light. And he needed to fight his way back from the hell he'd been in, to claim it.

"Daniel." She kissed his cheek, nipped at his chin. "I've tried to give you the space you needed, but I've missed you. I've missed us."

Oh, yeah. He'd missed this, too.

But the shadows had lived in his head for all these months for a reason.

"G.I. Joe?"

"No, kid. Captain Stone to you."

Suddenly his hands were full of blood. And a happy, trusting boy...

The darkness might have temporarily lifted, but one kiss couldn't make it disappear. This might be what he wanted, but he couldn't let that want become a need. As much as Kylie's patience, strength and stubborn love could heal him, it was too much of a gift to risk losing.

"Baby… Kylie…" Daniel wrapped his hands around her wrists and pulled her fingers from his skin. He caught her palms against his thundering heart and forced some space between them. He dipped his forehead to touch hers. "We've got to stop."

She was breathing as hard as he was. "I know. Wrong time. Wrong place."

"Wrong man."

Her blue eyes opened mere inches from his. "Daniel—"

"Don't argue with me." He looked deep into the sea

of blue and willed her to understand. "Call me whatever name you want for letting that kiss get out of hand. You've always been irresistible to me." Desire still pulsed through his blood. "But I don't want to feel this way. I don't want to feel. It's too much."

Instead of slapping his face or retreating, Kylie wound her arms around his neck and hugged him. "So you care, but you don't *want* to care. Am I understanding you correctly?"

"Call me a coward—"

"I would never."

"—but I don't think I'm strong enough to fail anyone I care about again. Maybe not for a long time. Maybe never." His arms tightened like a vise around her. "If I disappointed you, if I hurt you, if I let anyone else hurt you…"

She shook her head, the soft waves of her hair catching in the two-day stubble of his beard. "You wouldn't hurt me or lose me. It doesn't have to be perfect. It just has to be you. I'm not as innocent as I used to be, Daniel. I know relationships aren't easy."

He untangled her hair from his face and tucked it behind her ear as he leaned back. "I don't want to give you false hope that we could make something work, or ask you to wait for me to get my head screwed on straight. It wouldn't be fair to you. And you're so strong and full of life and hope—I don't ever want to be the man who crushes that beautiful spirit of yours."

She nearly crushed his neck as she hugged him again. She was such a fighter. She turned her lips to his ear and whispered, "What if I've got enough hope for both of us?"

Daniel was pulling away from that hug when Winston Cooper knocked on the door and came in. The hammering of the workmen down the hallway was a welcome cover for the guilt, passion and regret still drumming inside him.

"Sorry." The lodge manager cleared his throat. "I didn't know you two were still…? Sorry."

Daniel pushed himself to his feet, faintly alarmed by the man's shallow breaths and pallor. "What is it, Winston?"

His eyes darted to Kylie. "I think your plan backfired. I'm trying to keep everyone together in the main room, like you said. But when the crew went out to bring in plywood and start the plows, there was a lot of movement. And then the diesel engines were running and there was hammering and no one was listening to me—"

"Winston." Kylie touched the older man's arm and urged him to take a breath. Other than the pinkened abrasions from Daniel's beard around her kiss-stung lips, she gave no sign of the passion and raw emotions they'd just shared. "What's wrong?"

"I can't find Victoria."

CHAPTER SIX

KYLIE DASHED OUT to the lobby with Daniel on her heels and Winston hurrying behind them. She nimbly climbed atop the front desk. "Victoria Cooper! Are you here? Has anyone seen Victoria Cooper?"

Conversations abruptly halted. Hammers and saws went silent. The maids who were handing out more blankets and pillows to anyone who was ready for some sleep stopped and stared.

Kylie scanned the long, tall room for a glimpse of auburn hair. No sign of Victoria. The silence echoed in her ears and in the pit of dread opening in her gut.

Kent appeared from the nearest hallway with a flashlight, the sober expression on his face adding to her fear. She squatted down to hear him, out of earshot of the guests.

"Good. You're already here," her brother said. "I located Winston to ask about the list, but he was already looking for his daughter." Kent shook his head as Daniel came up beside them. "I just checked every room and closet in the hotel wing. She's not there."

Kylie's worst fear had come true. "He's got her."

"Who?" Kent asked.

Daniel's tone was equally grim. "The strangler's partner."

Kylie rose to her feet and took control of the room again, before the buzz of speculation could drown her out. "False alarm. She's been located," she lied. She tried to summon a smile, but couldn't. "Nobody leaves this room. Understand? That's an order from the Granite County Sheriff's Department. It's for your own safety." She scanned the groupings of people again. "If an avalanche hits us directly, it could wipe out the hotel wing. Go on about your business, but you have to stay here where the stone walls can protect you."

From the dangers outside this lodge.

But what about the danger lurking within?

As the guests relaxed and the crew went back to work, Kylie spotted Mike Osterman lounging on a couch in front of the fire pit. The young brunette he was chatting up seemed more taken by his charms than Kylie had been. He'd come to Montana looking for snow bunnies, and apparently, had finally found one.

He'd made Victoria Cooper laugh easily, too.

Victoria was always ready for a smile or a laugh.

Wait a minute. Kylie was going about this backward. She hunched down to speak to Daniel and her brother. "Forget Victoria for a sec. Are there any men missing?"

"I've got the list in my pocket." Kent pulled the rolled-up papers from the back of his jeans and flattened them on the desktop. "You want me to have them sign their names again?"

Daniel shook his head. "I don't think we could come up with another excuse that wouldn't send everyone into a panic. Right now, Barb Hughes is the only person besides our staff and Winston who knows what really happened to her roommate. But they've all heard about her being missing. If they think someone else has disappeared..."

Kent nodded. "I can go through the crowd, make sure everyone has what they need for the night, and ask some casual questions to see if anyone has wandered off for any reason. I'll get somebody to talk. I can be real friendly." He waved over a couple of members from the ski patrol team and they quickly started working their way around the room.

Tony Marchek sat up from the sofa where he must have been dozing as Kent approached him. He yawned and stretched, then shook his head at whatever her brother had asked him.

I can be real friendly.

Her brother's tossed-off statement turned a switch inside Kylie's brain as every observation she'd made over the past twelve hours fell into place.

"Lou Sullivan looked me right in the eye. He joked with me." He'd never been that confident before. "He was flirting."

"What?" Daniel grasped her waist to help her down from the desk.

The imprint of his large, strong hands that had held her so desperately just a few minutes ago barely registered. "Forget head counts. Let me see that."

She dragged the stack of papers in front of her and flipped through the list. There. The clue was so simple that she'd overlooked it. "He didn't sign his name."

"Who?"

"Lou." Kylie pointed to the blank spot beside the printed name. "It's Lou. Lou Sullivan is Burney Novak's partner."

Daniel's shoulder brushed against hers as he verified the omission they'd all missed.

"He never once took off his gloves, not even to write his name. What if his hands are scratched up? And he always has that scarf wrapped around his neck. And those glasses? The man's hiding himself from head to toe. If he has any marks or blood on him, we wouldn't see them." He'd even made a joke about his autograph. "I was so intent on finding the killer, I wasn't really listening to what he was saying at the time—or how he was saying it." Kylie latched on to the arm of Daniel's sweater and the strength she felt beneath. "Lou Sullivan is trying to be Burney now that his partner is out of the picture. Lou is Stacy Beecham's killer."

Kent rejoined them at the check-in counter. "My men counted heads twice and asked some questions. Everyone's here for except for Victoria and—"

"Lou Sullivan," she and Daniel answered in unison.

"How did you know—?"

"Don't ask." Daniel's muscles bunched beneath her hand before he pulled away and faced Kent. "Do you know where he was last seen?"

"Maintenance crew said he was outside, driving the snowplow."

Daniel swore. "Clearing the path for his own escape."

"Well, he didn't get very far." Kent's tone was less harsh. "The engine seized up with the cold. The plow is broken down and blocking the parking lot exit."

Kylie glanced over her shoulder at Daniel's stern, surprisingly cold, expression. "That's probably what set him off and made him come after the woman who was easiest to get to. Someone he works with—a friend like Victoria, who wouldn't question it if he asked for some kind of help."

Winston chose the wrong moment to eavesdrop on their conversation. "My baby? This is about the Big Sky Strangler, isn't it? That note in the freezer. He's going to kill my baby."

"No, he won't." Kylie turned to Kent. "Calm Winston down. Don't let anyone else leave the building." Then she turned and hurried down the hallway toward the ski patrol office, where her winter gear was stowed.

Daniel was right behind her. He walked straight to the ski cabinet and pulled on his orange ski patrol gear as Kylie tugged on her hat and coat and adjusted the bulky warmth over her holster and utility belt.

Gun, check. Ammo, check. Flashlight, check. Boots, gloves, resolve—check.

Kylie no longer had any doubts that the Big Sky Strangler's partner was here in Ice Lake. Shy, stuttering Lou Sullivan made the perfect submissive for a dominant partner like Burney Novak. Lou could blend in to a crowd without being noticed. He could scout out an area for Burney's potential victims ahead of time, without anyone being the wiser. Burney and Lou were two sides of the same murderous coin. The FBI had it wrong. Lou hadn't abandoned his partner at all. Not in life. Or death. Instead of fleeing the area when he could, he'd stayed to carry on his partner's work.

Kylie had to find Lou Sullivan before he killed again.

If she wasn't already too late.

The door was blocked by a tall, golden mountain man with deadly intent stamped in his gray-green eyes. Her heart broke apart at the tight clench of his jaw and the resolute determination that flattened his beautiful mouth. "Ready?"

Kylie reached out to stroke her fingers across those tight lips that had kissed her so thoroughly. She wanted to spare him any more pain and regret, and the guilt she didn't fully understand. "I don't know if you should go. What if something's happened to Victoria? Another dead body might—"

"Nobody knows that mountain like I do." He pulled

her hand away, refusing her comfort. "It's the middle of the night. Who else can track him?"

"But you seem so…"

"Unbalanced?"

"Angry."

"Yeah, I'm angry. I'm angry that innocent people are dying on my watch and that the bastard killing them has been right under my nose for two months." Daniel shrugged into his pack and reached for hers. "A hell of a fine guardian I am. I couldn't protect that little boy or my men or you—"

"What little boy?"

But that was still a nightmare he wouldn't share. "I'll carry the gear. You carry the gun." He was calm, focused, determined—every bit the Marine going off to battle—as he stepped aside and ushered her through the door.

THE SNOW HAD FINALLY stopped. But even with everything around them painted white, the sliver of moon in the clearing sky gave them little visual advantage beyond the scope of their flashlights. But the scents of gasoline and exhaust fumes, and two sets of boot prints, led Daniel to the snowmobile shed.

It looked to have been a quick stroll across the parking lot, judging by the spacing of the prints. Victoria had no qualms about keeping up with Lou Sullivan—until the shed door opened. Daniel pointed his light to the swath cleared through the snow that went straight down to the pavement, then knelt down to pick up the pink mitten that lay half buried beside it. "Looks like there was a struggle here."

"He probably had to knock her out or tie her up, once Victoria realized the excuse he'd used to get her out here was a ruse." Kylie's light swept the same area before she pulled open the unlocked door. "I don't see any blood. That's good. Chances are she isn't dead yet."

While she searched inside, Daniel's ears tuned in to a distant, rhythmic sound coming from far up on Mount Atlas. He stood, held his breath and listened for the enemy in the darkness.

"No one's inside. But one of the snowmobiles is missing." Kylie's voice dropped to a whisper as she rejoined him. "What is it?"

"Shh."

"Is that...?"

Daniel's release of warm breath clouded the air between them. The distant, evenly timed clacking noise of the lift chairs passing over each tower. "He's cranked up the ski lift."

"Why would he do that?"

"Besides draining the generators?" Daniel circled the shed. The base of the lift was a good fifty yards beyond them. And while there was a set of deep boot prints leading in that direction, the dimness of the moon and massive drifts of snow prevented him from seeing the entry platform, to know whether or not those tracks went all the way to the lift. "If Victoria is unconscious, once he got her onto the chair he wouldn't have had to carry or drag her."

"He could be taking her up to where he killed Stacy. Most killers like familiar territory."

"I'm guessing his familiar territory is buried under about five feet of snow by now. He'd have a hard time finding it in the dark." Daniel hiked back through the thigh-deep snow to the front of the shed. "It could just be a diversion, too, to make us think he's gone up the mountain."

Kylie unzipped the top pocket of her coat and pulled out her walkie-talkie. "I'll radio Kent to turn off the lift."

Daniel stopped her hand. "No. If Lou has taken her to the top of Atlas, that's the quickest way for us to get there. But hold on…" He shone his flashlight along the pair of parallel tracks that headed toward the lake. "The snowmobile went that way."

"To the cabins?" Kylie put away the walkie-talkie and took a few steps along the path. Their powerful flashlights barely made it to the edge of the trees, where the tracks disappeared. "But the gravel road around the lake circles back to the main lodge."

"And the terrain is too rugged and steep to go cross-country to get to the more remote cabins or the highway. A snowmobile is too heavy to get far in snow this deep, when it hasn't been packed down yet."

"So which way did he take her, and which is the diversion?" Kylie backtracked over her steps. "Lou's smarter than I gave him credit for."

Bad memories were crawling inside Daniel's mind. There was nothing about this setup he liked. Two trails. Deep snow. Limited vision. Freezing temps. Missing young woman. Crazy bastard who wasn't right inside his head. Tonight was going to end badly for someone. Daniel could feel it in his bones.

But as much as he dreaded the possibility of losing someone else, he was equally determined to do whatever was necessary to keep Kylie from losing an innocent victim on her watch. "Which way do you want to go?"

Her decision was far too easy, and way too risky. "We have to split up."

"No."

Damn that stubborn Webber spirit. "If Victoria's hurt, she'll need your EMT skills. And if there's any chance of saving her, you can get up the mountain faster than anyone I know. I'll check the lake cabins."

"What if she's hurt down here?"

Kylie's answering smile illuminated the darkness. "You can come down the mountain faster than anyone I know. Or I can radio Kent. It wouldn't be that much farther for him."

Daniel didn't need daylight to see the determination in her eyes. No matter what he chose, she was going the other way.

"You'll need these." He pulled the snowshoes off his pack and dropped them at her feet. Then he pulled out his skis and poles. "Radio the second you spot anything. With the snow stopped, the walkie-talkie should carry over a longer distance."

"You, too. The moment you see anything suspicious, let me know."

Ah, hell. One way or the other, they had to ferret out the enemy. The sooner he got up that mountain, the sooner he could get back to Kylie. As soon as she straightened, he palmed the back of her neck and pulled her to him for a hard, quick kiss that conveyed everything he felt, yet wasn't nearly enough.

He released her and jabbed his poles into the snow. "We'll meet up back here, right?"

He had to see her again. There was no surviving this world without her.

"Right."

KYLIE WATCHED Daniel's powerful legs carry him up and over the first tall drift before she lost sight of him in the trees.

Her own feet didn't want to move at first. She was still reeling from the power of that kiss. Daniel felt everything so deeply, so powerfully.

And it was that reason, the need to protect him from any more pain and loss, that got her moving. With the beam of her flashlight leading the way, she jogged beside the snowmobile's tracks as quickly as her snowshoes and the chilled air filling her lungs let her. With her ears tuned for any unusual sounds beyond animals and birds stirring back to life now that the blizzard had ended, and her eyes straining for any unexpected movement in the shadows, Kylie kept alert for any signs that this was the path Lou had taken.

The snowmobile runners went right past the first cabin, but veered off before they reached the second. After a quick 360 scan, she left the road and followed the tracks up the small incline at the shoulder of the road, then looked down toward the frozen lake below. "Oh, my God."

Kicking off her snowshoes to negotiate the rugged drop-off through the trees, Kylie climbed down over the rocky, snow-studded slope. She stopped to check out the gouge that had been made in the trunk of a pine tree, verified that the sticky trail of dark liquid in the snow was oil and not blood. She picked up the runner that had snapped off when the vehicle hit the rocks and spun out onto the lake. Dropping it, she braced a hand on a granite boulder and leaned out as far as she could to follow the skid marks across the ice with her light.

She unhooked her holster before unzipping her walkie-talkie and getting Daniel on the line. "Daniel. This is Kylie. Do you read me?"

There was an answer of static, the whine of wind over the receiver and then a clear, "This is Daniel. I'm up at the roundhouse. It's clear. I've got tracks into the trees, but haven't had a chance to follow them yet. What is it?"

Although the lake remained frozen through the winter, she was still tentative about stepping out onto the solid surface and testing her weight on it. "I found the snowmobile. It went off the road and crashed into the lake."

One step, two. Those little crackles of sound must be the static over their connection, because the ice felt firm as she slid her feet across it. But wait, the broken runner support had carved a pretty deep gouge in the ice. It must have finally caught and flipped the vehicle, which it was resting on its side about twenty yards out from shore.

"Kylie?" A few more crackles. "Kylie, answer me!"

"I'm fine. There's no one here." She started again toward the snowmobile, but something beneath her feet seemed to give way and she jumped back. "Whoa. Is that supposed to happen?"

"Kylie? Report."

She backed up another step. "I think the heat from the engine must have softened the ice."

"Kylie, get off the lake! I'm coming down."

"No. We stick to the plan. Victoria's counting on us to be smarter than Lou." Once Kylie felt firmer footing, she swung her light around. "I've got tracks going out to the north."

"One set or two?"

She hurried over to follow them off the lake and onto the rocky bank. "It's hard to tell. One, I think, but he's doubled back at least once."

"Sullivan was probably making sure he could save himself before he went back to get Victoria."

Kylie pulled herself up over the rocks and tried to

make sense of the patterns in the snow. Were there two sets of footprints now? Someone had fallen here. Or had Lou set down Victoria's body? Man, Kylie wished she could read a trail the way Daniel did. "Maybe this is a wild-goose chase down here and you're on Lou's track. Watch your back."

Wait. There. Through the trees. Definitely two sets of boot prints. One made by someone either too drunk to walk, or fighting every step of the way.

"I think I've got them, Daniel. Heading up toward the second cabin. I need to go to radio silence in case this trail's legit."

"No! Do not—!"

With the turn of a button, she silenced the walkie-talkie and zipped it back into her coat. Then she pulled her gun, braced the flashlight on top of it, and made the steep climb up to the cabin.

The boot prints led right to the door with the busted lock.

This was it. Leaning her back against the door frame for a few seconds to steady her breathing, she steadied her Glock and her flashlight and swung around, pushing the door open and sliding inside in one swift movement. The entryway was clear.

She shone her light inside the first door. Bathroom, clear.

Bedroom, clear.

She turned the corner into the main living area. Nothing seemed disturbed from the last time she'd been in here with Daniel. She was about to lower the beam of her flashlight when she heard the soft scuffle of sound to her right.

Instantly on alert, she walked a wide circle around

the stools and island that separated the kitchen from the living room. Slowly. One step. Two.

And then her light hit the reflection of wide, frightened eyes. “Victoria?”

Bound and gagged with duct tape, the startled young woman scooted back against the refrigerator. Her hair was a mess, her jacket was torn, her cheek was bruised and she’d been crying. But she was alive.

Kylie holstered her weapon and hurried to her side. “You’re safe. Let’s get you out of here.”

Victoria screamed beneath the tape. Her eyes darted to the side.

Lou Sullivan.

Kylie leaped to her feet, reached for her gun. She saw the rush of a shadow from the entryway behind her. But she turned too late.

Something hard slammed into her temple, knocking her off her feet. A Tilt-A-Whirl spun inside her head as she tried to get her hands beneath her and push herself up. The object struck her again. Darkness swallowed her as she crumpled to the floor.

CHAPTER SEVEN

THE FLOOR WAS SO COLD, like ice beneath her cheek.

Kylie tried to wake up, but her eyelids were heavy steel curtains. A headache buzzed like the grind of a chain saw carving through the ice to drop a fishing line.

Ice.

So sleepy. Her bed was hard, icy.

Ice Lake.

Ignoring the chain saw, she opened her eyes to a grayish light. Everything around her was white, yet somehow dark. She struggled to shake the cobwebs from her brain and bring her surroundings into focus.

Snow. Sky… A Cheshire cat smile of a moon overhead reflected an eerie light off the wintry scene around her. Why was her bed outside?

She rolled over onto her back to look straight up at the moon. The ball bearings pinging around inside her skull cleared away the last of her grogginess.

Not her bed.

Outside.

Search for a killer.

Victoria found.

Lou Sullivan.

"Lou?" She pushed herself up onto her elbows, and the night spun round her. What had he done to her? Hit her from behind. "Where's Victoria?" Kylie rolled over onto her hands and knees, ignoring the lurch in her stomach. "Lou?" Where was she? And why could she still hear the snaps of ice cracking? "Lou?"

"There's no Lou here."

She froze at the man's voice behind her. She placed it immediately—add a stutter and raise the tone half a pitch and it was her former friend Louis Sullivan. The voice didn't surprise her.

The fact that she was kneeling out on the surface of Ice Lake did.

"Oh, my God." The swaying she felt wasn't entirely in her head. He'd dragged her out here next to the wrecked snowmobile. And the snapping sounds weren't in her head, after all. The ice might be thick here, but it was weak, cracking beneath her knees. Gingerly, minding the treacherous ice and her shaky balance, she got her feet beneath her and stood. Turned.

And looked straight into the barrel of her own gun.

Lou stood on the bank twenty feet away. He'd traded his big orange parka for a formfitting ski outfit. The thick scarf that normally wound around his neck hung open over his chest, exposing his throat and revealing the angry red marks of a dying woman's hand.

Rage burned inside Kylie. "Stacy Beecham put up a hell of a fight, didn't she, Lou?"

His glasses reflected the dim moonlight, masking the focus of his eyes. But there was no mistaking the contemptuous set of his mouth, or the steady aim of a gun she knew held fifteen bullets.

The cracking sounds beneath her feet picked up a rhythm like a distant drumroll.

"Where's Victoria, Lou?" Kylie had to get him to talk, to put down the gun. She had to get off this ice. "Is she all right?"

He didn't answer.

"How long was I out?" The bastard just stood there and stared at her with those glasses that kept her from reading his expression. "Damn it, Lou. You don't want to do this."

He shifted his stance, diverting her attention to the cross-country skis and backpack at his feet. Smart move. Now that the blizzard had died down, he could follow the highway out of here. And if they couldn't get phones or long-distance radio back before a sympathetic road crew picked up the stranded man, Lou would be dropped off in the nearest town before she could get an APB out on him. Very smart move.

Of course. He wasn't thinking like Lou Sullivan anymore. She was trying to reason with the wrong man.

"Burney?" she asked. "Burney Novak?"

He grinned. "Yeah, D-Deputy?"

She looked at Lou Sullivan, but spoke to the man inside his head. "You don't want to hurt me, Burney."

"Oh, but I d-do. And I have to d-do it before your boyfriend figures out where we are."

Daniel. Oh, God. If something happened to her here, and he found her…? *Fight, Kylie. Do not let this man win.* She needed to live. For Daniel's sake as well as her own.

So get the man talking. And while he was distracted by a little conversation and the extra voice in his head, she'd slide a subtle step forward. "Where's Victoria?"

"I left her in the c-cabin. She can freeze to death for all I c-care. I knew you'd come to save her. You're the one I really want. I don't c-care about her. She's too freaked out to fully c-c-comprehend what I can do to her." When Kylie took another step, Lou shook the gun, aimed right at center mass of her chest. Even though the Kevlar she wore beneath her coat would stop a bullet, it couldn't prevent her from getting knocked off balance and hitting the ice hard enough to crack it. So she stopped. He was definitely a more observant, more ruthless entity than meek Lou Sullivan had ever been. "But you understand, Deputy. You know just how d-dangerous I am."

She raised her hands, respecting the gun if not the man. "But you like to strangle your victims, Burney."

"You think I'm an idiot like Lou? You're a professional, trained in hand-to-hand combat, I'm guessing. You think I'm going to get c-close enough to you to let you g-get the drop on me?"

"Lou would let me get off the ice." She risked another step. "He and I could talk."

"Lou isn't here. That w-w-weak idiot isn't here."

This was her chance. "Lou? I need your help. The ice is thin here. I need—"

"Stop!" He raised the gun and fired a round off over her head. "Stop moving!"

Kylie jerked at the loud report. But she stopped. Burney was back. And he might just have silenced Lou Sullivan forever.

"Why didn't you strangle me when I was unconscious?" she asked.

"Because your eyes weren't open. I couldn't see the fear in them. I c-couldn't hear you beg for your life."

Kylie lowered her arms. "I won't beg."

He steadied the gun. "You will."

"Shooting me won't give you the satisfaction you crave."

He looped the scarf around his neck and licked the evil smile on his lips. "Who said I'm going to shoot you?"

He pointed the gun down at the ice. The breaking ice suddenly cracked like thunder in her ears. "Burney?"

"That's the fear I'm lookin' for, bitch."

Bang. She tried to run to safety, but the shots were too close to her feet. *Bang. Bang.* The hard surface of the lake groaned in protest.

"Burney!"

Two more shots drove her back from the shore. If she was going down… She unzipped her coat and yanked it off her arms. If it got wet, the weight would surely drag her under. More shots rang out like thunder in the night. A crack raced across the ice from the snowmobile toward her feet. She tossed the coat. Three more shots and the snowmobile exploded behind her. A wave of heat knocked her off her feet. Flames shot up into the sky. Roiling black clouds of oil and gasoline stung her nose.

"Burney!"

The bastard was climbing up the hill, sticking the gun into the waist of his pants, shrugging into his pack as he found one handhold after another to pull himself up to the road.

Kylie's feet slipped when she tried to stand. Her knees came down hard on the ice. The fire burned. Her world tilted.

Crawl, Kylie! Move!

The distant, low-pitched roll of a kettle drum echoed in her ears, surrounding her, engulfing her.

Get on your feet!

She stumbled back to her aching knees. Another crack in the ice. He was up on the road now, sliding his feet into the clamps of his skis.

"Burney!"

The ice opened up beneath her and gravity sucked her down into the icy waters of the lake.

The drenching cold shocked her into stillness as she sank into the freezing darkness. And then the instinct to live shocked her again. She reached with her arms and kicked back up to the surface.

But her hand hit ice. Where was the hole she'd fallen through?

She reached up again. *Frozen solid.*

Circling in the water, her lungs protesting in her chest, she kicked one more time, swimming toward the thin spot where she could see the moon's half smile through the ice. But she bumped her hand.

Don't panic.

She'd grown up here. She knew the dangers of ice and winter and water. *Think!*

She pressed her lips up beneath the ice and inhaled the last pocket of oxygen there. And then she punched at the ice with her fist. But her muscles were getting so stiff.

The hole was already freezing over and she was already so cold. So tired. Every cell of her body could feel the frigid tomb that claimed her. She gulped in a mouthful of water, which hastened the chill from the inside out. It was hypnotic, really.

The last thing she saw was the moon.

The last things she heard were the drums, and the wind shouting her name.

"KYLIE!" DANIEL CROUCHED over his skis and straightened his run, picking up speed over the choppy snow as he neared the bottom of the slope.

Flying snow bit into his cheeks beneath his goggles. The spotlight anchored to the hat he wore gave him some idea of where he was heading. But he was moving too fast to make out landmarks beside the trees to his left and the ski lift to his right. He was relying on memory and instincts and twenty some years of skiing this mountain to guide him down in one piece to reach the woman he loved.

"Kylie!"

He'd hit the slope at the first gunshot. He'd heard nine more since. Ten gunshots in the space of a minute, reverberating through the crisp, clear air on Mount Atlas. Sending shock waves into the snow and deep into his heart.

Bringing the world down on them all.

Ending his world if even one of those bullets had struck Kylie.

The slope flattened out and he skipped over drifts as the lodge, outbuildings and parking lot came into view. He spotted a short figure coming out of the trees by the cabins, pumping his arms and legs in the slow, familiar rhythm of a cross-country skier. Lou Sullivan. That bastard. Kylie had found him. Or he'd found her.

"Kylie!"

The instinct to fly at the man burned through Daniel. He'd have the advantage of speed and surprise. But he'd already chased one dead-end trail where Sullivan had led him astray. And the need to get to Kylie was stronger.

With his downhill speed still carrying him along at a swift pace, Daniel angled his skis toward the lake, where she'd been when she'd last made contact.

He spotted the fire on the ice immediately. The ghosts of his past tried to lure him in different directions. But the blaze burned like a beacon in the night, calling him straight to it.

Once his skis became more of a hindrance than a help, he kicked them off and ran toward the flames. The boots made it awkward to climb down the rocky slope to the lake, but he didn't slow. Most of the frozen lake was solid white, covered with the recent snow. But the bluish tint of a patch about ten feet out from the shore told him the ice had broken there.

He pulled out his flashlight to track the strip of thin ice from the rocks to the burning snowmobile, and prayed his instincts were wrong. But he saw her pale face come up beneath the surface. Oh, no. Hell, no.

"Kylie!"

He pulled the pickax from his pack and slid out as close as he dared. "Kylie, baby, you stay with me. You hear?" He brought the ax down once. He swung it again and water bubbled up over the surface. "Kylie!"

Lying on his belly, Daniel crawled forward and thrust his arm deep into the hole he'd made. The ice wobbled beneath his weight. The water soaked into his glove and sleeve and the front of his coat.

"Kylie! See my hand. Come to me, baby. I'm here for you." He splashed the water to keep it from freezing over again. *Please, baby. Please.*

The mountain rumbled with an ominous omen behind him.

But this was not the Middle East. This was not some innocent boy. This was Kylie Webber. His strong, brave, beautiful Kylie. The woman didn't know how to give up.

She swam a little closer, and as soon as Daniel felt the brush of her fingers against his, he latched on to them and pulled. He hooked her arm onto the edge of the ice as she surfaced with a loud gulp for air. She sputtered, spit water, shivered and jerked, until her other arm was out of the water, too.

"Kylie? Babe?" He touched her pale cheek and turned her eyes to his. Oh, man, she was way too cold.

Her lips were blue. She was shivering hard. "D-D-Daniel?"

"I've got you." Staying flat on his belly, he backed across the ice, pulling her a little farther out of the icy water.

"Lou?"

He shook his head. "I had to save you."

And then he was on his knees, pulling her free. He crawled to the shore and carried her onto the rocks. He pulled her sopping hat off her head and tossed it aside, replacing it with his own warm, dry stocking cap.

"Where's your coat, babe?" he asked, knowing he had to get her talking.

She was shaking hard, going into hypothermia. "Too heavy."

Daniel unzipped his own coat and wrapped her inside. He needed to get all those wet clothes off her and get them both inside, someplace warm. But they didn't have that kind of time. "Can you walk?"

The thunder grew louder.

Holding tightly to his arms, wrapped tightly around her, Kylie nodded. "I can try."

He slipped the spotlight off the hat she now wore, and looped it over his own head, freeing his hands to help her up the slope onto the road. But her knees gave way and she collapsed after a few steps.

Daniel knelt down and pressed his lips against her icy mouth, blowing his warm breath into her lungs and keeping her alert enough to focus on him. "Don't you die on me, Kylie Webber." He kissed her again just to kiss her. "You promised."

"I w-won't."

He scooped her up into his arms and carried her through the snow. The ground shook beneath his feet and he turned his eyes toward the mountain. Night hid the top of the peak from him, but he knew what was coming. He felt it in his bones.

Kylie's shivering arms tightened around his neck. "What's that sound?"

"The wrath of Mount Atlas."

He was already moving. But with Kylie in his arms and ski boots on his feet, Daniel knew they'd never make it to the lodge in time. He could see Lou Sullivan nearing the first of the outbuildings now. The man might think he'd outsmarted them all. But nobody was smarter about this mountain than Daniel Stone.

Reading the trembling beneath his feet, he switched course and plunged into the deep snow off the side of the road. Kylie tumbled from his grasp. But he quickly had her back on her feet, back in his arms, and then he stretched his long legs out, moving them through the drift to higher ground.

"Can you get the walkie-talkie from my coat?"

"I think s-so." It took her several tries to get her fingers to lock on to the zipper. "My hands are so cold."

"I'll get you someplace warm. I promise." She held the radio up to his mouth and pushed the call button. "Avalanche! Kent!" Daniel cried. "Answer your radio. Get everyone away from the north windows of the lodge. Eagle One to home base. Avalanche!"

Static crackled in response. "Home base to Eagle One. Daniel?" Kent's voice sounded justifiably concerned. "Did you say avalanche?"

"Roger. Get everyone away from the windows."

"Did you find Victoria? Where's Ky—?"

Kylie's fingers shook and the radio dropped into the snow. Daniel didn't stop to pick it up.

"Where are you going?" Her hold on his neck was slipping. "We need to get to safety."

"We will. Just hang on, baby. We will."

He hit slightly shallower snow once he reached the open space of the ski run. Swinging Kylie behind him piggyback-style, he caught her thighs beneath her frozen pant legs and climbed at a diagonal across the slope.

The rumble above them was picking up strength, getting close enough to start throwing up bits of snow.

"Daniel?" Kylie wasn't too far out of it to realize the danger they were in. "Let me go." Her teeth chattered against his ear. "I'm slowing you down."

His legs burned with the effort to keep moving. His chest heaved with every breath. "You don't get your way this time. I'm not losing you." He spotted the steel crossbeams of the ski lift tower. "Not to a wannabe serial killer. And not to this mountain."

The snow blew past them as though the blizzard was starting up again as he set Kylie's feet on the first rung of the tower. Daniel stepped up right behind her. "Come on, baby. Climb."

First one foot, then another. Reach. Grab. Hold on tight. When Kylie slipped, he caught her and put her hands back on the steel.

He heard the clack of a seat pass over the tower above them. The mountain was coming at them like a speeding freight train now.

"Almost there."

"I can't—"

"The Kylie I know doesn't say *can't*."

They were high enough now that he could see the next chair coming at them. The tower swayed back and forth. He could see the wall of snow racing toward them out of the darkness.

Digging deep, he summoned a final burst of strength to lift her up onto the chair as it passed by. “Hang on!”

Snow from the top of Atlas dusted his feet as Daniel swung himself onto the chair beside her.

Kylie turned her chilled face into the warmth of his neck. He wrapped his arms around her and held on tight.

“Victoria?” she whispered.

“It’s veering away from the cabins. It’s gonna hit the lodge.”

“Kent’s there.” Daniel could feel the protest in her muscles, but she wasn’t strong enough to pull away.

“They’ll be fine. He’ll keep them safe.”

“Lou?”

Daniel glanced over his shoulder at the shrinking speck of a man trying to outrun the reach of the snow. “He’ll never make it.”

CHAPTER EIGHT

KYLIE AWOKE FROM HER LONG, deep sleep feeling toasty and warm and deliriously pleased to be alive.

Now if her brother would just stop shouting in the next room…

"Yes, Agent McCade, that's right. It'll take us another couple of days to dig out from under all this snow. But it's probably easier to get to us from where you are than to try to make it into town. I know exactly where the north-face cabin is located. I've got a team already on its way to bring you in, so sit tight. Two more souls here isn't a problem. Food and water are good, and the sheriff's department dropped in a new supply of fuel that should keep us powered up for a week. What's that? It'll take Winston a few months to get everything back in order for the next tourist season. But somehow, I don't think he minds. He's just glad we're all safe. He'll be relieved to hear you and Agent Gray made it through the storm, too."

Kylie moaned and squished her face back into the pillow.

"He is kind of loud, isn't he?"

One eye popped open at the familiar gravelly voice. Kylie rolled over, smiling, and opened both eyes to take in Ice Lake Resort's infirmary and the golden-haired hero sitting in the chair beside her cot. "Daniel."

He braced his elbows on his knees and leaned forward. "Your color's a lot better today. Vitals were good yesterday. Temperature's normal. You get to keep all your fingers and toes."

"So I'm okay?"

"Dr. Big Brother said that once you got enough sleep to treat the exhaustion, he'd be willing to release you into my custody."

Her smile widened. "I thought I was the law around here."

"Maybe. But it's my job to *protect* the law around here."

"You saved my life," she said, thanking him. But he looked so tired, and even though it was his civilian style to keep his wheat-colored stubble on the shaggy side, the man needed a trim. Kylie reached out and laced her fingers with his. "Are you all right?"

"I lost a good pickax in the lake, but I came out of the whole thing without a scratch."

She tightened her grip and sat up. "I meant on the inside. How are you feeling?"

Kent's strong voice came through the door again. "My men can take you to Stacy Beecham's body and bring her down the mountain as soon as the snow has fully settled and it's safe."

Kylie released Daniel's hand and combed her fingers through her hair. "Who's he talking to out there?"

"The FBI agents who took out Burney Novak," Daniel explained. "Apparently, they were almost to Graniteville when they got word that Novak's partner was still in the area. When they tried to make it back to the lodge to look for him, they got stranded by the storm and had to take refuge in one of the remote cabins, to ride out the worst of it. We got radio communication back this morning. Agents McCade and Gray called in first thing. I think they were ready to hike in—"

"It's too deep. And the avalanche will have buried roads and changed landmarks. They could get lost."

"Exactly. But once they found out we had the situation under control, they agreed to do the safe thing and wait for search and rescue." Daniel glanced toward the closed door between them and the office. "From the sound of things, though, the FBI is anxious to wrap up their case. Kent also got ahold of Sheriff Quick, so the department knows you're in one piece and that the remaining guests are out of danger from both the storm and the killers."

"All that happened this morning?" The brightness of the sun outside the windows told her it was already midafternoon. "What time is it? I feel like I've lost a day out of my life."

"That's about how long you slept. The avalanche was night before last."

"More than twenty-four hours?" She pushed the covers back and swung her stockinged feet over the side. "I have things to do. Responsibilities. I should be the one reporting in to Sheriff Quick and the FBI."

"Relax." Daniel's gaze slipped down to where her nipples pearled up beneath the long-underwear shirt she wore. *His* shirt, if she remembered correctly. "Kent gave you a good report. And rightly so. You figured out Lou's identity and kept anyone else from dying."

Feeling a little warm under Daniel's unabashed scrutiny, Kylie spotted the jeans and flannel top one of the guests had loaned her, and quickly dressed. "How's Victoria?"

"Physically, she's all right. But she had a pretty good scare." The chair creaked behind her as Daniel stood.

"I know a good therapist I can recommend if she's got some trauma issues to deal with."

Kylie buttoned the flannel shirt as she turned to face him. "You never answered my question. How are you feeling?"

He pulled a key to one of the lodge's guest rooms from his pocket and dangled it in front of her. "That's something I'd like to discuss in private, if you don't mind."

Her temperature rose another notch in embarrassment as she looked around Daniel's shoulder to see Barb Hughes working on a crossword puzzle over on her cot. "Okay." Whatever Daniel wanted to say to her, wherever and whenever he wanted to say it, she would listen. "Privacy it is."

"Winston gave me a key to one of the rooms upstairs, and promised to heat it for us. I'm not taking any chances that you'll relapse into hypothermia."

Resting his hand lightly at the small of her back, Daniel guided her into Kent's office.

"That's right. We found Lou Sullivan's body in the snow. Broken neck." It sounded as if her brother was covering all the bases with Agent McCade. "We've already put him in the freezer with his partner."

"I'm checking this patient out," Daniel informed Kent as they walked by his desk.

"Hold on a sec, Alex," Kent said, rising to his feet and signaling for Kylie and Daniel to stop. He set down the radio and circled the desk to wrap his sister up in a tight hug that lifted her onto her toes. "I called the right person to come save the day for us, didn't I."

She hugged him right back. "I had a lot of help from Daniel and you."

He kissed her cheek and let her go, to open a drawer

in his desk. “Yeah, well, as a wise, determined, yet frequently annoying woman once said to me—you’re the cop and I’m the guy who keeps everyone healthy and safe. Here—” he tossed Kylie her badge “—you’ll need this.”

“And hey, Stone?” Kent grinned as he resumed his seat and picked up the radio. “That healthy and safe thing applies to my role as big brother, too. You break my baby sister’s heart and I’ll break your legs.”

“Kent!” Kylie chided.

But he was already back on the radio, and Daniel was pulling her out into the hallway. “C’mon. He knows he can get away with saying that, because I’d do the same myself if anybody ever tried to hurt you.”

A few minutes later they were within the reasonably warm, and definitely private, walls of room 214. Drawn by the bright sunlight shining outside, Kylie crossed to the north-facing window and looked out onto the monster drift of snow that came up to the second story. “Wow. Is that from the avalanche?”

Daniel tossed the key onto the dresser and joined her at the window. “We ended up with about twelve feet here. No major damage at the lodge, although Winston did lose a couple of sheds.”

Kylie closed her eyes and leaned back against his warm chest. “Who’d believe that I was drowning in a frozen lake two nights ago? Isn’t this heavenly?”

“Yeah.” Daniel’s husky voice danced in her ear. Shifting, she opened her eyes to read the rare uncertainty that narrowed his gaze. “After everything that’s happened over the past seventy-two hours—two dead serial killers, a blizzard, an avalanche, two deaths and a kidnapping—do you still feel hopeful?”

“About us? Of course.” She faced him, lifting her

fingers to sweep them across the taut line of his lips. "Unless you tell me to stop, I will always believe that you and I were meant to be together."

He caught her hand in his and pressed a tender, ticklish kiss into her palm. "Don't stop." His ragged plea touched her heart, reminded her of the young Daniel she'd once loved, and made her love the mature man even more. He leaned in and pressed a gentle kiss to her mouth. His face hovered near hers, close enough for his warm breath to fan her cheek, close enough for her to see the trust he had in her—the trust he was beginning to have in *them*—heating the granite sheen of his eyes. "Don't ever stop believing. I…I really need you to believe."

"I do, Daniel. I d—"

He silenced her with his lips. And when she stretched up on tiptoe and wound her arms around his neck, he thrust his tongue between her teeth and deepened the kiss. He backed her against the wall and kept coming until his hard chest flattened her soft breasts, and one sturdy thigh was wedged between hers.

There were no more words for a long time, only kissing and touching. Stroking and needing. Gasps and hums and guttural affirmations.

A firestorm licked through Kylie's veins, heating her up from the inside out. Pressure built in the weepy juncture of her thighs, which squeezed with helpless need around Daniel's leg. The tips of her breasts ached and tingled and grew heavy at the friction sparking between their bodies.

Daniel's sure hands made short work of her buttons, and with a feverish groan, he slipped his fingers beneath the hems and skimmed both shirts up and over her head. The air was cool against her skin, the wall at her back even cooler. But he dipped his head to capture the rigid peak of her breast in his mouth, and she was on fire. He laved, he teased. He gently touched his teeth around the distended tip and she spasmed in his arms. Kylie squirmed as he turned his attention to the other breast, suckling it with his tongue, brushing his beard over the sensitized nub and making her cry out as sparks shot a flaming arrow straight to her core.

When he finally gave her respite from the sensual overload, she turned the tables and explored his body with the same focused enthusiasm. She pushed up the sweater that was in her way and he shed the offending garment himself, giving her permission to reacquaint herself with his body.

He ran his hands up and down her back, from the flare of her hips to the nape of her neck, while she tasted the salty tang of his skin at his neck and shoulder. Her fingers worked their way down the hills and hollows of his chest, tracing the narrow trail of wheat-gold hair that ran down his stomach and disappeared beneath the snap above the bulge in his jeans.

When she swirled her tongue around a taut male nipple and pulled the snap apart, Daniel growled low in his throat. "No more."

He recaptured her willing mouth with his, and lifted her into his arms. He laid her across the bed and followed her down. In an ungainly, yet timeless ballet of hands and legs and stolen kisses, Kylie helped Daniel remove the rest of their clothes, slid a condom over his straining shaft and guided him inside her.

It had been so long that it was painful at first, but only for a moment. Daniel held himself still until her body stretched to welcome him, then clasp him tight. And it was she who looked up into his beautiful eyes, she who wrapped her legs around his hips and bound them even closer together as he moved inside her, she who tipped back her head and cried out as the fire exploded inside her.

Daniel's release came moments after. She hugged him with her arms, with her legs, with her whole heart as he whispered her name against her neck and flew apart.

Afterward, they snuggled skin to skin under the covers, dozing and talking. Daniel told her about the little boy who'd been killed by a sniper's bullet, and Kylie wept against his chest at the heartbreak she heard in his voice. He talked about the men in his unit dying in the same attack. He'd lost men before—he'd been in the Marines too long not to—but something about the deaths that day had changed him, damaged him inside.

But he was healing. Slowly. He couldn't always keep the nightmares and insecurities at bay, but the episodes where he flashed back were coming less often now, and when they did, he could usually control them.

Kylie's energy was spent, her body weary. But she felt closer to Daniel in these quiet moments on a snowbound afternoon than she had even before his fateful deployment. He dried her tears, then pulled her to lie on top of him, letting their legs and hearts tangle together.

"You're a miracle to me, Kylie. You had faith in me when I didn't have faith in myself. I can see the sunshine at the end of the tunnel through your eyes." He played with a curl at her temple. "I want you. I want to be with you. I want to be with you for the rest of my life. If you can put up with me."

"Seriously?" She brushed her palms against the short spikes of his hair. "Do you think there's any other woman out there who will?"

Kylie bounced up and down on his chest as Daniel's

face creased with a smile and he truly laughed. It was a sound she hadn't heard for far too long, and it did as much to reassure her that this was right—that *they* were right—as any word or promise could.

Daniel leisurely kissed his way across her mouth before stopping to frame her face in his hands. "I love you, Kylie Webber. You chase the shadows from my soul and make me feel good things again. I don't deserve you, but I'm not going to let you go."

"You're going to keep seeing your therapist?"

"Yeah."

"You're going to let me do my job without interfering?"

"Possibly."

"You're going to love me forever?"

He wound his fingertip into the curl and gently tucked it behind her ear. "Absolutely."

"All right. Then I'll take you on." Her future—their future—was finally turning out the way she'd always known it would. She rested her hand over his heart and smiled. "I love you, Daniel Stone. And there's not a blizzard or mountain or bad guy—or you—who'll ever change that."

* * * * *

Louisa Morgan loves being around children. So when she has the opportunity to tutor bedridden Ellie, she's determined to bring joy back into the motherless girl's world. Can she also help Ellie's father open his heart again? Read on for a sneak peek of

THE COWBOY FATHER

by Linda Ford, available February 2012 from Love Inspired Historical.

Why had Louisa thought she could do this job? A bubble of self-pity whispered she was totally useless, but Louisa ignored it. She wasn't useless. She could help Ellie if the child allowed it.

Emmet walked her out, waiting until they were out of earshot to speak. "I sense you and Ellie are not getting along."

"Ellie has lost her freedom. On top of that, everything is new. Familiar things are gone. Her only defense is to exert what little independence she has left. I believe she will soon tire of it and find there are more enjoyable ways to pass the time."

He looked doubtful. Louisa feared he would tell her not to return. But after several seconds' consideration, he sighed heavily. "You're right about one thing. She's lost everything. She can hardly be blamed for feeling out of sorts."

"She hasn't lost everything, though." Her words were quiet, coming from a place full of certainty that Emmet was more than enough for this child. "She has you."

"She'll always have me. As long as I live." He clenched his fists. "And I fully intend to raise her in such a way that even if something happened to me, she would never feel like I was gone. I'd be in her thoughts and in her actions

SHLIHEXP0212

every day."

Peace filled Louisa. "Exactly what my father did."

Their gazes connected, forged a single thought about fathers and daughters…how each needed the other. How sweet the relationship was.

Louisa tipped her head away first. "I'll see you tomorrow."

Emmet nodded. "Until tomorrow then."

She climbed behind the wheel of their automobile and turned toward home. She admired Emmet's devotion to his child. It reminded her of the love her own father had lavished on Louisa and her sisters. Louisa smiled as fond memories of her father filled her thoughts. Ellie was a fortunate child to know such love.

SHLIHEXP0212